Samuel,
   Thanks for being my student
and my friend. I hope you enjoy
your time in Fright House.
                          Fred

Fright
House

By
Fred Wiehe

October 1, 2015

Damnation Books, LLC.
P.O. Box 3931
Santa Rosa, CA 95402-9998
www.damnationbooks.com

Fright House
by Fred Wiehe

Digital ISBN: 978-1-62929-226-7
Print ISBN: 978-1-62929-227-4

Cover art by: Dawné Dominique
Edited by: Kiera Smith

Printed in the United States of America
Worldwide Electronic & Digital Rights
Worldwide English Language Print Rights

Praise for Fred Wiehe:

"Fred Wiehe...always delivers shocks and thrills."
—Jonathan Maberry, author of the Bram Stoker Award-Winning novel *Ghost Road Blues*

~

"Fred Wiehe has established himself as an important voice in a new age of horror fiction."
—Nicholas Grabowsky, author of *The Everborn* and *Halloween IV*

~

"Wiehe is out to make a name for himself in the horror field..."
—Barry Hunter, *Baryon Magazine*

~

"Wiehe's punchy prose pounds us with dementia, mis-adventure and enough multi-dimensional mayhem to KO Quinten Tarantino and leave him smiling as he hits the floor."
—Weston Ochse, author of the 2006 Bram Stoker Award-Winning Novel *Scarecrow Gods*

~

"Fred Wiehe knows what he wants with horror, and the imagination is of an author that doesn't exactly fit with the current trend. If he was alive in the 1930's he would find great company with the likes of H.P. Lovecraft and Algernon Blackwood."
—Nickolaus A. Pacione, *Renegade Horror Writer*

"Evil lurks in shadows
It lingers in hallways
Hides in corners
Awaits at the threshold
Pounds at the door

The key is all it needs
Once the door opens
It's ready to pounce
Eager to run amok
Fervent to kill

And only the key
That set evil loose
Upon the world
Can lock it away again
Ending the terror"

—The Collected Nightmares
by Fred Wiehe

For my family.
I love you all.

A special thank you goes out to Dave Reda of Elftwin Films. This story concept started as a feature length screenplay that I had written for Elftwin Films. During that process, Dave played an instrumental role in developing the storyline and creating that script. I also must thank Dave for his encouragement and agreement in turning this story concept and script into a full-length novel. The existence of this book wouldn't be possible without him. Thank you, Dave. Also, Dave and I both still hope to someday release Fright House as a feature film in theaters around the country. Be watching! A special shout out to Kiera Smith, my editor at Damnation Books. Without a doubt she is the best damn (pun intended) editor I've worked with so far in the business. She definitely helped my novel to be better, stronger. Thanks Kiera for all your hard work.

Chapter One

Penny Winters was blinded by the bright, fluorescent lights. Disinfectant assaulted her nostrils, brought tears to her eyes. Even through the dizzying effect of the disinfectant and the prism of tears, she could see that her surroundings were at once bizarre yet eerily familiar. She stood in the hallway of what was apparently a hospital. Surprisingly, it was one she had never been in before. She didn't understand how she had gotten there. She didn't even understand why she was there. Not only that, but the doctors, nurses, orderlies, and patients who walked the hallway didn't notice her or pay her much mind, as if she were invisible.

Something else wasn't right, either. Everyone, other than herself, looked and dressed as if they had stepped out of the distant past—the hairstyles on both the men and women, the style of glasses some of them wore, the nurses' uniforms, the doctors' clothes under their open lab coats. Nothing looked right. Everything and everybody reminded her of some old black and white movie on late-night TV.

An uneasy feeling suddenly churned her stomach. Hot bile erupted into her throat.

Without fully understanding why, she dared not move or make a sound. Instead, she watched, listened.

That's when she noticed that no one spoke or acknowledged each other as they moved along the hallway. The few patients there silently shuffled up and down the hallway in robes and slippers. Their eyes blank, lifeless, as if they'd been lobotomized.

Another eruption of bile burned the back of her throat. A chill blew through her like a frigid wind. Goose flesh crept along her skin and scalp.

That's even before she heard the electrical whine that set her teeth on edge. Followed by a scream. A little girl's scream. One that reminded her of her own.

Penny spun in circles, trying to determine the origins of the whine and the screams. To her amazement, no one else in the hallway reacted to either sound, even though the electrical whine remained constant, and the little girl's screams grew louder.

Without understanding, she stopped spinning. Instead, she began running down the hallway, dodging staff and patients alike, toward the elevator. Somehow, she felt certain that the elevator held some sort of answer.

Once at the elevator doors, she pushed the *down* button. The light above the elevator blinked on. A chime rang out, announcing its arrival. The doors swished open. She hurried onto the empty elevator, pushing the button for the basement as she did so. Breathing hard, heart racing, she listened to soft, piped-in music while waiting with urgency for the elevator to reach the basement. It jolted to a stop after what felt like an eternity but was probably only a few seconds. Again, the chime sounded.

She ran into an empty hallway. The whine of the electrical instrument heightened, reminding her of a dentist's drill. The little girl's scream rose to a fevered pitch. She raced toward an imposing iron door at the end of the hallway. She didn't know how, but she was sure the sounds came from there. As she reached the door, the electrical instrument whined on, but the girl's screams died.

"No," Penny shrieked.

She slammed into the iron door, surprised that it wasn't locked, that it opened so easily. Once inside, though, she wished she hadn't gained access. Inside, a doctor held a rotating saw, bloody blade spinning, cutting at the air. The headless body of a little girl was strapped to an operating table. Blood spurted from her neck. Her lifeless body still spasmed as if it didn't know death had already come. The girl's head lay on the floor next to the table. Her pigtails flopped backward into an ever-growing pool of blood.

"No," Penny shrieked again.

With that, as if being called back from the dead, the girl's eyes opened. A macabre smile crept across her blood-splashed face.

"Welcome," the little girl's severed head croaked. "We've been waiting for you. Won't you come and play with us?"

Penny screamed.

* * * *

The scream was still on Penny's lips when she bolted upright in bed. Seconds later, she hacked up her undigested Big Mac and fries onto her lap.

She sat in darkness. Blankets drenched in her own vomit. She choked on disgorged matter. Spittle hung from her mouth. Sweat plastered hair to her head, nightgown to her skin.

Trembling and breathing hard, she gasped, "God, help me."

Chapter Two

Penny had taken the bus to Fright House. Unlike other seventeen-year-olds, she didn't have a driver's license and never learned to drive. Since the nearest bus stop was a mile down the road, she walked from there.

Once she entered Fright House's parking lot, she stopped to take in the monstrous building. She stared wide-eyed at it, awestruck by her new place of employment.

At first sight of the place, a gasp escaped her lips. Goose flesh crept along her skin and scalp, much like in her nightmare last night.

Not only was the sheer size of the building monstrous, but the look of it was, as well. Yellow lights on and around the building and parking lot cast a sickly, eerie glow in the darkening gloom. The lighted sign on the front depicted maniacal, screaming faces and read *Fright House: California's Largest and Scariest Halloween Attraction.* Except for that, the grey, institutional building looked every bit the hospital it had once been. She noticed the iron bars on all the windows. That was odd. Maybe they were added for effect after the hospital became a Halloween attraction.

Taking it all in, she thought, *this is the last place I should be. Considering everything, the last place...*

She had no choice, though. She knew that.

Against all odds, she had finally escaped—her physical prison, anyway. Her past, however, wasn't about to let go of her without a fight. People were surely looking for her. If found, she would just as surely be taken back. She couldn't allow that. She wouldn't go back for anything.

Being underage and having no identity, she'd discovered that finding a place to live and finding employment was difficult to nearly impossible. Most places that rented rooms were way too expensive, wanting first and last month's rent plus a security deposit. She couldn't come close to affording anything like that, or much of anything, for that matter. Besides, even if she could afford a nice place, no one would even consider renting to her without her first being employed. Prospective employers wanted background checks, social security numbers, references. She had no references. She couldn't allow background checks. She couldn't use her real social security number. She couldn't use her real name.

Luckily, she had found a small market run by a Vietnamese family that was willing to hire her. They paid her off the books, under the table, as they said it. They didn't pay much, but it had been a start. They also rented her a small room, above the store, for very little. They never asked questions, either. Never wanted to know why she found herself on the streets, with no money, no place to live. Maybe they understood. Maybe they had been where she was now.

The problem with this arrangement was she couldn't save enough money to get out of California. She desperately wanted to get out of California and go somewhere no one knew her. That's why she lied about her name, her age, and her past when she started looking for another, better paying job. She even made up a phony social security number, hoping no one would check. At least not for a while. At least not until she made the money she needed and could move on again and disappear.

She found the job to manage Fright House on Craigslist and dared to answer the ad. It was perfect, a dream come true. At least she had thought so at the time.

Now, eyeing the monstrosity before her, she shivered. Goose flesh again attacked her scalp, her skin.

Finally seeing the place, she understood why Mister Peabody was willing to hire her on the spot, at a great salary too. Probably no one else was willing to take the position, to work every day in such frightening surroundings, no matter how much money. It was, however, an offer *she* couldn't turn down. It truly was perfect. Mister Peabody was desperate because the Halloween season was already in full swing. The job was temporary too—a holiday position—which was probably another reason her new employer was a bit lax about doing background checks. She'd have her money. She'd be gone before Mister Peabody, or anyone else, was the wiser.

Still, perfect opportunity or not, Fright House riveted her gaze. Finally, she looked away.

Opening her purse, she took out a small mirror and checked her reflection. Haunted, brown eyes stared back at her. She ignored them, checking her makeup, running fingers through her shoulder-length brown hair. She looked twenty-something, she guessed, she hoped. Anyway, Mister Peabody hadn't questioned it at the time of her interview. She hoped he wouldn't now.

The faraway, frightened look in her eyes again caught her attention. It was a look she hadn't seen staring back at her for some time. She didn't like it.

She threw the mirror back inside her purse.

She had put off her first night at work long enough. Mister Peabody was waiting for her. Soon, the crowd would show up for a night of scares and thrills.

She took another deep breath to settle her nerves, then set off across the gloomy parking lot. Unknowingly, she hurried toward a destiny in which this time she couldn't possibly escape.

No matter what.

Chapter Three

A man in his fifties, looking like a funeral-parlor salesman, waited for Penny outside the front doors of Fright House.

The heels of Penny's shoes clicked rapidly against the pavement as she approached. "Mister Peabody," she said in a breathless hush, "I'm sorry I'm late."

Cyrus Peabody fumbled with a set of keys. "I saw you standing out in the parking lot," he said. He gave Penny a tight smile. "I hope everything is okay. It took you awhile to come forward."

Penny didn't answer. Instead, she concentrated on catching her breath, slowing her heart rate.

Mister Peabody continued with that tight smile. He waved off his suggestion that it took Penny some time to get up her nerve. "It's okay, Miss Winters. Fright House has that effect on some people the first time they see it. Wouldn't be a great Halloween attraction if it didn't." Finally managing to find the right key, he unlocked the iron doors. "I'm really quite glad I found you," he continued, speaking over his shoulder at Penny, who stood silently behind him. "You're a gift from Heaven."

Penny brushed brown hair away from her face with a nervous hand. She felt the heat of a blush on her face. "Thank you, I guess."

"Oh, I'm being quite sincere. My manager quit..." Mister Peabody snapped his fingers. "...just like that. No explanation. Just a week after opening. Just a few weeks before Halloween, too. I was desperate."

She had been right. The person who had the job before had abruptly quit, and no one else wanted it for any price. That's why Mister Peabody had hired her so readily, without checking her background—at least so far—or asking for references.

Penny snickered. "Desperate enough to hire *me*?"

That's why he had offered such a high salary, too. Good for her. At the money she was making, she'd be able to leave California and start a new life in no time.

Mister Peabody turned around, a pained look of embarrassment on his face. "I didn't mean it quite that way. I just meant you came to me at the right time. I think you'll make the perfect manager for this place."

Penny thoughtfully scanned her morbid surroundings. "I'm not sure how to take that."

Mister Peabody waved the remark off, ignoring Penny's obvious reservations. Turning back to the iron doors, he opened them, the rusted hinges squealing in protest. He turned back to Penny with that tight-lipped smile. "Come, let me show you Fright House."

Forcing her own smile, Penny nodded.

Not for the first time she thought, *This is the last place I should be...*

Reluctantly, she followed her new boss across the threshold.

Chapter Four

Mister Peabody and Penny stood in a large, hospital reception area, full of dark corners, gloom, and despair. Penny's new boss switched on the lights, but they—like the lights around the building and in the parking lot—only succeeded in casting a sickly, yellow glow across the room, giving everything a jaundiced look.

Penny took in her surroundings. Like in her nightmare last night, the scene was both bizarre and eerily familiar.

The ceiling was low, giving the rather large room an unusual, claustrophobic feel. A multitude of cracks and chipped paint covered the walls. They stood on a tiled floor—chipped, cracked, bloodstained. A television was mounted on one wall, up by the low ceiling. A few metal folding chairs, along with a couple of old wooden benches, were arranged for optimal TV viewing. A reception counter stood in front of the far interior wall. An imposing iron door stood behind it. A thick layer of dust clung to every surface. Genuine cobwebs hung in every corner.

Mister Peabody and Penny's footsteps echoed against the tiled floor as they walked around the reception counter to the iron door. Mister Peabody pressed a button on the wall, and a buzz answered. The iron door clicked when it unlocked. As he pulled the door open, it squealed just as the front doors did moments ago.

Mister Peabody led the way, crossing the threshold. He said, "This place was actually an insane asylum at one time, you know."

"Oh?" Penny gasped.

She froze, desperately wanting to turn away, desperately wanting to run from the place. She knew it had been a hospital of some sort, but she hadn't known *that* dark tidbit of important information. It not only explained the iron bars on all the windows but many other things as well. Apparently, her boss had forgotten to mention important facts when he interviewed her in his lush, downtown office.

She had only herself to blame, though. She had acted like the three monkeys—see no evil, hear no evil, speak no evil. Thinking only of the money to aid her in her flight, she had covered her eyes, ears, and mouth. She hadn't asked to see the place, hadn't really listened to what Mister Peabody had told her about the place, hadn't asked any questions about its background before accepting the job.

She guessed they both had something to hide.

Well, there was no turning back now. Reluctantly, she followed her boss across the threshold. They stood in a long, dark hallway. Cold air blew down it like the breaths of a thousand ghosts.

"We've tried to maintain the asylum theme throughout," Mister Peabody prattled on. "On the main floor, as patrons are escorted inside, the lobby is full of medical staff and mental patients being admitted or watching TV. Sometimes, these bizarre patients get up close and personal. Very fun stuff."

"Sounds awesome," Penny muttered, barely able to hide her sarcasm.

If Mister Peabody heard the sarcasm, he ignored it. "We then buzz them through the locked iron door and slam it closed behind them." He chuckled. "That always gives them a start."

"Sure it does."

Behind them, the iron door slammed shut.

Penny spun toward the sound, letting out a squeal.

Mister Peabody laughed. "See what I mean." He switched on the lights.

The hallway instantly turned red, as if Hell's fire awaited them at the other end.

Penny almost choked on her own spittle.

Mister Peabody chuckled again. "Red light bulbs," he said. "Great effect, huh?"

Penny swallowed hard. "Awesome," she mumbled. "Just awesome."

The macabre glow lit up old, cracked walls made of cinder blocks. Rusty, exposed water pipes zigzagged across and down a low cement ceiling from which rusty, metal light fixtures dangled. Padded cells with iron bars lined the walls on both sides of the hallway. Old cots without mattresses occupied the empty cells.

Mister Peabody turned. He began walking down the hallway. "Follow me."

Penny followed a step or two behind. Again, she thought, *This is the last place I should be...*

Their footsteps echoed throughout the hallway.

Mister Peabody continued, "During performances, actors playing mental patients occupy each cell. They reach through the bars at the patrons. They scream. That sort of thing."

"Fun stuff," Penny responded.

Apparently again missing her dripping sarcasm, Mister Peabody responded, "Exactly." Not skipping a beat, he continued, "In the basement, we have rooms where mad scientists conduct unsettling experiments on their patients. Electric shock treatment and the like, you know."

As they continued down the hallway, a faint but steady heartbeat began.

Penny stopped cold, listening intently. Her own heart felt as though it had stopped. Her breath choked her throat.

Mister Peabody stopped too, apparently realizing that Penny no longer followed. He turned around, a perplexed look on his face. "Miss Winters?" he called. "Is there something wrong?"

Penny didn't move or breathe. "Do you hear that?" she whispered.

The heartbeat stopped.

Mister Peabody cocked his head, listening. "I don't hear anything."

"It sounded like something beating."

"I think you're letting your imagination run wild. This place can do that to a person."

Penny could've sworn she heard the heartbeat, but her boss was surely right. Her imagination had taken control. She was hearing things not there. Even that realization, however, caused her heart to skip a beat and her hands to tremble. She squared her shoulders. With renewed determination, she gathered herself. "You're probably right," she relented.

Concern etched itself across Mister Peabody's face. "Shall we continue?"

In the red light, Penny couldn't help seeing Mister Peabody's face as demonic. She couldn't help feeling as though he were leading her toward eternal damnation. Still, she nodded her affirmation to continue.

The two started walking again, footsteps echoing.

"We'll take the elevator to the basement to look at the

torture rooms," Mister Peabody said.

Oh great, Penny thought, *torture rooms. Maybe this hallway does lead to Hell.*

Mister Peabody continued, "We also have a Cemetery Room down there. It's really quite a scary..."

Penny stopped again. She no longer listened to Mister Peabody's chatter.

The faint but steady heartbeat was back. This time joined by another heartbeat. Another...then another...and another. Each additional heartbeat grew louder until sounding like a hundred simultaneously beating hearts.

Penny covered her ears.

Mister Peabody stopped. He turned. "Miss Winters," he called, "are you coming?"

The beating hearts grew louder, her hands unable to muffle the sound. The ghosts' breath blew hard down the hallway, planting cold kisses on her face, rustling her long, brown hair. Everything around her began to ripple as if coming alive.

Soon, the ripples in the walls and ceiling began to take shape, began to form. Faces and hands pressed outward as if the surrounding walls and ceiling were made of nothing more than latex, with people stuck behind them, trying to push their way through. The faces wore expressions of pain and agony, like grotesque Halloween masks.

Penny clamped her eyes shut. She screamed.

"Miss Winters," Mister Peabody yelled.

The echo of his footsteps as he hurried back down the hallway mixed with the steady heartbeats. Suddenly, Penny felt someone grab her by the shoulders and gently shake her.

"Miss Winters."

It was Mister Peabody.

"You must get a hold of yourself."

Penny opened her eyes. Mister Peabody's red, frightened face loomed before her. The walls and ceiling had returned to normal. The cold gust of air was again just a soft current from the air conditioning vents. The heartbeats stopped. She frantically searched Mister Peabody's shaken expression for any indication that he had seen or heard anything out of the ordinary except her scream.

There was none.

"Maybe you being the manager of this place isn't such a good idea—"

"No," Penny quickly interrupted. "I'll be fine."

No, I won't. I won't be fine. This is the last place I should be.

Penny steadied herself, caught her breath. With false bravado, she said, "Just my imagination running wild, like you said." She smiled, hard and thin. "Really, I'm fine now."

Mister Peabody gave her a doubtful but resigned stare. "Very well," he said. "Shall we continue then?" He turned abruptly away, continuing down the hallway, his footsteps echoing.

Penny scanned the hallway. Everything remained normal. She willed it to be so. She wasn't about to let sanity slip through her fingers, not without a fight.

"Miss Winters?" Mister Peabody called. "Coming?"

Behind Penny, a human form pushed out from the ceiling. The face contorted with evil intent. Arms reached out to grab her but just missed as she raced off to join Mister Peabody for the rest of the tour.

Unaware.

Chapter Five

Three Weeks Later:

Tory Jackson, the young director of *Paranormal Scene Investigations*, had his doubts that the house he was investigating was truly haunted. His cynicism stemmed from the fact that on every job, he and his team always hoped to find an authentic haunted locale. They hoped to actually see or hear ghosts. They even managed to sell their ghost hunting exploits to a small cable television station where they enjoyed a somewhat large cult following; however, after countless televised investigations involving private homes, hotels, castles, hospitals, amusement parks, stores, cemeteries, and more, they had never been able to prove without a doubt that there was actual ghostly activity of any kind.

Anywhere.

There was usually either insufficient evidence to support the claim or these so-called haunted places proved to be the fanciful imaginings of inane people. Even worse, they sometimes proved to be outright hoaxes perpetrated by parties wanting to boost popularity of their establishments.

It's not that he didn't believe in spirits, ghosts, or demons. He did. He had his own inexplicable, supernatural event from his childhood that still haunted him to this day. The effects of that event were behind his decision not to go to college after graduating from Pasadena High School a couple of years ago. It was the effects of that event that was the driving force to use his trust fund to create PSI so that he could be in constant search of otherworldly activity.

Still, he remained skeptical throughout every investigation, including this one.

At least on this job he didn't suspect a hoax. He didn't doubt that Gloria Howe truly believed a spirit or demon plagued her home. What he hadn't ruled out was the possibility of the sixty-eight-year-old woman's overactive imagination. That's why they were there, though—to disprove or prove her claim. Also, if there was even the slightest indication of possible paranormal activity, it was their job to cleanse her home, rid her of the disturbance.

He took this responsibility seriously.

The PSI team chose to start the investigation in the basement, because according to the client, this was where most of the strange occurrences took place. The basement was dark, except for the white votive candles in clear glass holders already lit. Three were set on top of a small, round table and the rest interspersed throughout the room. A Sangean AM/FM radio had been converted into a ghost box for two-way spirit communication. That, and a small digital audio recorder were on the table, set within the circle of the three votive candles. Infrared motion detectors were set up about the room to pick up possible movement invisible to the naked eye but giving off an IR heat signature. Infrared video cameras were set up for video documentation. A full spectrum camera recorded still pictures at five-second intervals. The room was also equipped with electromagnetic field detectors, ambient air thermometers, vibration monitors, and three wireless microphones for additional voice recording. Snakes of gray cable covered the floor, wiring everything to computers, monitors, audio recorders, and a four-channel DVR in another room of the house that PSI dubbed Tech Central.

Tory and Mrs. Howe sat around the small, round table. Other members of the PSI team were also there. Occult Specialist Lizzie Goodwin, Reverend Gabriel Dent, their intern Isabel Gold, and Independent Consultant and Medium Tony Scout. The only two members of PSI missing were Tech Specialist Tom Chong—nicknamed Cheech—along with Team Documentarian Morgan Jones. Both of them were manning Tech Central.

Tory ran a hand through his cropped, blonde hair. He turned to Mrs. Howe, a steely gaze in his gray eyes. "It's almost 3:00 a.m.," he whispered. "Jesus died at 3:00 p.m., the exact opposite time. In the occult world, 3:00 a.m. is considered a mockery of his death. It's when paranormal activity is supposedly at its peak. Many paranormal investigators refer to this as *Dead Time*."

Mrs. Howe bit her lower lip and wrung her arthritic hands. She nodded nervously.

Tory continued, "As you know, Tony Scout is a medium who we occasionally call on to help with cases such as these."

Mrs. Howe turned her attention toward the medium.

Whereas Tory was just short of twenty, intense and brooding, Tony was forty something, with kind, blue eyes and a comforting smile. "You just relax, Gloria," Tony said, patting Mrs. Howe's shoulder. "I'm an old hand at this."

Mrs. Howe relaxed a bit. She gave Tony a slight smile, albeit the corners of that smile twitching nervously.

"Mrs. Howe, Tony is going to conduct a *séance* of sorts," Tory said, trying to command their client's attention again. "He's going to attempt to contact the spirit or demon that you say is haunting your home." He paused. "Do you understand?"

Mrs. Howe nodded. "I understand," she croaked.

Tory tried to smile but failed. He was not a people person. He knew that. Even in high school, he had been a loner, a geek with not many friends. He was certainly no better with old people than he was with his peers. He was no good at giving comfort, though somehow, he was pretty good at instilling confidence with his clients in his and his team's abilities.

Still, Mrs. Howe looked downright petrified.

"Gloria," Tony interjected, a sincere smile on his kindly face, "do we have your permission to proceed?"

Mrs. Howe again smiled that little, nervous smile at Tony. "Yes," she said, nodding.

A bit jealous of Tony's people skills, Tory grabbed a small two-way radio from in his shirt pocket. Into it he barked, "Cheech, are you and Morgan ready?"

Nothing but static answered.

Tory barked louder, "Cheech, take that Twinkie out of your mouth. Are you ready?"

Through the radio, as if around a mouthful of Twinkie as Tory had suggested, Cheech finally answered, "Did Pinocchio have wooden balls?"

Okay, who's supposed to be the mature one here? Tory thought.

He so wanted to punch his Tech Specialist in the nose right then and there. Cheech, though, was in another part of the house—physically impossible. Besides, it would've been as unprofessional as Cheech's response. Tory sighed. Looking and sounding professional was always important to him. It helped clients, and the team, accept him despite his age.

Calmly, Tory said, "We'll take that as a yes."

Putting the radio back in his pocket, Tory turned to Mrs.

Howe. He winced. "Sorry," he said. He turned to his medium. "It's time. Are you ready?"

Tony smiled. "Yes, sir," he responded, always professional, always respectful.

Looking around the table, Tory asked, "Everyone else ready?"

No one spoke. They only nodded in affirmation.

Tory turned on the Sangean AM/FM radio. The LCD display screen lit up. He set the radio to sweep down the AM band waves. White noise hummed in response.

"What's that for?" Mrs. Howe asked.

"We converted this radio into what we call a *ghost box*," Tory explained. "It creates raw audio and white noise to better help bring ghost voices through. It's called EVP or Electronic Voice Phenomena."

Mrs. Howe gasped. "You mean we could hear a ghost speak through the radio?"

Tory nodded. "Not only that, but with this model, a ghost can hear us as well," he said with some pride, even though it was Cheech who had modified the standard radio. "It's a two-way communication."

Mrs. Howe looked at Tony for comfort.

Tony smiled. "There's nothing to worry about. We hope to make contact with the ghost, so we can find out why it's here, what it wants. If we know what it wants, then maybe we can help it move on."

Mrs. Howe nodded. "I understand." She sat up straighter. "I'm not afraid."

"Good," Tory said. "We're also going to record everything that's said by us and, hopefully, the spirit with this recorder." He turned on the small digital recorder. "We set up a few wireless microphones around the room, too. Anything said will be picked up by those and recorded on audio equipment in Tech Central."

Mrs. Howe clasped her hands together, wringing her arthritic fingers. "Okay," she whispered, "I'm ready."

"Tony?" Tory said as way of giving the command to begin the *séance*.

Tony closed his eyes as if entering a trance. When he spoke, it was not to his associates or to Mrs. Howe, but to the supposed entity possessing the home. "We call upon the spirit or demon who haunts this house, who troubles this fine woman.

Come to us. Talk to us. Show yourself. Make yourself known."

The only response was the white noise of the ghost box as it swept down the AM stations.

"Speak to us," Tony commanded. "We're listening."

White noise answered.

Mrs. Howe gasped. She whispered, "I feel a coldness on my neck. I think it touched me."

"I feel it, too," Tony confirmed. "A chill. Deep in my bones. I'm not sure we should continue. I think we're dealing with a demonic presence. Pure evil."

Gabriel scoffed. "Wooden or not, at least Pinocchio *had* balls. Could we please get a medium with some?"

Tony shot Gabriel a look of disdain. "Talk like that from an ordained minister?"

Gabriel scoffed again. "I'm a minister, not a chicken-shit. A little demon's not going to make me drop my balls."

Isabel giggled.

"Isabel," Tory snarled. He might have to take this kind of unprofessional behavior from Cheech or from Gabe or even uncharacteristically from Tony, but not from his seventeen-year-old intern who had a tough-girl attitude, still thought looking Goth was chic, and who had a penchant for witch-craft. "That's enough." He looked around the table with his best steely gaze. In a more hushed tone, he said, "That's enough from all of you."

As always, Tory turned to Lizzie in his time of need. They'd been friends since sixth grade. Her devotion to him would never waiver. Besides, when it came to knowledge of the supernatural—whether historical, mythological, paranor-mal, demonic, or urban legend—she was like an encyclopedia. That's why she was the Occult Specialist. That and the fact that she'd always been a bit out there when it came to crystals, incense, tarot cards, and all that new age stuff.

"Lizzie, what do you feel or think?" Tory asked.

What *he* was thinking, what *he* was feeling, was too bad Lizzie was so mousy and nerdy looking in her thick, black glasses. Not his type at all. If she were just brainy *and* ath-letic, she'd be perfect. Still, she was definitely his girl when it came to everything but romance. Always would be, too.

Lizzie looked down at her hands. She shook her head. "I'm sorry. I don't feel anything." She paused thoughtfully, push-ing her sliding glasses back up the bridge of her nose. "But my crystals protect me against negative spirits and psychic energy."

Gabriel *humphed* and said, "Damn Pagan."

Tory shot Gabriel an annoyed look. He said, "I don't feel anything either, and I'm not carrying crystals like Lizzie." He paused. "Or a Saint Michael medal for protection either, like you."

Gabriel looked away, jaw clenched.

Tory continued, "We've had no proof of a spirit or of demonic possession. Yet." He turned to Tony. "Continue."

Gabriel *humphed* again.

Tony cleared his throat. "Demon or spirit plaguing this home, show yourself. Talk to us. Make yourself known. I command it."

Suddenly, every infrared motion detector began to chime at once.

Everyone jumped.

Mrs. Howe screamed.

Isabel giggled. "Awesome," she whispered.

Tony turned to Gabriel. "Did that drop your balls?"

Gabriel clutched the Saint Michael medal around his neck. Nervously, he scanned the dark basement, the dancing shadows. My balls are fine," he said, "thank you."

The chimes stopped. Again, only white noise filled the room.

"I still feel nothing," Lizzie said. "No noticeable change in temperature or anything. But again, I have—"

Cutting off Lizzie, Tory took out his two-way radio. Into it he barked, "Cheech, Morgan, anything?"

Chapter Six

The room picked out for Tech Central was well-lit. It was full of electronic equipment such as computers, monitors, and DVRs, as well as cables snaking across the floor.

Biting down on the Twinkie sticking out of his mouth, Cheech took a quick slug of Mountain Dew to wash it down as he checked his equipment for readings. He scratched at his unkempt beard, looked at Morgan, and shook his head.

Morgan picked up a two-way radio and spoke into it. "No change in the Electromagnetic Field. Nothing from the vibration monitors to indicate movement of any kind. Nothing on any of the monitors, video or full spectrum. No unusual sounds recorded here that we can tell, just the white noise from the ghost box and the motion detectors going off."

Cheech gulped down the last chunk of Twinkie. He chased it with a slug of Mountain Dew. He too picked up a two-way radio and spoke into it. "We'll clean up the sound recording with the Audacity Editor software then get back at you. If anything's there, we'll hear it. I'll bet my ponytail on it." He paused, looking at his partner with a smile. "Better yet, I'll bet Morgan's muscles on it."

Morgan grinned. He shook his head. "I can cut that ponytail of yours off," he said to Cheech. "How do you suppose taking my muscles away?" He pushed up the short sleeve to his T-shirt and flexed a muscle-bound arm at his partner.

Cheech grinned back. He held up a Twinkie. "About a hundred or so of these ought to do the trick, my friend."

Morgan laughed. He spoke into his radio. "No reason for those motion detectors to go off. No sign of movement or activity of any kind. Normal or paranormal. Out."

He put the radio down and nudged Cheech. "Hostess went out of business. How are you still getting those?"

Cheech shrugged. "Dude, eBay. Cost a small fortune, but I got enough to last more than a year."

"What then?"

"Cold turkey." Cheech shivered. "It'll be dark days, for sure."

Morgan grinned. "Hand me one."

Cheech did so. "That's one. Only ninety-nine more, big fella, and the muscles are gone."

Morgan took a bite. "Mmmm. I'm hooked now. You better hope your cache holds out."

Cheech shivered again. "Crap. Keep the muscles. The rest are mine."

Morgan swallowed. Grinning, he said, "Relax. I just read another company bought Hostess. Twinkies are back on the shelf."

Cheech sighed. "Dude, you scared the crap out of me."

Morgan shook his head. "Ghosts don't scare you, but not being able to get Twinkies does?"

"Priorities, dude. Priorities."

"Well, you wasted that small fortune, bro. Does that scare you?"

Cheech bit into a Twinkie. Around a mouthful, he said, "Money well spent."

Chapter Seven

Tory pocketed the radio.

"Proof enough for you?" Tony asked.

Gabriel shook his head. "No."

"Something set off those motion detectors."

"You might be way older—"

Tony cut Gabriel off. "And more handsome."

Even Tory had to grin at that. Tony was as homely as an old hound's butt. Whereas Gabriel, minister or not, was only about thirty and Hollywood handsome—tall and dark like Hugh Jackman.

Gabriel just sighed. "You might be a lot older," he continued, "but not smarter. I need absolute proof before I believe. I'm not just going to jump to conclusions because some motion detectors malfunctioned."

Tony started to respond, but Tory cut him off. "I agree with Gabe," he said. "We've encountered no undeniable proof of paranormal activity. I'm not convinced we have a true haunting here." Now Tory sighed. "But Dead Time is over." He turned off the ghost box and digital recorder. "Considering everything, I think it best to side with caution."

"What does that mean?" Mrs. Howe asked.

Tory looked at his client with what he hoped was a reassuring expression. He said, "A spiritual cleansing." He turned to Tony. "Are you up for it?"

Tony closed his eyes and nodded.

Tory turned his attention on Gabriel next.

Gabriel clutched his Saint Michael medal. He said, "Born ready."

Tory rolled his eyes. "Do we have your permission to proceed?" he asked Mrs. Howe.

Mrs. Howe straightened. Still wringing her arthritic hands, she said, "I want this thing out of my home."

"Awesome," Isabel whispered.

Chapter Eight

A depression or darkness haunted Cyrus Peabody. Call it what you would, but he couldn't ignore it any longer. He couldn't shake free of it. Even within the comfort of his spacious living room, sitting on and amongst the expensive furniture, surrounded by lush trappings, and with every lamp in the room brightly lit, he couldn't hide from it. It lived within him now. He could no more get away from it than he could run from his own shadow. He had searched the depression or darkness within him for answers but found none, either intellectually or emotionally. Now, he looked for answers outside himself. He needed help. He knew that much. Surprisingly enough, maybe a TV show could provide it.

He leaned forward in his wing-backed chair, gaze riveted to the television, as if it were simultaneously salvation and damnation.

On the screen, Tony Scout stood in the middle of a dimly lit bedroom. He sprinkled Holy Water in all four directions—north, south, east, and west. As he did so, he said, "I command you, demon, to leave this room. To leave this house. In the name of the Father, of the Son, and of the Holy Spirit."

The picture on the screen switched to the kitchen of the same house. Gabriel Dent stood in the middle of that room. He too sprinkled Holy Water north, south, east, and west. He said, "I command you, demon, to leave this room. To leave this house. In the name of the Father, of the Son, and of the Holy Spirit."

The television showed Lizzie Goodwin kneeling on the floor of the home's living room. On a coffee table was a bowl filled with Frankincense. She pushed her glasses back in place as she lit the incense. Smoke wafted upward. She said, "The elements of life—earth, wind, water, and fire—command you, demon, to leave this room. To leave this home. Never to return."

Tory Jackson's young but serious face filled the screen. "Although paranormal activity in the home of Gloria Howe was never confirmed," he announced, "the client reported that there has been no further unexplained, malicious activity in her home after the cleansing performed by our experts. Furthermore, she claims she's personally more relaxed and confident that she's in no further danger."

An outside shot of Gloria Howe's home replaced Tory's face on the television screen. Titles and credits began to roll over the shot of the house:

> *Paranormal Scene Investigations*
> *A Close Encounter Production*
> *Tory Jackson: Director*
> *Tom (Cheech) Chong: Tech Specialist*
> *Lizzie Goodwin: Occult Specialist*
> *Reverend Gabriel Dent: Cleansing Specialist*
> *Morgan Jones: Team Documentarian*
> *Isabel Gold: Trainee*
> *Special Guest: Medium, Tony Scout*

As the credits continued to roll, Tory's voice-over said, "If you or a loved one is experiencing paranormal activity in your home or business, contact Paranormal Scene Investigations at 1-800-555-6661. We're here to help."

Cyrus Peabody sighed, rubbing at his burning eyes. He still couldn't decide whether the program meant salvation or damnation; however, he was desperate. So, he resigned himself to do something he hadn't wanted to do, that just three weeks ago, he would've found preposterous to do. He truly didn't believe in ghosts or paranormal activity. Nevertheless, he climbed out of his wing-backed chair. With slumped shoulders, as if he carried the weight of the world on his back, he stumbled to the phone on a nearby table. With some reluctance, he punched in the phone number Tory Jackson recited on the TV. As he listened to the PSI theme song play on the other end of the phone, he felt like vomiting.

Chapter Nine

This night, the grounds of Shadow Brook Cemetery were an eerie mixture of life and death. Far off, an owl hooted. Night birds hiding in the treetops chirped. All around, cicadas spoke to one another. Tall, full trees, lush foliage, and blooming flowers surrounded headstones and monuments to the dead that poked out of a settled mist. Above, the sky was devoid of moon and stars.

The only beacon slicing through the deadly combination of dark and fog was the built-in LED light on Morgan's Sony XDCAM handheld video camera. He aimed that light and camera at Tory, who stood in the gloom without fear of the unknown or of the dead.

When Tory spoke, it was to the camera. "My team and I are at Shadow Brook Cemetery on the outskirts of LA. We're here at the request of the caretaker, James Brodie. He lives on the property in that house." Tory pointed to his right.

Morgan took the light and camera off Tory. He aimed them at the house.

Tory continued, "Mister Brodie has reported strange occurrences ever since he took over as caretaker after his father's death. The senior Mister Brodie had been the caretaker here for the past fifteen years but never indicated to his son anything about paranormal activity; however, as the current caretaker, the younger Mister Brodie says he has seen strange lights. He's heard bizarre noises in the graveyard at night. His investigations, however, have turned up no plausible explanations."

Morgan put the light and camera back on Tory.

"We're here," Tory continued, "to discover whether these lights, these noises, are the result of pranks by outsiders, an overactive imagination on the part of Mister Brodie, or actual paranormal activity."

Lizzie joined Tory in the shot.

"This is our Occult Specialist, Lizzie Goodwin," Tory said. He turned to Lizzie. "Have you found anything that might indicate there's an actual haunting going on here?"

Lizzie adjusted her glasses. She faced the camera. "Not yet. But—"

"Shhh." Tory cut Lizzie off. "Do you hear that?"

They both strained to hear over the night noises.

"Is that running water?" Tory asked.

"It could be," Lizzie responded. "It sounds—"

"Shhh." Tory cut her off again. "Listen. Where's that coming from?"

Again, they both strained to hear. The sound of water running definitely invaded the chatter of the cicadas and night birds.

Suddenly, Tory announced, "Follow me."

He took off at a steady jog, Lizzie and Morgan right behind. Morgan still held the camera up, shooting shaky video. Somehow, even he avoided tripping over headstones and monuments in the settled pall.

Running, with breathless excitement, Lizzie warned, "Be careful. This could be a water demon. Moving through the undergrowth. Trying to make it back to the pond on the other side of the grounds."

Tory pushed through foliage. He zigzagged around grave markers. Scoffing, he said, "We can only hope."

The sound of water, running and splattering, grew louder as Tory and Lizzie pushed past some overgrowth, into a clearing. Morgan followed close behind with his camera, still shooting footage. Once in the clearing, all three put on the brakes.

Lizzie let loose with a high-pitched squeal. Yanking off her glasses, she immediately turned, pushed past Morgan, and ran back the way she had come.

The LED light on Morgan's camera illuminated Cheech, who had his pants halfway down. He stood peeing at the base of a big oak tree.

Tory yelled, "Cut." He stood as straight and stiff as that old oak tree Cheech was peeing on, hands fisted at his sides, mumbling obscenities.

"Hey, ditch the light, dude," Cheech said. "You know I can't do it when someone's watching." He looked sheepishly over his shoulder, jerked sideways. "Now see what you've done," he cried. "I peed down my leg."

"Zip it," Tory ordered.

Morgan had stopped shooting footage but still aimed the

light at Cheech. He laughed. "Maybe you should save some of that for your probation officer."

Cheech finished and zipped up. Walking toward Tory and Morgan, he shook his leg like a cat with a wet paw. "I only give him my sister's pee."

Morgan laughed again. "Isn't she pregnant?"

"Yeah, I'm due in three months."

A buzzing noise suddenly rose above Cheech and Morgan's prattle, as well as the night noises.

"Shhh," Tory commanded. "Hear that? What is that?"

The steady buzz continued.

"Uh, it's your phone, bro," Cheech said with a grin. "It's vibrating."

"Might want to answer it," Morgan offered.

"Maybe it feels too good to stop," Cheech jabbed.

Tory stiffened even more. "Idiots. I'm surrounded by idiots."

Cheech turned to Morgan. "Can he talk to us that way?"

Morgan shrugged. "He pays the bills."

Ignoring the two, Tory reached into his jeans pocket, pulled out his cell phone, and looked at the screen. "Numbers restricted," he mumbled. Answering the call, he put the phone to his ear. He said, "PSI. Tory Jackson."

As Tory listened to the caller on the other end, Lizzie returned. All three investigators gathered around their leader.

"What can I do for you, Mister Peabody?" Tory said into the phone. As he listened, the group closed in around him, straining to hear.

"Fright House?" Tory asked, his mood brightening. "That's the Halloween attraction in the Bay Area that's supposed to be truly haunted, right?" He listened. The others gathered closer.

"Yeah, I heard about it," he said. "A little bit on the news, but mostly through contacts in the business." He paused before continuing, "Don't believe it, though." He fell quiet again, listening intently. He nodded as if the caller on the other end could actually see him.

"We could do that," he said. A grin spread across his face. "How much?" he asked, repeating Mister Peabody's question. He shrugged. "Money's not the important issue here."

"Speak for yourself," Cheech mumbled.

Tory waved at the Tech Specialist to be quiet. "We'll talk

money when we get there," he said. "Thank you, Mister Peabody. See you soon." He hung up and pocketed his cell. "Boys and girl, call in the others," he announced. "There's not much going on here. We'll do a quick cleansing. Call the job done."

"We're going to Fright House?" Cheech asked.

Tory nodded. "Yep, we're heading to the Bay Area in the morning."

"Cool," Lizzie said.

"Cool is right," Tory echoed. "This is the biggest job we've ever had." He paused before continuing, "Besides, there was something in the guy's voice. Even though he protested the rumors."

"What do you mean?" Lizzie asked.

Tory shrugged. "I'm not sure. Maybe it's because he protested those rumors a bit too much." He thought a moment. "Fright House just might end up being the real deal," he said, walking away.

Morgan mumbled, "Yeah, probably end up just pissin' in the dark again."

"Funny," Cheech replied. "Very funny."

Chapter Ten

Penny opened the iron door, hinges squealing. It was several hours before opening time. Fright House's first floor hallway stretched out before her. Long, dark, and vacant. The silence was deafening. She took a deep breath to steady her nerves as she crossed the threshold. Flipping the light switch, the hallway lit up in that horrid red that scared the willies out of her.

Behind her, the iron door clanked shut.

Startled, she gasped. "Nothing here can hurt me," she whispered the mantra she had started to recite to herself more than three weeks ago—the same mantra she had used in the distant past. Like before, it helped calm her frayed nerves. A bit. "Nothing can hurt me. Nothing here can hurt me."

Even as she said those calming words, her mind spun out of control, imagining all sorts of horrible dangers and pitfalls.

This is the last place I should be, considering everything. The last place...

"Nothing here can hurt me," she continued the mantra, starting down the hallway. "Nothing can hurt me." The echo of her footsteps answered her, along with her thoughts.

This is the last place I should be...

A coldness hatched within her.

"Nothing here can hurt me."

...considering everything, this is the last place I should be...

She continued her lonely trek down the crimson hallway.

"Nothing can hurt me."

The sound of a bell chiming not only stopped her mantra but also halted her cold in her tracks. The elevator light at the opposite end of the hallway blinked on, and the doors swished open.

Her breath caught in her throat. Shivers, like hundreds of snakes, slithered up and down her spine, across her scalp.

Someone—a man, shrouded in shadows, carrying *something*—stepped into the hallway. The elevator doors swished closed behind.

A heart somewhere began to pound. Penny looked around,

her first thought that the place was again coming to life. She then realized the beating heart was her own. She put her hand on her breast as if that could quell the pounding.

Taking a breath, she called, "Hello?"

Her voice echoed down the hallway.

"Who's there?"

The man hefted the object in his hand. The silhouette of the thing looked like a large, bizarre handgun.

"Who are you?" Penny cried.

The high-pitched screech of a motorized drill answered.

Penny cried, "Who are you?"

"Death," the man bellowed, running toward her, boots echoing, drill screeching.

Screaming, Penny turned. She ran back the way she had come. Back toward the iron door. Back toward the safety of the lobby.

The man was gaining. His footsteps came faster. Louder.

The iron door loomed just up ahead.

Penny fell.

She flew through the air face first, landing with a thud on the floor. Hurting, lying on her stomach, she slithered down the hallway like those imaginary snakes had done on her back, clawing her way to safety.

It wasn't to be.

A hand grabbed her ankle. She came to an abrupt stop. As the hand released her, she tried to squirm away. The hand quickly grabbed her by the shoulder and flipped her over, onto her back.

A man dressed in a bloodstained surgical gown stood over her. A surgical mask covered half his face. He held up the screeching drill, pointing it downward.

Penny screamed. Her hands reflexively went up in a useless, defensive posture.

The drill suddenly cut off. The man yanked down his surgical mask. "Miss Winters? You okay?"

Penny took down her hands. She stared up at the guy she had just hired days before. Slowly, pure terror turned to volcanic anger. "Jake," she yelled, "you asshole." She kicked Jake in the leg.

Jake cried out in pain. He dropped the drill. It clunked to the floor, just missing Penny. Groaning, Jake hopped around on one foot.

Penny struggled to her feet. "What were you thinking?" She punched Jake in the arm.

Jake hopped on one leg, rubbing his arm. "Stop beating on me," he pleaded. "Jeez, I'm sorry. I was just practicing. Getting ready for tonight, ya know."

Penny punched the guy again. "Well, you scared ten years off my life, you jerk. Besides that, I could've been really hurt."

Jake stopped hopping but continued rubbing his arm. He gave Penny a sheepish look. "I'm hecka sorry. Really. Are you okay?"

Penny shot Jake a disgusted look as she massaged her own sore muscles. She sighed, conceding, "I'll be fine, I guess. But you aren't allowed in here when we're closed. You know that."

The look on Jake's face remained sheepish, apologetic.

Penny took a deep, calming breath. Happy that it wasn't all in her mind, she shook her head and laughed in spite of herself. She said, "Jake, if that drill was real, I'd make Swiss cheese out of you right now."

A devilish grin replaced the sheepish, apologetic look on Jake's face. "You have to admit, though," he said, "I'm hecka good."

Penny laughed again. "Yeah...as much as I hate to, I have to admit that you're hecka good."

Jake's grin widened. He asked, "Say, Miss Winters, where were you heading, anyway?"

Penny shook her head. She wondered how Jake would feel about calling her *Miss Winters* if he knew she was three years younger than him. She said, "Honestly, I can't remember." She punched Jake's arm again. "Thanks a lot."

"Ouch," Jake rubbed his arm. "You gotta stop doing that."

Penny shook a finger at the guy. "You deserve it," she scolded. With a shrug of relief, she turned away, walking back the way she had come. "See you tonight," she called.

Chapter Eleven

Jake watched Miss Winters leave. When he heard the iron door slam shut, he grinned from ear to ear. His supervisor had been hecka mad, but it was worth every kick, every punch he received from her in return.

To himself, he said, "I love this job."

Something behind yanked Jake off his feet. He slammed to the floor, face hitting with a sickening thud. Groaning, he raised his head. Blood oozed from his forehead. He spat blood from his mouth. "What's going on?" he mumbled. He pushed up onto his knees and looked behind him.

Nothing was there.

"Hello," he called, voice echoing. "Who's there?"

He struggled to his feet. He wiped blood out of his eyes and spat more onto the floor. On wobbly legs, he stared down the red-glowing hallway.

A cold breeze slapped him in the face. A heart pounded. Everything around him began to ripple, like the air above distant blacktop on a hot summer day.

Jake cried out. He turned, limping as fast as he could toward the iron door Miss Winters had gone through just moments before. That's when cold, invisible hands grabbed him from behind. Arms flailing, hands reaching for something to grab onto, legs kicking helplessly, he was pulled down the hallway, unable to stop whatever was taking him.

Soon, he and his scream both disappeared.

Chapter Twelve

Tory startled awake. He sat up and rubbed his eyes. He gasped. Someone was in the room with him. Soon, his eyes adjusted to the dark. It was only his mom. She sat at the foot of his bed, watching him.

"Mom?"

Tory's voice sounded small. As small as he looked.

"Mom?"

His mom watched him. She smiled. "Be a good boy, Tory," she whispered. "Always make me proud."

Before Tory could respond, the door to his bedroom opened. The light from the hallway washed over the room. Tory's dad was framed in the doorway.

His mom looked over her shoulder at his dad, then back at him. She smiled before whispering, "I love you."

* * * *

Tory startled awake. He sat in the side seat at the front of the PSI bus. Gabriel drove. Lizzie sat in the side seat behind Gabriel, across the aisle from and facing Tory. She quickly looked away when he woke, as if caught watching him sleep. She sat sideways, staring out the window behind her at the passing scenery.

Tory blinked. He rubbed his eyes as he had in the dream. Looking around the bus, he tried to regain focus, tried to shake the cobwebs from his mind.

Cheech, Isabel, and Morgan sat at the back of the bus, huddled together around a laptop, talking and eating. Between the two groups, loose clothing, luggage, and large equipment cases filled the aisle and seats. Everything looked the same as always when they traveled to a haunted locale in the old, converted school bus.

Familiar, Tory thought. *Eerily familiar. A déjà vu moment.*

He tried to shake the feeling off but couldn't rid himself of it. He always felt this way after dreaming of his childhood, of his mom. A dull ache started in his head, throbbed at his temples. He hated dreaming of his mom. He closed his eyes and massaged his temples. He dreamt of her often.

"You okay, kid?" Gabriel asked.

Tory opened his eyes and stopped the self-massage. He sat up straight, blinked, and refocused. The *déjà vu* moment passed, but the headache remained.

Lizzie glanced at him before looking away.

"Yeah, fine," Tory lied.

He hated being called *kid*. Okay, Gabriel was about ten years older. Still...

"What about you, old man?" Tory asked. "How are you? Getting tired? Nodding off? Want me to take over?"

Gabriel shook his head. "Me and the Lord are wide awake," he said.

Tory grimaced. "Well, if you need a break, let *me* take over. The Lord can't drive."

Gabriel grinned. "Sure, you don't mind calling on the Lord for a cleansing ceremony, but you don't want to let the *Big Guy* drive. Hypocrisy runs deep."

"I'm no hypocrite," Tory insisted. "Me and the Lord are fine."

Gabriel shrugged. "So says you."

Tory ignored the knock. Instead, he checked out the group at the back of the bus.

Noticing, Gabriel checked for himself in the rearview mirror. "What do you suppose they're up to?" he asked.

Tory studied the three in the back, still huddled around a laptop, talking, laughing, and snacking on junk food. "Hopefully something more productive than playing *Ghost Tales* or even worse, *Angry Birds*." He turned his attention to Lizzie. "Why aren't you back there with the party?"

Lizzie shrugged as way of an answer.

Gabriel said, "Pagan girl has other things on her mind." He laughed. He then sang, "The power of love is a curious thing. Make one *girl* weep, make another *girl* sing."

Lizzie blushed behind her thick, black glasses. Turning back to the window, she stared out it.

Tory sighed. "Stop with the '80s music already."

Gabriel frowned. "Hey, I grew up on Huey Lewis. My mom loved them."

Tory glanced at Lizzie. "Pick another song then, old man. Or at least get the lyrics right."

Gabriel smirked. "I changed them to fit the moment."

Tory rolled his eyes. "You're not only old, but sometimes, you can really be a butt-face."

Gabriel laughed. "No, you got me mixed up with Tony."

That made Tory laugh. "Okay, then just a butt."

"The way I see it," Gabriel said, "I'm just doing the Lord's work." He chuckled before singing, "More than a feeling. That's the power of love."

Now, Tory felt the heat of embarrassment rush into *his* face. "Gabe." He shook his head.

Gabriel stopped. His grin spread from ear to ear.

Lizzie ignored it all, gaze glued to the scenery outside the window.

After a long, awkward silence, Gabriel got serious. He said, "Be honest, kid. Why do you think this Fright House gig might be the real deal?"

Tory stiffened. He hated it when any member of his team, especially Gabriel, questioned his decisions, leadership, or authority. No matter his age, he should be the undisputed leader. Besides, it was his money that paid the bills. "Why shouldn't I?" he snapped, furrowing his brow. "No reason to think otherwise, is there?"

Gabriel shrugged. "Guess not," he said.

"Actually, I don't truly know what to think about this job," Tory admitted after a while. He hated explaining himself but tried desperately to shake off that defensive nature. "Just something in the guy's voice, is all." He gathered his thoughts. Shrugged. "It's probably a scam. Peabody probably just wants the publicity, so he's concocted this whole haunted business."

"Why take the job, then?" Lizzie asked, her gaze suddenly riveted on Tory.

Gabriel's jaw dropped. "Trouble in paradise," he mumbled.

Lizzie ignored him. Her sights were set on Tory. "Aren't we just playing into his hand? I don't like helping con artists. You shouldn't, either."

"Sorry, Tory," Gabriel chimed in. "I have to agree with Pagan girl on this one."

Tory tensed at Lizzie and Gabriel questioning his integrity. Why were these two suddenly ganging up on him? Especially Lizzie. She so seldom, if ever, did. Taking a deep breath, he counted to ten. Rather than getting defensive, he put his hands up in a placating posture. "I don't," he pleaded his case.

"I do like exposing them, though."

Lizzie pushed her glasses up. She breathed easier. A thin smile of satisfaction spread across her face.

Tory grinned back. They were *simpatico,* again. Suddenly, his headache was gone, as well.

Gabriel chuckled at the two. He sang, "And that's the power of love."

Simultaneously, Tory and Lizzie said, "Shut up, you butt."

Gabriel shook his head. "The Lord works in mysterious ways," he mumbled.

Chapter Thirteen

At the back of the bus, Cheech stared intently at the laptop's screen. He researched the history of Fright House while systematically munching on potato chips and drinking Mountain Dew.

Morgan peered over his friend's shoulder, eyeing the screen, desperately trying to ignore Isabel's unwanted advances.

"I like you, Morg," Isabel prattled. "You have the darkest eyes." Cocking her head, she suddenly asked, "You don't mind if I call you Morg, do you? It has such a ring of death to it." She giggled.

Morgan didn't answer, didn't know how to answer. He wasn't at all interested in the crazy chick. Sure, she was cute under all that Goth makeup, but again, there was all that Goth makeup. Besides, she was too young, underage to boot. He was twenty-five. That made her jailbait, put him at risk of doing jail time. No way was that going to happen. Even if Isabel were eighteen, there was the fact that she was crazy, into witchcraft, into death.

Morgan eyed Isabel. He liked the paranormal and all, studying it, filming it. He was into working out, though, into life, into living. He wasn't at all into Goth, witchcraft, or death. No, Isabel wasn't his type at all, no matter how cute.

Isabel reached over. She plucked a few loose hairs from Morgan's shirt. "You're shedding, Morg," she said, discreetly tucking the hairs into a pocket of her black jeans.

Morgan ran a nervous hand through his thick, dark hair. Other than that, he didn't know what to do or say. He didn't like the attention.

Cheech swallowed a mouthful of chips and chased it with soda. Never taking his eyes off the computer screen, he asked Isabel, "What do you see in this muscle-bound stiff, girl?" He didn't wait for an answer. "I mean, seventeen or not, you got me if you want."

Isabel rolled her eyes. "Better that you just keep jerkin' solo, geek boy. You couldn't handle me."

For the first time, Cheech looked away from the laptop, right at Isabel. "I'm in my prime, only a couple of years older than my young, muscle-bound friend here. Just give me a chance, witchy woman."

Isabel gave the Tech Specialist a hard stare. "Be careful," she warned. "Don't ask for the thunder if you can't handle the clap."

Isabel, Cheech, and Morgan stared in silence at one another. Seconds later, all three cracked up.

"Oh my God," Isabel squealed, "I can't believe I just said that."

Cheech answered, "You can keep the thunder and the clap, girl. At least my hand's clean."

"Is it," Morgan deadpanned. "Is it really?"

They all three cracked up again.

Joking and laughing, Morgan breathed a sigh of relief. He was free of the crazy chick's unwanted attention, even if only briefly.

"Shhh." Cheech suddenly silenced them. "Tory's staring at us."

Morgan and Isabel both stifled their laughs.

"Probably thinks we're playing *Angry Birds* or something," Cheech whispered.

Morgan shook his head. "*He's* been one angry bird lately."

"Yeah," Cheech agreed. "He's the one in need of some thunder and clap."

"Lizzie will have to handle that little chore," Isabel said.

All three choked back more hysterical laughing.

"Settle down," Morgan croaked. "We don't want to piss Tory off. The kid pays our salaries." He shrugged. "Besides, I like the guy. Angry bird or not, he's cool."

"I agree on both counts, bro," Cheech said. "So, back to work."

"Ah," Isabel complained, "we were just starting to have fun."

Cheech again concentrated on the computer screen. He also went back to munching on potato chips and drinking soda.

Uneasy silence ensued, with Isabel's lovelorn gaze returning to Morgan.

Not able to take it anymore, Morgan turned his attention to Cheech. He asked, "What do you think of this Fright House gig? It's a scam, right? Pure and simple."

Cheech took a drink of Dew and looked up. He absent-mindedly scratched his beard and eyed his friend. "I'll admit it sounds crazy," he said, "but after reading some of this historical stuff on the place, I'm not so sure it's a scam."

Isabel's eyes lit up. Like a little girl, she clapped her hands together. She pleaded, "Ooo, read some of it to us. *Please*."

"Yeah, read some of it," Morgan agreed, delighted that the crazy chick's attention was on something other than him.

Cheech consented. "Okay, dig this." Scratching at his beard, he stopped and looked expectantly at his two cohorts, a mischievous look on his face.

Morgan rolled his eyes. "Get on with it," he demanded. Using his hand to simulate scissors, he added, "Or in the middle of the night, the ponytail comes off. Accidentally, of course."

"Okay, okay. Never touch the ponytail," Cheech warned. He lowered his voice, as if he were telling a ghost story around a campfire at night. "Before Fright House became a Halloween attraction," he continued, "it was Ludlum Insane Asylum."

Isabel whispered, "Awesome."

"Awesome is right," Cheech agreed.

"You two are sick," Morgan said.

Cheech ignored his friend. "I've been on the Internet reading old newspaper clippings," he continued. "Doctor Malcolm Ludlum opened the asylum in 1918. At the height of its success, it had forty-six buildings, covering more than 671,000 square feet, on eighty-one acres of land, and housed over 1,000 mentally ill patients. Apparently, back then, the laws weren't as stringent on what constituted as mental illness, either. Families dumped unwanted members there. You know, like aging grandparents and parents, people with Alzheimer's or dementia, as well as children with Down syndrome, autism, developmental delays, and mental retardation."

Morgan sighed. He whispered, "Out of sight, out of mind, right?"

"Right," Cheech agreed.

Morgan thought of his brother Shaun. Shaun had Down syndrome. He died at the age of eight, after running out in front of traffic and being hit by a pickup truck. Morgan's hands fisted, his body tensed. The memory of it haunted him to this day, not only because he had lost a brother, but also because *he* was supposed to be looking after Shaun when the accident occurred.

Grief and guilt proved a deadly combination.

"That's not the half of it," Cheech continued. "Besides discarded family members and true patients with mental illness at Ludlum's, there was the criminally insane. We're talking the dredges of society—pedophiles, rapists, sociopaths, murderers. Real bad people. Dumped there by the courts. Forgotten."

Morgan's entire body went taut. He didn't want to hear anymore. The haunting images of the innocent victims being preyed upon every day in that asylum replaced the memory of Shaun's accident.

Cheech wouldn't relent. "It turns out, Ludlum himself and his staff were far worse than any of the patients."

The haunting images paused. Still, Morgan's muscles didn't relax. "What do you mean?" he asked, not sure he wanted to know the answer.

"Here, let me read it to you," Cheech answered. He scrolled down the screen. "Here it is. 'The place had a long, sordid history of patient abuse and dark, unorthodox experimentation into mental illness.' What do you think of that?"

"I don't know what to think," Morgan mumbled, his mind again haunted by Fright House's past.

"Cool stuff," Isabel whispered.

Morgan eyed Isabel with new wariness. She really was crazy. How could she think any of this was actually *cool*?

Cheech looked at the laptop screen again. "Apparently, they did everything from electric shock treatments, experimental drug testing, lobotomies, brain transplants, head transplants, live autopsies, and everything in between."

Isabel giggled. "That's freakish."

Freakish is right, Morgan thought. He shook his head in disbelief. "How could they get away with it?"

"Ludlum had free reign," Cheech said. He took a drink of soda. "Families seldom, if ever, visited. Remember, out of sight, out of mind. No one cared about the criminally insane. They were off the streets, best forgotten. Besides, there was no governing, independent body to oversee the place. Ludlum was actually much respected. In some corners, he was even considered a genius. No one had the guts or the knowledge to go up against him. It wasn't until the 1960s, long after Ludlum was dead, that people started questioning the asylum's methods, looking into its practices. The governor of California appointed an independent task force to investigate. The place finally shutdown in 1989. After that, it sat vacant for years. Acreage sold off, out buildings demolished. Most of it was redeveloped. All that was left was the main hospital on about twenty acres that's now Fright House. Get this, there were a lot of patients, even some staff members unaccounted for. Records destroyed. Graves unmarked."

Isabel giggled. Hardly able to contain a display of excitement, she squealed, "This is so awesome."

Awesome wasn't the word that came to mind for Morgan. He believed the implications of this newfound information possibly disastrous. "That's a lot of pissed off ghosts," he mumbled.

Cheech nodded. "You said it, brother."

Morgan stood on wobbly legs. "Tory's gotta hear this."

Chapter Fourteen

The second-story office Mister Peabody used at Fright House was well-lit with overhead fluorescent lights. It was also spartan in its decor, with just the essentials. No pictures hung on the gray walls. The brown carpet was threadbare, stained. There were metal file cabinets and a printer/fax/photocopy machine. The only furniture was a metal desk and an old, upholstered chair on rollers. A computer rested on the desktop, along with a phone and a desk lamp. Comfort was obviously not a consideration.

The owner was not in his office.

Instead, Penny sat at Mister Peabody's desk. Even if the room had been lavishly decorated, she wouldn't have felt at all comfortable. The air was frigid. She could see her breath. It was the sight of the little girl in pigtails, however, sitting on the floor and playing Jacks that froze Penny to the chair. She saw the little girl, plain as day. The bounce of the rubber ball, the jingle of the metal jacks both sounded real enough, too. The girl couldn't be real, though. It was the same little girl from the nightmare just a few weeks ago. An imaginary character from a dream couldn't truly be there in the room now. No, she knew in her heart of hearts that the entire scene before her, right down to the chilly air, was just an elaborate delusion, a trick of the mind.

Penny's shallow breath sent out frosty plumes as she watched the girl play. Self-doubt plagued her tortured thoughts. Terror of the unknown gripped her, holding her hostage behind the desk.

"Nothing here can hurt me," Penny muttered. "Nothing can hurt me."

Even as she said those words, she no longer was sure she believed them. This wasn't pretend, as it had turned out to be with Jake earlier that day. This time, sanity truly seemed to slip away.

This is the last place I should be, considering everything, the last place...

Physically, she could run from her past. In fact, she had. Deep in her heart, though, she had always known she'd have to someday confront that past. In running away, she had tried to ignore it, pretended it hadn't happened, behaved as if she had always been normal, even convinced herself she *was* normal. Normalcy itself had apparently been nothing more than an illusion, however, induced by therapy, drugs, and hypnosis.

The little girl giggled. The rubber ball bounced. The jacks jingled.

...considering everything, this is the last place I should be...

Horror-stricken by not only the vision before her but also by the dangerous implications of the foreseeable future and just how fragile her mind still really was, she was helpless in stopping her thoughts from drifting back to when she was thirteen.

Back to when the hallucinations had first begun.

* * * *

Penny hurried into school, late as usual. The bell for first class was already ringing. Sally, Meg, and Tilly waited impatiently in the hallway while other students rushed to their classrooms all around them.

Catching sight of Penny, Tilly cried, "Hurry up, Pen. You're going to make us late."

"Again," Sally added.

Meg shook her head. "She may always be late," she said, "but like a bad Penny, you can't get rid of her."

The three girls waiting for Penny giggled at the familiar joke.

Penny caught sight of her friends. She stopped cold. Someone was with them today. An old woman stood next to Tilly, hovering over the girl. Who could the woman be?

"Come on, Pen," Tilly yelled.

"We haven't got all day," Sally added.

"Return, bad Penny, return," Meg said with a giggle.

Penny approached the three girls and the old woman with inexplicable apprehension. As she got closer, she finally recognized the old woman. It was Tilly's grandmother. Why would Tilly's grandmother come to school?

"What's with you?" Tilly asked.

"Looks like she's seen a ghost," Sally commented.

"Even worse, Mister Wood," Meg said, looking over her shoulder for their teacher.

Ignoring her friends, Penny instead gazed intently at Tilly's grandmother. She didn't understand why the girls ignored the old woman standing next to them.

Penny said, "Hello, Mrs. Gnome. How are you?"

Tilly's grandmother didn't answer.

Sally and Meg looked at Penny as if she'd grown donkey ears and a tail.

Tilly's brow furrowed. Her face grew red.

None of the girls even turned in the direction of Penny's gaze.

"What did you say?" Tilly demanded.

Penny faced her friend. Innocence clouded her vision of Tilly's simmering anger. "Tilly, why did your grandmother come to school with you?" she asked.

Sally and Meg gasped in unison.

Tilly's face grew as red as blood. Her eyes narrowed. Her jaw clenched.

Penny's eyes widened. "What's wrong?" She looked from Tilly to Tilly's grandmother and back again. "What's wrong?"

"That's just mean," Sally said.

"The meanest thing ever," Meg agreed.

Penny looked from one friend to another. Innocence, along with confusion, still clouded her vision, making her incapable of really seeing how upset Sally and Meg were, how angry Tilly was becoming.

"I don't understand," Penny insisted. She turned to Tilly's grandmother. "Mrs. Gnome?"

"You're either really mean," Tilly hissed, "or you're some kind of *freak*." Her hands fisted at her sides.

"What?" Penny asked.

"Mean," Sally confirmed.

"Freak," Meg insisted.

Penny's entire world was spinning out of control. "What?"

That's when she remembered. How could she have forgotten? Tilly's grandmother had died over the summer. Wait a minute. If Mrs. Gnome was dead, how could she be standing next to Tilly in the hallway?

Bewildered and scared, Penny hadn't even seen Tilly swing. The punch landed squarely on her eye. Her butt landed squarely on the floor.

Tilly loomed above, face contorted into something grotesque. "You're not my friend anymore, *freak*," she hissed, shaking a fist.

Whimpering, Penny sat on the floor. She held a hand over her hurt eye and, with the other, watched through tears as her friends marched away down the hallway.

"Freak," Sally and Meg yelled back at her as they left.

Mrs. Gnome hovered around a moment longer, concern etched on her ghostly face. She too finally turned away, following her granddaughter to class.

After climbing to her feet, Penny ran crying down the hallway, out the doors, away from school. She spent the day wandering the streets, hanging out at the park, afraid to go back to school, afraid to go home.

By four in the afternoon, she had to go home. When she got there, her mother was waiting. The school had called. Her mother acted more scared than angry and didn't punish her. Instead, her mother made an appointment to see their family doctor. That appointment led to the doctor sending her to a therapist. After countless therapy sessions, plus more inexplicable occurrences such as the one with Tilly's grandmother, she went to Emerson Hospital where she spent more than two years in lock down. There, she received intense therapy and countless drugs.

* * * *

Penny breathed hard. Plumes of frosty breath blew out then dissipated before her. She was still frozen, unable to pull her gaze away from the little girl who sat on the floor, playing Jacks.

This is the last place I should be, considering everything, the last place...

"Nothing here can hurt me," Penny muttered. "It's all in my head. Just as Doctor Rosenthal said. Nothing can hurt me."

It was Doctor Evan Rosenthal's arrival at Emerson and his taking over of her case that turned the tide. He was the one who finally convinced her that these *ghosts* were only in her head. Imaginings, he called them, explaining that they had to retrain her mind. After taking her off all drugs, he began hypnosis therapy to do just that. After just one year, her mind was retrained. She was finally free of further hallucinations. She was finally free of Emerson Hospital too, for she was deemed cured and released.

"Nothing can hurt me," Penny continued the mantra.

Neither her parents, her teachers, nor her classmates ever again truly accepted her, though. They all still thought of her as a *freak*. She heard the late-night, tearful conversations between her parents. They were actually afraid she might hurt her little sister. She read the mean, spiteful postings of former friends on Facebook and Twitter. Her classmates cyberbullied her with threatening text messages, too. Her teachers were no better. They acted as if she might go crazy in the classroom at any given moment.

After several months of being treated like a *freak*, she couldn't take it anymore. That's when she decided to run away, change her name, escape her past, make a new life. She stole her dad's ATM card, cashed out two separate transactions of three hundred dollars each, threw the card away, and hit the road, taking a Greyhound from So. Cal to the Bay Area.

"Nothing here can hurt me."

She had truly believed she was cured of her hallucinations, as Doctor Rosenthal had stated. She had forgotten all about her past, so-called *ghostly* experiences. Instead, she concentrated on making her way in the world. That and the physical—food, a place to live, a job. Finally, everything in her life seemed truly to return to normal.

Until now.

"Nothing here can hurt me."

The little girl giggled. The rubber ball bounced. The jacks jingled.

This is the last place I should be, considering everything, the last place...

Until coming to Fright House. Here, the illusion of normalcy hypnosis had temporarily offered completely shattered.

The little girl stopped playing Jacks. Without moving her body, her head turned on her neck as if detached.

Penny went quiet. She gasped, her hand covering her mouth.

This is the last place I should be, considering everything, the last place...

A macabre grin spread across the little girl's face. "We're so glad you're here," she said in her little girl voice. "We've been waiting for you." Her voice deepened. "You must stay," she said, voice now definitely masculine. "Forever," she boomed demonically.

Penny screamed and jumped to her feet. Terror of the unknown no longer froze her, but instead, like electric shock, jolted her into action. She ran from the room as she had run away from school so many years ago, as she had run away from home just four short months ago. She didn't stop running until she was in the parking lot.

Free of Fright House.

Chapter Fifteen

Fright House loomed up ahead. Searchlights shot rotating beams of light into the night sky. Eerie, yellow lights twinkled like demented fireflies all around the parking lot, all along the silhouette of the large, institutional building. On the front of the building, the Fright House sign with its maniacal, screaming faces was a mass of blinking and rotating lights, as well. People ran about the parking lot and grounds. Yells, screams, and laughter, along with bizarre sounds, echoed into the night. A long line of customers stretched from the ticket booths into the parking lot. A few security guards with flashlights directed traffic. They tried to control the crowd, but pandemonium reigned. The Halloween attraction was in full carnival mode.

The yellow PSI bus found itself stuck in a long line of traffic that snaked its way into the jam-packed parking lot. After what felt like hours to the passengers within, the bus finally pulled into a spot and parked.

The front and back doors of the bus clanked open. Tory, Gabriel, and Lizzie piled out the front. Isabel, Morgan, and Cheech stumbled out the back. The six ghost hunters met at the middle of the bus, in front of where it once read *Pasadena School District,* but now read *Paranormal Scene Investigations* in black paint.

Everyone gathered around Tory, but their attention was on Fright House itself and their surroundings.

"Awesome," Isabel squealed.

"Holy crap. This place is crazy," Cheech announced.

Tory couldn't agree more. For an instant, he wondered what kind of circus, what kind of insanity, he had gotten them all into. Was it worth it, coming here? He had to remind himself that the haunting of Fright House could be for real, that finally they might actually find undeniable proof of paranormal activity. He felt especially positive that this one-time insane asylum could be a true haunted locale after what Cheech had found out on the Internet about the place, its history, and Doctor Malcolm Ludlum.

He wouldn't admit that to his team, though. Instead, to them, he said, "Forget everything Cheech told us about this place. We don't want the history of this place or Doctor Ludlum's biography to cloud our judgment. We need to go into this investigation with unbiased perceptions."

"Yeah," Cheech said, "we don't want to see spooks behind every corner, within every shadow."

"Or do we?" Morgan deadpanned.

Tory sighed. "What we don't want," he said, "is to see spooks that aren't there." He looked at each member of his team. "We don't want our imaginations running wild."

"Agreed," Gabriel said. "We should treat this investigation like every other."

Still, they couldn't help being affected by the pandemonium all around them. They all looked as if they were in shock.

"Gabe's right," Tory said. "We treat this just like all our other investigations." He wasn't getting through. No one paid him any mind. "As always, bear in mind," he continued, "'that when we have eliminated the impossible, whatever remains, however improbable, must be true.'"

"Uh-oh," Morgan muttered. "We're in trouble when the kid starts quoting Sherlock Holmes."

Cheech scoffed. "You said it, bro."

Tory tensed at being called *kid*. Still, he let it go.

Gabriel cleared his throat. "Tory, where are we meeting Peabody?"

"We're not meeting Peabody," Tory answered. Now he'd show them who was boss. Kid, huh. "Not tonight," he continued.

Lizzie turned on Tory. "What?" she asked. "Why not?"

"Yeah, what gives, kid—" Cheech began. After turning his attention on Tory, he apparently saw the look of annoyance. He stopped and stuttered, "Uh, I mean, what gives, *boss man*?"

Tory sighed. He wondered if he'd ever get the respect or approval he knew he truly deserved, despite his age. Rather than get mad at Cheech, he took control of the situation, like any great leader would. He said, "Calm down, everyone. Tonight, we're just paying customers like everyone else. I want us to see Fright House for ourselves, as a Halloween attraction. With no one looking over our shoulders. Before we talk to Peabody." He grinned, adding, "Tonight, we just have fun."

"Awesome," Isabel said.

Cheech shrugged. "We could use some fun." He turned to Gabriel. "Right, preacher man?"

Gabriel raised his hands in a defensive posture. "Me and the Lord are not against fun," he said. "If it's fun you want, fun you'll get."

"Just a minute," Morgan said. He scrambled back onto the bus. He returned with a Sony Digital HandyCam and a hand-held dual infrared-ambient air thermometer that looked like a small pistol tucked in his waistband. "Can't have fun without some toys."

Tory's grin grew wider. "Good thinking. We'll get some exterior shots, do an opening in front of the place," he said. "After that, keep the camcorder out of sight."

"Gotcha, k—" Morgan started, but corrected himself in mid sentence. "Uh, boss."

Tory sighed again. His grin, though, never faded.

"Should we bring anything else?" Cheech asked.

Tory shook his head. "No, I don't want to draw too much attention to ourselves with a bunch of equipment. There's time for that later. Like I said, right now, let's just see what we see."

Everyone else nodded in agreement, grins on their faces, too.

"Let's go get in line, *boys* and *girls*," Tory said, with pretend scorn. "Let's try to have some fun."

The ghost hunters walked off across the parking lot, toward Fright House.

Oblivious of the real *fun* ahead.

Chapter Sixteen

With Fright House as his backdrop, Tory looked into the lens of the camcorder. "My PSI team and I are standing in line to see Fright House, a Halloween attraction billed as being California's largest and scariest Halloween experience. Rumors of this place being truly haunted have brought us here to prove whether paranormal activity is taking place. Tonight, we're going to see for ourselves. First, as paying customers just for fun. Later, as investigators determined to get to the bottom of all the rumors. Come join us." He gave the camera a wry grin, then said, "Cut."

Morgan turned off the small camcorder and hid it under his jacket.

The team gathered excitedly around Tory. They were next in line to go inside.

The ghoulish-looking man who guarded the front door, asked, "How many in your party?"

"Six," Tory answered.

The iron door squealed as the ghoulish man opened it. "Welcome to Fright House," he said. "A place where many enter but few escape."

Chapter Seventeen

Penny crept along the private walkway behind Fright House. The roped off walkway looked deserted, no patrons allowed. The carnival noise that drifted through the air from the front of the building muffled the clop of her heels against pavement. Yellow lights on the building and nearby poles cast that all-too familiar, sickly glow across the place that she had come to despise almost as much as the red lights inside. Thanks to those yellow lights, her elongated shadow walked alongside her, against the wall, following like a stalker in the night.

It had taken all of her willpower, all of the courage she could muster, to return after what had happened in Mister Peabody's office earlier. She had spent two hours trying to convince herself that coming back was not only the right thing to do, but also the responsible thing, the *adult* thing to do. It was also the only thing she could do if she had any hope of piecing back together her quickly shredding sanity.

As if schizophrenic, she had argued *against* returning, too. She wasn't stupid. After years of therapy, she understood that the real danger was within her own mind. This place, however, incited her dark imagination. She could definitely lose her sanity within those red hallways. Coming back meant risking emotional and mental stability. Coming back meant risking everything. There was no doubt about that.

Still, if everything happening at the Halloween attraction was nothing more than the breakdown of Doctor Rosenthal's hypnosis, as she suspected, then wouldn't the danger follow wherever she ran? Fright House may have acted as a catalyst. It may have been the knife ripping through the thin veil of normalcy in her life. Now that the illusionary veil was ripped apart, could she effectively ignore it, hide from it, from herself?

No, the hallucinations would pursue her wherever she ran. She was sure of that. She decided this was where she had to make her stand. She needed to face the aberrations, not run from them. She needed to control them, not let them control her. Hypnosis in the end hadn't given back her sanity. At best, it had only camouflaged her mind's instability. She needed to somehow reclaim that mental and emotional stability, reclaim normalcy. In the end, it was the only way she could live with herself, the only way she could survive. Otherwise, although physically alive, she wouldn't be living. She'd be without a soul. If that were the case, she might as well be an unfeeling, unthinking zombie.

Worse, she might as well be dead.

Penny and her shadow stopped in front of an outside elevator that would take her to the top floor, back to Mister Peabody's office, back to whatever waited for her there. She rummaged through her purse for the plastic passkey that would gain her access. Finding it, she pulled it out and started to slip it into the slot next to the elevator doors.

A breath of cold air lightly touched her face, played through her hair. A faint, faraway heartbeat thumped rhythmically.

She held her own breath. Her own heart pounded in her chest. She tried to slip the passkey into the slot, but tremors racked her hand.

A shadow appeared on the wall before her, a twin to her own. It was not her twin, though. She couldn't cast two. Besides, this shadow was bigger, bulkier.

No one stood behind her. It was her imagination. She was sure of it.

Screwing up her courage, she whirled around to face her would-be stalker.

No one was there. As she suspected, she was alone.

The cold breeze faded, too. The faint heartbeat stopped.

Her held breath came out in a rush of relief. The entire event had only been a fabrication. She knew it as sure as anything.

Yet, she stood there alone, gasping for air and struggling to stop the tremors that traveled throughout her entire being.

What if it hadn't been a trick of her mind?

Self doubt crept into her thoughts.

She whirled back to the elevator. Somehow, in spite of the tremors, she managed to slip the passkey into the slot.

What if Doctor Rosenthal had been wrong all along? What if *she* had been wrong all along? What if ghosts really *did* exist?

She hadn't even considered those questions before now. At least not for a long time.

The elevator doors swished open, and she rushed on, turning quickly around to protect her back.

Maybe—just maybe—her illusions were not inventions of a broken psyche. Maybe monstrous forces really did exist in this place.

The elevator started to ascend.

Maybe Fright House wanted the very things she was trying to save by coming back: Her sanity. Her life. Her soul.

She gripped the metal rail within the elevator as if it were a mental and emotional lifeline. Her thoughts, her beliefs, were inexplicably spiraling out of control.

Maybe the place had already claimed her sanity. Now only her life and soul were left for the taking.

Chapter Eighteen

The ghost hunters stared in appreciation and amusement at their morbid surroundings. The hospital lobby they stood in was lit in that same, sickly glow as outside. The low ceiling, the cracked walls, the bloodstained tiled floor all added to the creepy ambiance. The thick layer of dust looked real enough. The cobwebs hanging everywhere looked real, too. Fake mental patients crowded around, all wearing hospital gowns, pasty complexions, sunken eyes, and blank stares. Most were silent, but some moaned or muttered incoherencies. Some of the patients wandered aimlessly about. Others sat in corners, rocking back and forth. A few stood like statues, frozen in bizarre poses. Some patients sat in wheelchairs, on metal folding chairs, and on wooden benches, watching a TV mounted to the wall.

Morgan opened his jacket and turned on the camcorder. Blindly, he recorded the best he could.

Cheech glanced up at the television. It played an old episode of *Paranormal Scene Investigations*. "Hey, look guys. We're on TV."

Everyone looked.

"Great," Tory mumbled sarcastically.

"I look good," Cheech commented.

Morgan chuckled. "A regular movie star."

Gabriel shook his head. "Are you sure that isn't *Woodstock* on the TV?"

"Wish I was old enough to have been there, preacher man," Cheech said. "Besides, when you find a look that works, you stick with it."

Morgan nudged Gabriel. He grinned. To Cheech, he said, "You're stuck, all right...in 1969."

"If only," Cheech said. "If only." He took one last glance at the TV screen. "I look good."

A male orderly stepped out of the sea of mental patients to greet the ghost hunters. A forced grin and a maniacal expression played with his face. "Welcome to Fright House," he said. "I hope your stay with us will be *pleasant*."

A young, female patient wandered over. She stopped in front of Lizzie, just inches away, staring blankly. Without saying a word, the girl slowly reached out with both hands. She started picking at Lizzie's clothes and hair, like a monkey grooming her mate.

Lizzie squealed, "Get away." She smacked the girl's hands away and moved into the middle of her group. Almost losing her glasses in the process, she adjusted them.

The others circled protectively around their friend.

"Don't mind Millie," the orderly said. "She means no harm." He turned around to face the reception counter.

A voluptuous nurse stood behind the counter. Her smile was warm and friendly, but the glint in her eyes screamed *evil*.

Behind the nurse stood an imposing iron door.

"Nurse Gillian," the orderly called, "we have new patients to process."

The voluptuous nurse winked at Cheech.

Morgan nudged his friend. "She wants you," he whispered.

Cheech gulped. "No way, dude. She's hot, but she's spookier than Isabel."

"Follow me," the orderly commanded. He stepped toward the counter.

Tory and his ghost hunters followed, Lizzie keeping to the middle of the pack for protection.

A small group of mental patients followed, too. They crowded, jostled, touched, picked, mumbled, and moaned, just like zombies smelling blood and readying themselves for an attack.

Nurse Gillian pushed a button. A buzz answered. The iron door clicked open. Screams, frightened laughter, banging, and other strange, indistinguishable noises thundered from inside.

The orderly pushed the iron door open wider, hinges squealing. He stepped aside, bowed, and motioned with his arm toward the open doorway. He said, "It's time to get acquainted."

With Tory in the lead, all six ghost hunters stepped into the bowels of Fright House.

Chapter Nineteen

Red light possessed the hallway the PSI team stepped into. Padded cells lined both sides. Mental patients occupied each cell. A few wore straitjackets, sitting in dark corners, their heads thumping rhythmically against the padded walls. Most were free within the confines of their prison. Some paced frantically around their cells while others threw their entire bodies against their prison's padded walls or iron bars. Still others grabbed those iron bars, rattling the doors to their cages.

All of them screamed and screeched wildly.

"Stay together. Keep toward the middle," the orderly warned just before slamming shut the iron door to the lobby.

Every one of the six ghost hunters gasped and jumped. They all shook their heads, laughing at themselves.

"Get a hold of yourselves, guys," Tory warned. "Remember, it's all just in fun."

"Or is it," Morgan deadpanned.

"I don't like this," Lizzie muttered, pushing her thick glasses back in place.

Gabriel *humphed*. "Don't have your crystals with you for protection, Pagan girl?"

Lizzie shot Gabriel an *I hate you* look. "Yeah," she answered. "Got that Saint Michael medal around your neck, preacher man?"

Gabriel nodded with a grin. "We're good to go then," he said.

At that, Lizzie grinned, too.

"I think it's awesome," Isabel shrieked, looking around excitedly.

"Feeling at home, witchy woman?" Cheech asked.

"Yes."

"I'll bet," Morgan mumbled under his breath.

Tory wanted his team to have fun, but he also wanted them to focus. "Morgan, get a quick shot of the hallway," he commanded.

Morgan slipped the camcorder out from under his jacket. He shot the hallway.

Tory continued, "The rest of you keep your eyes open for anything strange, out of the ordinary."

Gabriel gawked. "Really, kid? Out of the ordinary? For real?"

For once, Lizzie agreed with the minister. She added, "Boss, you *are* kidding, right?"

Tory sighed. He shrugged. As much as he hated to admit it, Gabriel and Lizzie were right. How could anyone spot something strange in all this *strangeness*? "Just do the best you can," he relented.

They began their journey down the crimson hallway. Even though they knew the mental patients around them were just actors and wouldn't really harm them, they still kept together, toward the middle of the hallway as the orderly had warned.

As if on cue, screaming like wild banshees, all of the mental patients rushed their prison bars. The ones not in straitjackets reached out through the bars, clawing and ripping at the air in their efforts to get the intruders venturing down the hall. Some of the patients even spat at the ghost hunters.

Morgan kept shooting footage the best he could. "They're good," he muttered.

"Really good," Cheech agreed.

"Yuck," Lizzie shrieked. A big goober hit her in the face. "A bit too good if you ask me," she added, wiping the mucus from her face with her sleeve and cleaning her glasses with her shirttail.

"Spit on me," Isabel cried, jumping up and down as they moved along the hall. "Spit on me."

"For God's sake," Gabriel yelled, "someone spit on the girl."

Cheech worked up some spit. He complied.

"Yuck, not you," Isabel complained. She wiped spittle from the back of her hair.

"My spit's not good enough for you?" Cheech complained back.

"Everybody stop spitting," Tory commanded.

"Tell them," Cheech shot back.

"Idiot," Tory mumbled.

Everyone except Isabel and Lizzie were older, supposedly more mature. Still, here he was baby-sitting, again. He didn't have the patience for it right now. He had other things on his mind. Like Lizzie, he couldn't help but think that these actors were a bit too good, a bit too convincing. He didn't, however, have time to dwell on that thought for long.

The plaintiff wail of a siren broke his concentration. Flashing lights that were dark and undetected moments ago suddenly splashed blue across the red walls. If possible, the patients in their cells banged, screamed, and yelled even louder.

Everyone stopped. Morgan stopped shooting. He hid the camcorder. The team gathered together, as if mere closeness would serve as a protective force field.

"Stay calm," Tory commanded.

That's when pandemonium truly broke loose.

A tall, lanky guy wearing a hospital gown and confined to a straitjacket emerged out of nowhere at the far end of the hallway. He ran full tilt toward the PSI team. His bare feet slapped against the hard floor as he zigzagged down the hall like a pinball hitting bumpers. His high-pitched screech echoed over the wailing siren, over the ranting and banging of the confined patients.

Two more guys wearing white, bloodstained lab coats gave chase.

The escapee rapidly approached the huddled group. Wearing a crazed expression on his young face, he slapped on the brakes directly in front of Tory. "Save me," he cried, "I'm not part of this."

"Move out of the way," one guy giving chase yelled, rushing forward.

"We're doctors," the other pursuer claimed, keeping pace with his colleague. "We order you to get away from him."

The young escapee looked frantic. "They're going to kill me," he insisted.

The doctors kept coming.

"He's dangerous," one doctor yelled.

"Get away from him," the other doctor concurred.

Dazed and confused, Tory didn't know what to do. Was this all an act? It had to be. Whether it was an act or not, he could only gawk at the escapee in silence. Indecision and shock froze him.

None of his team reacted, either.

The escapee took off running again, pleading, "Save me. Save me."

Without another word, the two doctors raced past the ghost hunters, in hot pursuit of their *patient*.

Everyone watched in shocked amazement as the escapee and the doctors somehow disappeared into the gloom before reaching the iron door at the other end of the hallway.

The siren stopped. The blue flashing lights went dark.

The mental patients all around continued ranting, banging, and spitting.

"Awesome," Isabel whispered, "so *freaking* cool."

"They're good," Cheech admitted again. "Really good."

Too good, Tory thought, not for the first time.

"That was all for show, right?" Lizzie asked.

"Sure," Tory answered but wasn't sure. The three *actors* vanished just before they reached the iron door, much the way they had emerged from nowhere when the siren began wailing. How could they have achieved that effect?

Before he could give that question much thought, a chime broke his concentration. It came from the opposite end of the hallway, where the escapee and the doctors had emerged.

He and everyone else in his group turned toward the sound.

A small, round light flashed on. Elevator doors swished open. A white glow illuminating from inside the elevators beckoned to them.

"I think that's for us," Morgan said.

"I think you're right," Tory agreed. "Let's go."

The group hurried the rest of the way down the hall, eager to leave it. They crossed the threshold of the elevator with no hesitation, crowding inside, basking in the white glow of its fluorescent lights.

The doors swished closed. Haunting music softly played.

"Going down," an elevator operator said.

In their eagerness to escape the horrors of the hallway, not one of them had noticed the insane-looking man who operated the elevator. That man eyed them with a maniacal, evil expression.

The elevator descended.

No one spoke. Only haunting music and heavy breathing filled the warm, confined space.

The elevator jerked to a stop. A chime announced its arrival in the basement.

"Everyone off," the maniacal operator announced as he pushed a button.

As eagerly as they had gotten on, the group clambered off.

The PSI team stood in a large, narrow room. Rather than the hellish red that lit the upstairs hallway, this room had an eerie, green glow. The floor was nothing but concrete. The walls looked to be made of cinderblocks. Huge, gaping cracks spiderwebbed those walls. Rusty, exposed pipes ran in a complex pattern overhead, just below a low, concrete ceiling. Some of the pipes dripped water. The air smelled musty, and the room felt cold, damp.

There were other patrons already in the room. Their constant chatter, nervous laughter, and frightened squeals were deafening, almost overpowering the bizarre, electrical and mechanical noises that accompanied strange flashes of light. These unsettling noises and flashing lights came from smaller rooms built within this one big basement. These rooms were well-lit, made of what appeared to be Plexiglas on three sides, with the basement's actual cinder blocks as each room's back wall. As if the basement were a freak show, patrons stood around these smaller, glassed-off rooms—these display cases—watching disturbing performances taking place within.

"Everybody gather around," Tory said.

The team quickly complied.

"First impressions?" Tory asked.

Lizzie shivered. "It's cold down here," she said. "I wish we would've brought a temp gun to get a base reading. That way, we'd be able to better measure cold spots."

"I did," Morgan answered. He took out the IR-ambient air thermometer. He held it by its pistol grip. "I don't know why, though," he continued. "If you ask me, there are cold spots everywhere, all the time—paranormal activity or not."

Cheech sighed. "Just take the reading and get a baseline, Jughead."

Morgan shrugged. "Sorry, dude. Didn't mean to ditz one of your toys." He pointed the temp gun in different directions, checking the LCD display as he did so. He shook the gun as if it were broken, as if that could help. He checked the display, again. "I'm reading about sixty-nine degrees in all directions. Pretty normal for a damp basement or if they have the air conditioner running."

Cheech sighed again and said, "But now, you big ape, we got a baseline reading, and we'll be able to measure cold spots."

Morgan opened his mouth to protest.

"I know, I know," Cheech cut Morgan off, "there are cold spots everywhere, paranormal activity or not, so says you."

"That's enough debate about cold spots," Tory insisted.

Morgan shrugged. He put the temp gun back into his waistband.

"Morgan," Tory continued, "shoot some footage when you can, but be discreet."

Morgan nodded. "I'm on it."

Tory eyed his group of ghost hunters. In the green light, he couldn't tell if their complexions were pale or not, but he did recognize expressions of concern and disquiet on at least Lizzie and Gabriel's faces. Isabel just looked giddy, excited. Cheech was apparently still annoyed at Morgan. Morgan was all business with the camcorder.

"Let's move on," Tory said.

Tory started off. Everyone followed. They stopped in front of the first brightly lit display case and stared, awestruck, by what was going on behind the Plexiglas.

A woman wearing a hospital gown was strapped to a large, wooden chair. Her hair hung in brown, greasy strands to her shoulders, across her face. Under the greasy strands, her eyes were full moons, pupils dilated. She was biting down on a leather strap. Electrodes were attached to her temples. Wires ran from the electrodes to an electric shock treatment machine that rested on a hospital cart. A doctor wearing goggles and a white lab coat stood over the machine. He cackled as if more insane than any of the patients he treated.

Throwing the switch on the machine, he fired volts of electricity into the woman's brain. Biting down hard on the leather strap, the woman convulsed. Her body stiffened. Her head slammed into the back of the wooden chair. The lights within the glassed-off room dimmed with the surge of power from the EST machine. When the doctor switched off the machine, the lights within the small room again brightened. The woman slumped in the wooden chair. She looked comatose. Still cackling insanely, the doctor again flipped the EST machine's switch. The woman bit down hard on the leather strap. Her body stiffened. Her head slammed back against the chair.

"My God," Gabriel said. "I feel like I'm at a zoo in Hell."

Tory shook his head. "More like a freak show in Hell," he muttered.

"Cool beans," Isabel hissed.

Lizzie looked away.

Morgan continued to shoot footage.

Cheech could only stare.

"Cheech, you worked on a movie set once, didn't you?" Tory asked. "Could that possibly be real?"

"I worked on one sci-fi movie," Cheech said with a shake of his head. "I'm no SFX expert by any means." He paused, scratching at his beard like a dog with fleas. "The special effects are good. It would take a lot of money, though, to pull this off. The acting's good, too. Too good." He paused, still scratching. "But dude, obviously it can't be real."

Tory wasn't so sure. He had no reason to think otherwise except for the realistic acting and effects, but he wasn't sure.

In the background, the elevator chimed, the doors swished open, and the operator announced, "Everyone off." People scuffled off the elevator, chattering, squealing nervously.

Morgan stopped shooting. He hid the camcorder under his jacket.

Tory took one last look. The scene looked so real, but it couldn't be. "Come on, guys," he announced. "Let's move on."

The ghost hunters turned away as the newcomers approached the glassed-off room with screams of horror and nervous giggles on their lips.

At the next display case, Morgan took out the camcorder. He began shooting. Everyone else gawked, more horror-stricken by what they saw happening within this room than even the last one.

Within the confines of the Plexiglas walls, three prisoners sat on a blood-soaked, cement floor. They each had both wrists chained and shackled to the back cinder block wall. Screaming and crying uncontrollably, two young girls desperately fought against their iron constraints. Insanity clearly marked the leering, blood-smeared face of the third prisoner, a young man. Although he had one arm still shackled to the cinder block wall, the prisoner had already somehow managed to chew off his other arm at the shoulder in an attempt to free himself. Blood spurted from the gaping wound, splattering the Plexiglas within the room. The mangled arm dangled from the iron manacle. Blood dripped from the arm to an ever-growing pool of red wetness on the cement floor.

"Holy, Mother of God," Gabriel exclaimed.

Isabel giggled. "Freaking awesome," she whispered. "Freaking, freaking cool and awesome."

Tory's brow furrowed. He rubbed at his temples. He could feel an oncoming migraine. "Something doesn't feel right," he muttered. Everything appeared too *real*, but it couldn't be. He continued to rub his temples, hoping to at least soften the headache's attack.

With her face pinched in disgust, Lizzie offered, "Maybe the electromagnetic field? Maybe that's what doesn't feel right."

Tory rubbed at his temples. "Yeah, maybe," he said. "I'd give my right arm for an ELF meter right now."

Cheech pointed at the glassed-off room. "That guy already did," he cracked.

Morgan slapped the Tech Specialist upside the head.

"Hey," Cheech protested. "I'm just saying…"

Ignoring Cheech and Morgan, Lizzie asked, "Is it colder now?"

"Hey," Cheech said, "I do have the *Ghost Radar Classic* app on my cell phone. I could get an EMF reading with that."

The migraine rocked his brain, 7.2 on the Richter scale. "No." Tory winced. "Liz is right," he said. "It does feel colder. Morgan, get a reading."

Morgan pulled the temp gun from his waistband. He pointed it in different directions, concentrating mostly on the glassed-off room before them. "Temp's down to sixty-two," he said. "That could just be a variance in the AC." Morgan again shook the gun as if that might fix any problem with it. "No good piece of crap."

Cheech rolled his eyes. "If it's such a piece of crap, why bring it along?" he asked.

Morgan shrugged. "Looks cool. Chicks love it."

Now Cheech smacked his muscle-bound friend upside the head.

"Hey," Morgan protested. He winked and grinned. "I'm just saying…"

An aftershock hit Tory's head. "Would you two clowns quit," he demanded.

Cheech and Morgan gave each other a knowing look.

Tory tensed. He was sure those looks said, *Ooo, look out. Kid at work.*

Newcomers crowded around the PSI team, gawking at the room of horror and suddenly erupting into a sea of screams, followed by nervous giggles, nervous chatter.

Tory grimaced. He wanted so much to punch those two. Instead, he ordered, "Come on." He turned and stomped away. He knew something wasn't right with this place, with him. Thanks to the migraine, though, he couldn't think straight.

Tory and his team stopped at the horrid scene playing out within the next display case.

Dry blood spatter stained the Plexiglas walls. So was the cinder block wall in the back. A masked surgical team of two nurses and a doctor gathered around an operating table. Fully awake, a man was already strapped to the table by leather restraints over his forehead, waist, wrists, and ankles. He desperately struggled against those restraints, screaming for help, for mercy. None came. Instead, one of the nurses handed the surgeon a scalpel. The surgeon made an incision across the patient's forehead, just above the leather restraint. The patient's body stiffened under the blanket covering him. He cried out in agony as the surgeon peeled scalp away from skull. Blood spurted everywhere, splattering the glass with fresh carnage. With the patient's scalp peeled away, the doctor started an electric saw to open the cranium for an apparent lobotomy. The saw whined. Sparks flew as the rotating blade hit bone. The patient's bloodcurdling scream rose above it all.

People crowded in around the ghost hunters, all trying to see the macabre scene within the glassed-off room. Screams of fright and disgust erupted from the crowd. A few whooped and hollered as if it was the coolest thing they had ever seen.

Morgan stopped shooting. He hid the camcorder back under his jacket.

Gabriel was pushed in the back and jostled by the crowd. "I was wrong," he said. "This place isn't a zoo. It's a demented circus."

Isabel disagreed. "I think it's hecka awesome."

Gabriel scoffed. "That somehow doesn't surprise me."

Isabel narrowed her eyes. "Why?" she asked. "Just because I'm not a stick-up-the-butt priest?"

Gabriel stiffened. "I'm not a priest," he protested. "I'm an ordained minister."

Cheech laughed. "You notice he didn't correct you about the stick up the butt."

"Hippy reject," Gabriel shot back.

"Ooo," Cheech taunted. "Is that the minister talking or the stick?"

Tory turned on them. "That's enough," he commanded. He could feel the heat in his face. His ears buzzed as if annoying mosquitoes flitted around inside them. The migraine reached epic proportions, banging against the inside of his skull. Absently, he rubbed at the back of his neck, the side of his face. Things were quickly going from bad to worse. He could hardly think at all anymore. He felt out of control.

More people crowded around, bumping, jostling. The din from their reaction to the fake carnage within the room was deafening.

Without saying another word, Tory pushed his way through the onlookers to the next glassed-off, morbid display. The others followed in silence as the crowd parted for Tory like the Red Sea had done for Moses. Morgan took out the camcorder. He began shooting footage, again.

What looked like a dental office occupied this room. Except the decor and equipment looked archaic, from around the early 1900s. Like the last room, the glass on the inside was spattered with dried blood. A young woman was already strapped to the dental chair. She struggled against the leather restraints, but to no avail. Some kind of metal contraption that looked like a torture device the Nazis used forced her mouth open abnormally wide, choking her screams. A dentist dressed in a surgical gown and mask stood over his patient, drill in hand. The drill droned like a thousand bees when he started it. The lights within the room dimmed from the power surge. At the sight of the drill, the young woman's eyes rolled back in her head, showing only the whites. The dentist leaned in. He drilled into the patient's gaping mouth. Blood gushed forward. The young woman convulsed with seizure-like spasms. There were no screams.

Except from the crowd that pushed around the PSI team.

Morgan ditched the camcorder as the six investigators pushed their way through the crowd, away from the horrid scene within the display case. The basement had become jam-packed with people, overrun by adults, teenagers, and children alike. Tory and his colleagues fought their way to the next macabre play, where there was already a crowd. They had to strain to get a good view. Morgan held the camcorder up high. Blindly, he shot the scene.

An autopsy was taking place within this room. The fake cadaver was strapped down to the autopsy table. Dressed in a hospital gown and mask, the coroner took a scalpel. He began making a Y-shaped incision—two incisions that started at the tip of each of the shoulders and met in the center of the chest, with a single mid-line slice continued down to the crotch. The cadaver never moved or showed any signs of life, even as its blood spritzed the room, even as its insides spilled out onto the table and the floor.

"That's really good," Cheech said in appreciation. "Excellent special effects."

"Why would a cadaver, fake or otherwise, need to be strapped down?" Tory mumbled.

"I don't know, but God help me, I've seen enough," Gabriel answered.

Tory's head jerked. He tried to contemplate his own question, but his ears buzzed. Another aftershock played havoc with his skull. He winced at the annoyance and the pain.

"Maybe *you've* seen enough," Tory hissed, "but there's more." He turned, pushing free of the throng.

The others glanced at each other with questioning looks but followed. Silently, they made their way through the over-crowded basement until they all stood before the last, morbid display case.

Gloom occupied this glassed-off room. Within the dim light, a silhouette could be seen hanging by the neck from a rope. The body wore the surrounding shadows like a shroud as it swung back and forth, as if the suicide had just taken place. A knocked over stool rested on the floor, just below the dangling feet.

Tory gaped at the horrible scene. "Mom," he whispered. His ears buzzed. A quake rattled his skull. No tears came to his eyes. Still, anger welled in his heart as if ready to cry blood. He clamped his eyes shut, put fists to his head. "Mom."

Someone placed a hand on his shoulder. "Tory," a female voice said, "be a good boy, always make me proud."

"What." Tory opened his eyes. He whirled toward the voice.

Lizzie stood there, a shocked look behind her thick, black glasses.

"What did you say?" Tory demanded.

Lizzie looked around at her group of coworkers, a dazed expression on her face. She stuttered, "I—I was...was just asking...are...are you...you...ok-kay?"

Gabriel came to Lizzie's defense. "She was just worried about you, kid."

Cheech interjected, "Yeah, dude. We all are."

"*Are* you okay?" Morgan asked.

Tory looked from face to face. Lizzie, Gabriel, Cheech, Morgan, and even Isabel all stared at him with worry etched into their features. "I'm sorry," he muttered. He winced in annoyance, in pain. "I'm sorry," he repeated.

"It's cool, dude," Cheech assured.

Everyone else nodded their agreement.

Gabriel cleared his throat as if to change the subject. "I wonder why they didn't put anything in this last room," he said.

"Huh?" Tory asked.

Gabriel pointed to the room behind Tory. "There's nothing in this room."

Tory whirled back around. The room had gone black, nothing to see.

His ears buzzed. His head banged.

Tory winced. "Nothing in the room," he mumbled.

"Well, there's still the Cemetery Room," Morgan suggested, "might as well experience it all."

Tory stared at the darkened room behind the Plexiglas. "Might as well," he muttered. He took one last, disbelieving look before turning away.

At the far end of the basement, the PSI team stood under an archway that read, *Fright House Cemetery*. Venturing into the graveyard, they found what looked to be a night sky on the ceiling, complete with stars and a full moon. There was even dirt on the floor to help simulate the outside. An eerie mist traveled through the grounds, covering glowing headstones, fake trees, and mechanized vultures picking at discarded body parts. Ghostly projections drifted amongst it all.

Nervous squeals, laughter, and cries echoed all around.

"Ooo, creepy," Cheech said sarcastically. "Like we haven't seen a hundred real cemeteries."

"Disappointing," Isabel agreed, "after those awesome torture chambers."

"Yeah, not much here," Morgan added. Taking out his camcorder, he shot the graveyard anyway.

"Let's be sure," Cheech said. He took out his cell phone. "I'll check the electromagnetic field." He opened the app, *Ghost Radar Classic*.

Morgan stopped shooting footage. "You've just been itching

to use that," he mused, looking over his friend's shoulder.

A radar screen appeared on the display of Cheech's cell phone. A ghostly, green light circled continuously.

Morgan rolled his eyes. "Another toy."

"It's not a toy," Cheech insisted. "An EMF burst indicating paranormal activity shows up on the radar screen as a blip. Different colored blips—blue, green, yellow, red—indicate the intensity of the burst. Red means it's more likely to be ghostly activity."

"Really?" Morgan scoffed. "Did it ever occur to you, genius, that cell phones themselves give off EMF bursts? Therefore, they can't measure EMF."

A red blip showed up on the screen.

"See there," Cheech said.

Morgan shrugged. "Uh-huh."

"Penny," the cell phone's mechanical voice said.

"What was that?" Morgan asked.

Cheech grinned. "The app works like a ghost box too, receiving EVP."

"Penny," the cell phone app repeated.

Morgan rolled his eyes. "That random name is a ghost talking to us?"

Cheech shrugged. "Possibly."

"Penny."

Morgan laughed. "Sounds like the ghost wants a date. You better go out, find it a dead girl named Penny."

"Very funny." Cheech paused, thinking. "Maybe the ghost's name *is* Penny," he suggested.

"Put it away, dude," Morgan insisted. "That app is more useless than the temp gun tucked away in my waistband."

Cheech shut down the app. "Killjoy," he said, pocketing the cell.

"Like I said before," Morgan insisted, "not much here."

"I have to agree with Morg, geek boy," Isabel said, getting into the argument. "Your app sucks." She sighed. "After those awesome torture chambers, this is just disappointing."

Cheech *humphed.* "That's your hormones talking, not your brain."

Isabel made a fist and shook it at Cheech. "I'll hormone you right in the kisser."

Tory ignored the ongoing bickering between his cohorts. As he looked around, he wasn't so sure they were right. No, he didn't trust *Ghost Radar*. Morgan was right about cell phones giving off EMF. Something besides the ongoing migraine and the buzzing in his ears wasn't right. With *him*. He definitely didn't feel himself. He felt agitated, nervous, angry.

There was something not right with this room too, with this entire place. Even though it couldn't possibly be, everything in the upstairs hallway and in those torture chambers felt so real.

He blinked, trying to see past the gloom, the cheesy gimmicks, and all the patrons roaming around the simulated grounds.

Just the opposite in here. In here, it all felt fake. It didn't make sense that they'd cheap out with the graveyard after going full-tilt realistic everywhere else.

Something wasn't right.

He tried to concentrate, tried to see what it was that bothered him so, but the buzzing in his ears, the pounding in his head, kept logic and reasoning at bay.

He winced and shook his head, as if that could discard the mosquitoes he knew weren't there anyway.

Something else was here. It had to be. He knew it. He knew it like he knew that last torture chamber wasn't empty. He had seen the body hanging, swinging from the ceiling. He was sure of it. Just like he was sure there was something here besides fake ghosts, mechanized vultures, and glowing headstones.

He blinked, scanning the graveyard again.

That's when he saw it.

A little girl in pigtails stood under a fake tree, surrounded by glowing headstones. She grinned demonically as she removed her decapitated head and held it up for all to see.

Tory froze, mouth agape, unable to speak.

The little girl put her head back on her neck.

"Anyone else see that?" Tory asked, the words suddenly rushing out. "Anyone else see that little girl?" He was manic now—voice too loud, mannerisms exaggerated, mind whirling out of control. He knew it, could hear himself, could almost see himself, like having an out of body experience. He couldn't stop himself, though. "Does anyone else see that little girl?"

The little girl disappeared.

"Little girl?" Gabriel asked.

"Yes," Tory screamed. "A little girl. Over there. Did anyone else see her?"

"Where?" Lizzie asked. She adjusted her glasses for a better look.

"There." Tory pointed to the fake tree and glowing head-stones where the little girl in pigtails had appeared.

Everyone looked, trying to spy one little girl in a gloomy room full of other people.

Lizzie shook her head. "There's no little girl." She paused. Looked again. "Oh, wait. There? There's a little girl. Is that her?"

A little girl with flowing blonde hair ran out of the shadows where she'd been playing amongst the headstones. She ran to her parents and got a scolding from her father for apparently wandering off.

Tory blinked. Confused, disoriented, he stared after the blonde girl, watching her leave with her parents.

His ears buzzed. His skull pounded. Reasoning and concentration were held hostage. He couldn't think.

He blinked again, staring hard at the spot where the pig-tailed girl had stood before disappearing just moments ago.

"Was that her?" Lizzie asked again.

"Yeah," Tory mumbled unconvincingly. He couldn't admit to anyone that he had seen a little girl take her decapitated head off her neck before just disappearing. They'd think he was crazy. "That was her."

Lizzie looked skeptical. "Are you sure?"

The others put their heads together and whispered.

Tory eyed them with suspicion, sure they were talking smack about him behind his back. They didn't just think he was immature. They thought he was crazy, too. Either that, or they saw the decapitated girl and were trying to make him *think* he was crazy.

Everyone continued to peer at him, their heads together, whispering.

They were plotting against him. They *did* think he was crazy. He was sure of it. They probably wanted to put him in an asylum, like this one.

"I need to get out of here," Tory announced.

He turned, fleeing the faux cemetery. He rushed under the archway, into the torture room, nudging people out of his way as he went. The others were in tow, whispering behind his back, making plans, plotting against him. He could hear them even over the din surrounding him.

They did think he was crazy.

He knew he wasn't. He had seen the decapitated girl. He

had seen the hanging suicide. He had heard his mom's...

He winced, the migraine hitting him hard again, the buzzing in his ears growing louder, more annoying than ever.

The elevator up ahead chimed its arrival. The round light above it blinked on.

"Let's hurry," Tory yelled over his shoulder as he rushed ahead.

He had to get out of there.

The elevator doors swished open, bathing the eerily green basement in fluorescent white light. Amazingly, with the large crowd, the elevator was empty.

Tory and his team hurried on.

A few stragglers tried to join them, but the elevator operator blocked their path. "Sorry," he said, "just these six. *Please.*"

The doors swished closed. The elevator ascended. Haunting music played. Continuing to ascend, it passed the lobby.

Annoyed, Tory yelled, "Hey, we're still going up. I thought there were only two floors."

Now the elevator operator was against him, too. How far did the conspiracy go? Who was involved?

"Stop," Tory yelled.

Plumes of frosty breath exploded from his mouth. An icy chill drilled into his bones. Gooseflesh snaked across his pounding head.

That's when he noticed everyone breathed frost. Everyone shivered. They hugged themselves against the sudden cold.

"What's going on?" Isabel shrieked.

"I can't see," Lizzie cried. "My glasses are fogged."

Without warning, the elevator operator grabbed Tory by the throat.

He had been right, after all. They were all against him. They didn't just want to put him away in a loony bin, however. They wanted him dead. This guy was going to do it for them.

Tory gasped. He fell backward as he struggled against the sudden attack.

The elevator operator followed, hands still strangling the ghost hunter's throat.

"Help," Tory croaked. He struggled to pry the madman's hands free but couldn't.

Screams and cries erupted all around. Although Gabriel crawled to a corner and prayed, Cheech, Lizzie, and Isabel all came to Tory's aid, scuffling with the man trying to kill their boss. Morgan pulled the temp gun from his waistband, looking for an opening.

"Help me," Tory pleaded again. His team wasn't plotting against him. He could see that now. They didn't want to put him away. They didn't want him dead. Only this lunatic on top of him did. "Help me."

Screams and cries continued with the ongoing scuffle.

The more they fought, the stronger the elevator operator got. His strangling hands supernaturally tightened. Leaning in close, he said to Tory, "You can save us. You can save us all."

That's when Morgan found his opening. He cracked the madman over the head with the temp gun.

The elevator operator collapsed on top of Tory, rendered unconscious.

Tory pushed the madman off him. He sat up, holding his throat, gasping, coughing.

On their knees, Cheech, Lizzie, and Isabel surrounded their leader. Gabriel joined them as if fear hadn't held him hostage, as if he had been a part of the struggle all along.

Standing over them, Morgan held up the temp gun. He said, "Hey, Cheech. You were right. This thing does work." He tossed the broken ghost-hunting tool aside.

In spite of themselves, everyone grinned.

"Yeah, it's good for something," Cheech acknowledged. "Told you."

Tory calmed his breath, coughed. "What just happened here?" he croaked, still rubbing his throat.

"I don't know," Lizzie said, "but it's much warmer now."

She was right. They could no longer see their breath.

"Whatever, dude," Cheech said. "You okay?"

"I think so," Tory answered. Except for his sore throat, he meant it. Only a remnant of headache remained. No more invisible mosquitoes buzzed in his ears. Paranoia had been stamped out. He almost completely felt himself again.

"God be praised," Gabriel muttered.

A chime answered that prayer. The elevator jerked to a stop. The doors opened.

Chapter Twenty

Penny stood at the elevator, waiting for its arrival. Mister Peabody wanted her to go down into the bowels of Fright House. He wanted her to check on the activity, make sure everything was running smoothly.

After her meltdown in the elevator earlier in the night, she had somehow managed to calm herself. Convinced again that everything happening here was mere fabrication, her mind playing tricks, she remained on the job.

After all, ghosts didn't really exist. They never had. They still didn't.

Still, the mere suggestion of her walking the attraction at night, while the morbid playacting was in full swing, stabbed her with cold fear. She tried to avoid it as much as possible. It was, however, getting more and more difficult to do so in the last few weeks. Besides, Mister Peabody was getting less and less understanding of her trepidation. It was part of her job, after all. She was the manager. She had certain responsibilities. She didn't want Mister Peabody to question her capabilities or her maturity. The last thing she needed was for her boss to second guess his decision or to decide to run a background check.

Give him no reason, she thought.

Still, the thought of going downstairs during the performance slowed her heart to an abnormal rate, caused her knees to almost buckle.

It wasn't that the second floor, where Mister Peabody's office and the storage rooms were, was any less likely to harbor unusual, unwanted activity. After all, it was Mister Peabody's office where she had first seen the *little girl*. Besides that, it was all in her mind anyway. She couldn't effectively hide from herself, could she?

At least up there, though, it was well lit. It had a certain air of normalcy. She could at least pretend she had a regular job in an office and hide from the macabre surroundings downstairs. Maybe that in itself could stop the aberrations from occurring. She could hope anyway.

She pushed the *down* button again.

They must be especially busy tonight. The elevator was taking a particularly long time to ascend. Not that she was in any hurry. She was happy to remain upstairs, pretending, hiding, hoping.

The fluorescent lights suddenly dimmed. Brightened.

Gasping, she scanned her surroundings. Everything looked the same, looked *normal.*

The lights dimmed, again. An eerie chill filled the hallway, as if she were out in the night air. Not the balmy Bay Area night air, either. More like she imagined an East coast winter's night air. Her breath blew out in a panting frost. Gooseflesh scampered along her skin like thousands of tiny spiders, raising the hairs along her arms, on the back of her neck. She shivered, hugging herself against the cold.

The upstairs, after all, was no better than downstairs amongst the morbid goings-on. There was no hiding, no pretending. No hope.

"Stop," she whispered. "Please, stop."

The lights in the hallway flickered from bright to dim and back again. The cold air chilled her to the bone. Shivering, teeth chattering, hugging herself not only against the cold but also against her own fear, she begged, "Please, stop."

She no longer knew for sure whether she begged for her sanity to return or if she begged for the horrid place and its ghosts to leave her alone. She no longer cared. She just wanted it to stop.

Desperate, she continued begging, "Please, stop. Leave me alone." She paused, her mind in a panic. Suddenly, she was willing to try anything, even giving in to the possibility that the place she worked in was actually haunted. "I'll go," she promised her hypothetical ghostly surroundings. "If that's what you want, I'll go." Hot tears welled in her eyes, streamed down her cheeks. She sobbed. "Tonight. I'll go tonight. Please just leave me alone."

The lights brightened and remained on. The air warmed. The hallway returned to normal.

Stifling her sobs, she wiped tears from her eyes, from her face. "Thank you," she whispered to the bedeviled air, grateful only that the nightmare had stopped and not whether it was her mind that finally put an end to it or the ghosts. "I'll keep my promise," she claimed. Delusional or not, she had every intention of doing so. "I'll leave and never come back."

The small, round light above the elevator lit up. A chime announced the elevator's arrival.

She wiped away the last of her tears, choked back her sobs, and took a deep breath.

Forget needing the money to get away from California, away from her haunting past. It just wasn't worth it. She would get on the elevator, take it to the lobby, and walk out the front door, never to return. Just as she had promised. Whether she made the promise to her shattered psyche or to actual spirits, it didn't matter anymore.

The elevator doors swished open.

Her breath caught in her throat. To her amazement, the elevator was full of people. Samuel, the elevator operator, lay unconscious on the floor. Another young man sat on the floor next to Samuel, coughing, rubbing his throat. Others surrounded him. All but poor Samuel turned as one. They eyed her with expectant looks.

The lights in the hallway flickered. The air chilled. Her breath released in a rush of frosty plumes.

As she stared at these strangers, at poor Samuel in the elevator, she suddenly understood. It didn't matter anymore whether this was an elaborate illusion created by her mind or a true haunting. Her leaving was nothing more than a hollow promise. There *was* no turning back. There *was* no leaving. Neither her mental state nor this place would let her.

She then remembered what the little girl in pigtails had first said, *"Welcome. We've been waiting for you."*

Breathlessly, she whispered, "I'm screwed."

Chapter Twenty-One

The fluorescent lights in the hallway flickered slightly as Penny watched two uniformed police officers lead a sullen, confused Samuel away in handcuffs. All the others from the elevator waited in Mister Peabody's office, door closed. Mister Peabody stood by the elevator, talking with a detective as the police officers approached with their suspect. He shook the detective's hand. The police took Samuel on the elevator and descended to the lobby. Mister Peabody trudged back up the hallway, looking haggard, shaken, older.

As she watched her boss approach, Penny whispered, "If you want me to leave, I'll leave." She paused, hoping against hope.

The lights flickered.

She took a deep, hitched breath, whispering, "If you want me to stay, I'll stay."

The lights brightened, remained steady.

Her heart rammed against her chest. She choked back sobs. With a trembling hand, she quickly wiped tears from her eyes.

She had her answer. She was sure of it. As sure as she knew her *real* name.

She wasn't going anywhere.

Mister Peabody stopped. "Miss Winters," he muttered.

Penny didn't answer.

"Miss Winters."

Penny shook free of her thoughts. "Yes."

"It's time for you to meet our guests."

Penny straightened. With new resolve, she asked, "What do you mean *guests*?" She steadied herself. She dug deep within to find the courage to not only face her boss, but to face her newfound realization that she wasn't going to be able to run or to hide.

Mister Peabody sighed. "The people from the elevator who are now in my office are here by my request."

"What?" Penny asked, squaring her shoulders, standing

up to her boss. "Who are they?"

Mister Peabody paused before answering. "They're professional ghost hunters." His shoulders slumped a bit with that admission.

"Ghost hunters?" Penny squealed.

The lights in the hallway flickered slightly.

Oh crap.

"Professional ghost hunters? Really?" she asked. "Why didn't you tell me before now?"

"A need-to-know basis, Miss Winters." Mister Peabody shrugged. "Now, you need to know."

Penny took a deep breath. She not only had to decide whether she believed in ghosts but also whether she believed in ghost hunters. "Are charlatans really the answer?" she asked.

"How do you know they're charlatans?"

Penny cleared her throat. "Could they be anything else?" she muttered.

Mister Peabody studied her for a long time. "Why?" he finally asked. "You don't believe in ghosts?"

Penny stiffened and looked away. She didn't know what to believe in anymore. Her entire belief system, imposed upon her will by Doctor Rosenthal's therapy, was being called into question. The question of her sanity wasn't far behind. Her whole world was spinning out of control, crashing down. Maybe she was, after all, just a freak, like her classmates, teachers, even her family thought.

Clearing her throat again, without much conviction, Penny answered, "There's no such thing."

"Good." Mister Peabody nodded. "I agree."

"Why invite them here then?" Penny quickly asked. Sometimes, she felt as though she would never truly understand this old guy. "You're only encouraging..." She wanted to say, *her fantasies, her illusions.* Instead she said, "...the rumors."

"Something strange is happening here." Mister Peabody studied his shoes. "Just ask poor Samuel." He looked back up. "We need to find out what." He turned away and opened the door to his office. Over his shoulder, he asked, "You coming?"

Penny hesitated. She couldn't decide if matters just got worse or better with the emergence of these outsiders.

The hallway lights flickered.

Worse, she thought.

Mister Peabody paused in the doorway. "Miss Winters?"

Penny sighed with resolve. "I'm coming," she said. Following her boss across the threshold, she closed the door behind them.

In the hallway, the lights went completely dark.

Chapter Twenty-Two

Mister Peabody sat behind his desk.

Penny stood beside her boss, scrutinizing the ragtag group of paranormal investigators. The five who stood together, off to one side of the room, were an odd assortment, almost comical. Maybe not as individuals but definitely as a group. Their ages looked to vary from seventeen or eighteen to maybe thirty-something. Although she didn't have any real expectations, they were not at all what she expected of ghost hunters. Their leader, the one they called Tory, paced back and forth in front of Mister Peabody's desk, wearing away an already threadbare carpet. He didn't look more than nineteen, twenty at most. Still, except for his age, this guy fit the profile of how a ghost hunter or paranormal investigator might look, might act. Again, she'd never given ghost hunters a moment's thought. She really didn't know how one should look or act. This one, though, held her attention. The guy was intense, brooding. Okay, kind of cute too.

Tory suddenly braked. He wheeled and faced the two behind the desk. With his jaw clenched, his fists at his sides, he asked, "What the hell's going on here?"

Penny fidgeted. She looked down at the desk when Tory's steely gaze settled on her.

No one answered.

Tory continued, "I was almost killed tonight. I deserve an answer."

Mister Peabody cleared his throat. "My sincere apologies, Mister Jackson—"

"What about the police?" Tory interrupted. "You conveniently forgot to tell me during our phone conversation that they are involved in this *investigation*." He paused for only a beat, not enough time for either Penny or Mister Peabody to respond. "That they've been trying to shut you down, that people have gone missing."

Penny continued to stare at the desk, as if that held all the answers. She couldn't bring herself to meet this guy's intense, gray eyes.

Mister Peabody spoke up. "Missing?" His body tensed at the accusation. "To my knowledge, no one's gone missing because of my Halloween attraction."

"That's not how the police feel," Tory said.

Mister Peabody swallowed hard. "Yes, recently there have been some young people in this city that they say are missing," he admitted, "and yes, recently employees have not shown up for work or returned our calls, quitting with no consideration or notice." He paused, brow furrowed. "Forgive me, present company excluded," he continued, "but it's been my experience that *young* people, especially college students, are unreliable. They come and go. Don't get me started on runaways, hopping on buses to LA, hoping to make it big in the movies." He took a deep breath. "No one's proven foul play or that anyone is actually missing. As for the police?" He gave a dismissive wave of a hand. "We're just a convenient scapegoat for their incompetence." Finished, he slumped back in his chair.

Penny glanced up from the desktop to gauge the ghost hunter's reaction.

Tory eyed Mister Peabody with a mixture of what looked like cynicism and resignation. At least his jaw had relaxed. His fists were unclenched. He was definitely more calm, more collected. "I'll admit," he said, "I haven't heard anything on the news about missing people."

Mister Peabody leaned forward again. "My point exactly," he said. "The police have no proof of foul play. All of the people missing are of age. It's a big city. People come and go all the time." He gave another dismissive wave of a hand. "As I said before, they just picked up and left, with no consideration, no notice, as young people often do."

Tory put the palms of his hands on the desktop. He leaned close, almost nose to nose with Mister Peabody. "Why *then* are we here?" he asked.

Mister Peabody slumped back in the chair, either to get distance between himself and the ghost hunter or in resignation. "As I told you on the phone," he said, "because of the recent rumors that Fright House is truly haunted."

Tory straightened. He now looked amused. "I would think, Mister Peabody, that rumors of a Halloween attraction being haunted would help business, not hurt it."

Gabriel suddenly put in his two cents. He said, "Yeah, it was like a carnival tonight."

"You've got plenty of customers," Lizzie agreed.

Mister Peabody nodded. "Good for business, yes," he acknowledged. "Because of this silly rumor, we have more customers than ever this year. So far."

"What's the problem then, dude?" Cheech asked.

Mister Peabody turned to the Tech Specialist. "As I told Mister Jackson on the phone, what I've been trying to tell all of you tonight, is that it's employees we're losing. The ones I do have are mostly security for crowd control. We barely have enough staff to keep both floors open to the public."

The ghost hunters shared a look of confusion that Penny didn't fully understand, causing her to find her voice. In spite of herself, she said, "You took the tour. You saw firsthand how short-staffed we are." Expectedly, she eyed the entire group of outsiders, her gaze finally falling on their leader.

"Not really," Tory said.

"What Miss Winters means," Mister Peabody interjected, "is at one time, we had enough employees to fill the lobby with mental patients. We used to have a nurse behind the counter. We had an attendant that would greet customers. Now, as you have seen, the lobby's completely empty. Instead of actors, we have a video playing on the TV that tells people some history about the hospital. It also instructs them on where to go, what to do. We've even automated the iron door so it opens and closes by itself." Sighing, he shook his head. "All the fun's gone. Half the padded cells in the hallway are empty. We had to shut down some of the torture rooms in the basement too. Now, because of Samuel, we'll have to have the elevators on auto run, as well." He looked imploringly. "Everyone's scared, so they're leaving. We're running this place on a skeleton crew."

Isabel giggled. "Freaking awesome."

"I need a change of underwear," Cheech muttered.

Gabriel clutched the medal around his neck. "God help us."

Tory wheeled on his crew. He gave them a look that clamped them up.

That's odd, Penny thought, unable to comprehend what they had alluded to. In her mind, she sighed. There was so much these days she couldn't comprehend. She had no time to give it the consideration it deserved, though, for the group's leader again commanded her attention.

Tory turned back to Penny and Mister Peabody with that

steely gaze. "What do you want us to do?" he asked.

"Simple," Mister Peabody answered. "As I told you on the phone, prove the place isn't haunted." He paused, eyed the ghost hunters. "You said you could do that."

Tory didn't respond. Instead, he scrutinized Penny. "It's Miss Winters, right?" he asked.

Penny looked away. She fidgeted from foot to foot at the unwanted attention. "Penny," she whispered. "Please call me Penny."

"Huh," Morgan exclaimed.

Cheech grinned. "Your first name is *Penny*?" he asked.

Confused, Penny nodded. "That's right," she said.

Cheech turned to Morgan. "Told you."

Morgan just stared, slack-jawed.

"That's enough," Tory commanded.

"What does my first name have to do with anything?" Penny asked, a skullcap of fear gripping her scalp, as though someone had just walked on her grave.

"Nothing, Miss Winters...uh, I mean *Penny*," Tory assured.

Penny started to protest the brush-off, but she was interrupted.

Mister Peabody said, "Look, we believe that if PSI proves there's no paranormal activity at Fright House then our employees will have to believe it. They will then return." He gave the leader of the ghost hunters a beseeching look. "Mister Jackson, we need employees to keep up that carnival atmosphere you described tonight. People will stop coming if we have to keep cutting back on scares. Halloween is tomorrow night, a Wednesday. That means a long weekend of celebrating. All the nights leading up to Halloween are about breaking even. It's Halloween night and the long weekend that bring profit. We have to stay open through Sunday."

Tory took a deep breath. He looked from Mister Peabody to Penny then back again to Mister Peabody. He asked, "You both believe beyond a doubt that Fright House isn't haunted?"

"Absolutely," Mister Peabody readily answered. "With all due respect, there's no such thing as ghosts."

Tory nodded. "Uh-huh," he said. He turned his steely gaze on Penny. "What about you, Miss Winters? I mean, Penny...do you feel the same as your boss?"

Penny shifted nervously. *I don't know what to believe anymore,* her mind screamed. Without much conviction, she said, "There's no such thing as ghosts."

Tory sighed, apparently unconvinced. He turned back to Mister Peabody. "How long has Fright House been in operation?" he asked, suddenly businesslike.

"Four years," Mister Peabody answered.

Tory shrugged. "Any problems or rumors like this in the past years?"

Mister Peabody shook his head. Emphatically, he answered, "Never. Just good fun."

"What about employees quitting?" Tory asked.

"A seasonal business like this always has high turnover in employees," Mister Peabody admitted. "I've never had employees just plain too scared to show up or to even call in to quit, though."

"Uh-huh," Tory said. "So what's different this year?"

Mister Peabody shrugged. "Nothing," he claimed. "Some employees returned from past years, but most have been new. Miss Winters herself is new. She's only been here a few weeks."

"Really?" Tory said, eyeing Penny with a look of renewed interest.

Penny fidgeted.

"As I said," Mister Peabody continued, "there's always been a high turnover."

"Uh-huh," Tory said. He studied Penny.

Penny couldn't make eye contact. She wished they'd all just go away—Mister Peabody, the ghost hunters, the ghosts... if they really existed. Everyone. She just wanted to be alone. She just wanted to go back to the way things were before coming to Fright House, whether it was an illusion or not. In spite of being on the run, living hand to mouth, at least then life *felt* normal. She stared at her shoes. Now it was anything but.

"Anything else?" Tory asked.

Mister Peabody shook his head. "I've told you everything," he said. "Can you help us?"

Tory continued his study of Penny. "Can I have a few moments alone with my investigators?"

Mister Peabody stood on wobbly legs. "Certainly," he answered. "You and your team talk it over. We'll just be out in the hallway." He started around the desk, toward the door.

Penny remained rooted. Fidgeting, but rooted.

"Miss Winters," Mister Peabody called over his shoulder as he opened the door to leave. "Are you coming?"

Penny forced her legs to move. Without saying a word, she followed her boss to the door, out into the hallway, wishing she could keep on going and never return.

It was too late for that.

Chapter Twenty-Three

The PSI team closed ranks.

"Bro, he's jerkin' our chain," Cheech insisted.

"For once, kid, I'm forced to agree with the derelict hippy," Gabriel confirmed.

"Me, too," Lizzie agreed.

Morgan shrugged. "It's unanimous."

Tory turned to their Goth trainee. "Isabel?" he asked.

Isabel grinned wickedly. "I disagree," she said. "This place is definitely haunted. I just know it is."

"You just wish it was," Gabriel said. He turned to Tory. "You're not going to listen to *her*, are you? She's—"

"Entitled to her opinion," Tory interrupted.

Isabel giggled. "Thanks, boss."

"She's entitled to her opinion, but do *you* agree with her?" Lizzie asked, adjusting her glasses, staring at Tory as if she was an entomologist and he was a bug specimen.

Tory hesitated. "I'm not sure," he finally answered. "I'm not sure what to believe."

"Dude, I saw a nurse," Cheech insisted, "a hot nurse."

"She wanted him, too," Morgan added. "I could tell."

"Righteous, dude," Cheech agreed.

"There was an attendant, too," Gabriel argued.

"Plenty of mental patients," Lizzie added.

"*We* were on the TV," Cheech said, "not an instructional video."

Morgan nodded. He slapped Cheech on the back. "*He* looked good, too."

"There were plenty of employees," Lizzie added.

"Dude, the guy's lying like a dirty rug," Cheech insisted.

"How can we believe anything this guy says?" Gabriel asked.

There was a long pause, and everyone looking to their young leader for answers.

Just the way Tory liked it.

Finally, Isabel whispered, "It's haunted."

Everyone started their arguments, again.

"Shhh," Tory warned. "I don't want them to hear." He stared at the closed door. "I'm not saying the place is haunted," he whispered. "I'm not saying it isn't. I'm just telling you that something's not right."

Lizzie cocked her head. She adjusted her glasses. "What do you mean?" she asked. "What's not right?"

Tory didn't readily answer. Instead, he reflected on Lizzie's question. He thought briefly of telling them all about how he had felt agitated, nervous, and paranoid during the tour, all about the little girl in the cemetery, all about the *empty* torture chamber where he thought he saw the suicide, all about hearing his mother's...

Quickly, he decided against it. For now, he wanted it all to remain his secret. He wanted proof. Otherwise, they'd think him crazy. So, he decided to cast attention onto something— or better yet—*someone* else.

"What about *Penny*?" Tory asked. He turned to Cheech. "Didn't the *Ghost Radar* app continue to say the name, *Penny*?" He paused. "Have you considered that?"

Cheech gulped. "Yeah."

"Have any of you considered that?"

No one answered.

Tory shrugged. "Coincidence?" he asked.

Silence ensued.

"Cheech, you're the one who insisted that the app works," Tory reminded the Tech Specialist.

"I'll stand by that," Cheech said.

"So if we go on the assumption that Cheech is right," Tory continued, "that the app works, then we can't dismiss the EVP." He looked into the face of each team member. He had them hooked. "We can't chalk up the app repeating the name Penny along with the fact that the new manager's name *is* Penny as coincidence. Besides that, according to Mister Peabody this Penny Winters has only been here approximately three to four weeks."

"That's just about the time the rumors started," Lizzie acknowledged.

Gabriel looked troubled. "How do you figure she's involved?" he asked.

"That I don't know," Tory admitted. "I'd like to find out." He looked from member to member. "Wouldn't you?"

Everyone nodded in agreement.

Tory grinned. "Good," he said. "Tonight, we conduct Dead Time."

"Freaking awesome," Isabel said.

Everyone ignored her.

"As soon as Fright House closes for the night, we set up the equipment," Tory commanded. "Cheech, you're in charge."

Cheech nodded. "You bet, k..." He grinned. "...*boss man.*"

Tory grinned wider. That's what he liked. Total compliance to his authority, total commitment to the job. "Everyone helps," he said. "We only have a few hours. I want the whole place monitored. Use wireless equipment where you can. Where you can't, conceal the wires and cables out of the way. The equipment too, for that matter. It might need to stay in place for the next night or two during operating hours. I don't want to have to tear the equipment down and put it back up each night. Everybody got it?"

Everyone nodded.

"Where are we setting up Tech Central?" Cheech asked.

Tory shrugged. "We'll get Peabody to give us a room up here that's not in use."

"Got it," Cheech responded.

Tory cocked his head. Suddenly, a thought that he hadn't considered before struck him hard, like being plowed into by an eighteen wheeler. The impact of it left him reeling. How could he have missed it? It was so obvious. "Uh, everyone be careful," he warned. "If this isn't a scam, we have bigger problems than Fright House being haunted."

Gabriel flinched. A nervous shadow passed over his face. He asked, "If Fright House is haunted, what in God's name could be a bigger problem?"

"You remember the PSI episode playing on the TV in the lobby?" Tory asked.

"Yeah," everyone answered in unison, as if practiced.

"The attack in the elevator, too?" Tory asked.

"Yeah," everyone answered.

Gabriel fidgeted. "Of course, what about it?"

"Fright House knows we're here," Tory answered, lowering his voice to a quiet hush. "And it's not happy."

Chapter Twenty-Four

In the hallway, Penny waited impatiently for the PSI team to decide their fate. She hugged herself against the sudden chill.

Mister Peabody stood several feet away.

Standing next to Mister Peabody was an older guy, speaking in a hushed tone. He looked grandfatherly—kind and gentle, with wisdom creased into his face, hair the color of fresh snow. The old fashioned, tweed suit he wore made him look...

What was the old-time term?

...*dapper.*

Mister Peabody suddenly turned away from the old guy, breaking off the one-sided conversation. To Penny, he said, "Miss Winters, in the morning, call a repairman to look at the air conditioner. It's too blasted cold in here."

"Yes, sir," Penny answered.

Mister Peabody turned back to his visitor. The old guy quietly continued to speak.

Penny hadn't seen from where this guy had come. She had visited the restroom. When she returned, the hallway felt colder. The grandfatherly man was already there. He spoke in hushed tones but with emphatic, animated gestures.

Mister Peabody said nothing. For the most part, he stood fairly still, with his head down.

Who was this old guy? From where did he come? What could he be saying? Why didn't Mister Peabody respond in any way?

Penny inched her way toward the two men. She strained to hear.

"You should never have invited them here," the old guy whispered. "They don't belong. Send them away."

Mister Peabody remained silent, head bowed.

Penny eased closer. She didn't know who this guy was, but she wished Mister Peabody would heed the advice. To her, it sounded reasonable.

"We don't need them here," the old guy continued. "They

will only get in the way. Send them away. Immediately."

Mister Peabody said nothing.

The man with snow-white hair just shook his head. He looked up, glancing at Penny. There was concern sculpted onto his careworn face. His eyes, however, were dark, cold.

Penny shivered at the sight. She didn't know why, but this kindly old grandfather now frightened her. She eased back a few steps, back where she first had stood.

"If they remain," the old guy said, his voice no longer hushed, "there will be consequences."

Again, Penny shivered.

What did that mean? Consequences? Was it a threat?

The old guy smiled. It was not a benevolent smile as one would expect from a kindly grandfather. This smile reeked of evil intent. "Consequences," he repeated. "Awful consequences." With that, he turned away and walked down the hallway toward the elevators.

The door to Mister Peabody's office opened.

Both Penny and Mister Peabody turned their attention there.

Tory Jackson stood, framed in the doorway. He said, "Tonight, we'll conduct Dead Time."

The lights in the hallway flickered.

Penny gasped. She looked after the old guy, but he was gone. The elevator had never arrived—there was no chime. Where had he disappeared?

The lights continued to flicker.

Penny turned her attention back to Tory.

More importantly, what the hell was *Dead Time*?

Chapter Twenty-Five

Under the twinkling, yellow lights that surrounded the parking lot at Fright House, Cheech and Morgan unloaded large equipment cases from the bus. As usual, they did all the heavy lifting, hauling the cases across the now empty parking lot, piling them outside the front door.

Cheech sat down on one of the bigger cases to rest. Breathing heavily, he asked, "Why us? Why always us?"

Morgan flashed a grin and flexed his muscles. "I don't know why you, skinny boy," he answered, "but I'm pretty sure I know why me."

Cheech scratched at his unkempt beard. "Yeah, well, I'll take brains over brawn any day," he insisted.

Morgan laughed. "Too bad you have neither."

"Big ape," Cheech shot back.

Morgan laughed again. "Brainless toothpick," he jabbed.

Cheech opened his mouth to respond but stopped short.

"Good choice," Morgan said, "in a test of wits or muscles, you lose every time."

Cheech shook his head. He sighed in resignation.

Morgan grinned. "Now, let's get this stuff inside," he suggested.

Cheech made no move to comply. "So, dude, what do you think of this *Penny* thing?" he asked

Morgan stared at his friend. He didn't know what to think. He still didn't believe the *Ghost Radar* app actually worked. Still, it was a pretty big coincidence that the manager of Fright House turned out to be a girl named Penny. "I'm not sure," he said.

"Want to know what I think?" Cheech asked.

"I'm just glad to know that you still *can* think," Morgan retorted.

Undaunted, Cheech continued, "This Penny chick knows more than she's letting on."

"What do you mean?" Morgan asked.

"I'm not sure," Cheech admitted. "It's a feeling more than

anything else. I'd bet, though, that she's knee-deep into what-ever's going on here."

Morgan considered that possibility. "It does seem pretty coincidental that all the weird stuff around here started after Mister Peabody hired her," he admitted. "I—"

A sudden burst of music cut Morgan short. It came from inside the case underneath Cheech.

Hearing it, Cheech jumped off the case as if a ferocious beast just bit him in the butt. "What the—"

They both stared at the equipment case, listening.

> *Here's a story of a girl*
> *Who grew up lost and lonely*
> *Thinking love was fairy tale*
> *And trouble was made only for me*

"Open it," Morgan said.
Cheech gulped. "You open it."
The song continued.

> *Even in the darkness*
> *Every color can be found*
> *And every day of rain*
> *Brings water flowing*
> *To things growing in the ground*

Morgan approached the case with the same trepidation as approaching a poisonous viper. With caution, he snapped open the metal locks, lifting the lid. The ghost box, a convert-ed AM/FM radio, lay amongst the clutter of equipment within the case. Its LCD display was lit. Rather than sweeping up and down the bandwidth, creating white noise as it had been modified to do, it tuned in to one station, the volume turned up as high as possible.

> *Grief replaced with pity*
> *For a city barely coping*
> *Dreams are easy to achieve*
> *If hope is all I'm hoping to be*

"Why did it turn on?" Morgan asked. "Why is it tuned in to a station?"

Wide-eyed, Cheech shrugged. "Search me," he answered, "to both your questions."

"You're the specialist of all things techie," Morgan insisted.

Cheech opened his mouth for rebuttal, but no words came out.

Awestruck, they both listened.

> *Anytime you're hurt there's one*
> *Who has it worse around*
> *And every drop of rain*
> *Will keep you growing*
> *Seeds you're sowing in the ground*

"Dude," Cheech blurted, "I know that song." He paused. "Oh, dude. We're screwed."

Morgan didn't understand. "What? Slow down. Tell me what's going on in that addled brain of yours."

"Dude, that song's from *Dr. Horrible's Sing-Along Blog*."

> *So keep your head up Billy, buddy*

The song ended.

"So?" Morgan asked. "What about it?"

The radio shut itself off.

"That's weird," Morgan muttered.

Cheech fidgeted from foot to foot. He eyed their surroundings as if something in the night stalked them. "Oh, dude. We're really screwed."

"Tell me," Morgan barked.

Cheech froze. He stared at his partner. "The name of that song," he whispered, "is *Penny's Song*."

Morgan's jaw dropped. He had no time to react, because an instant later, a lightning bolt cracked open the night sky.

It startled both ghost hunters.

Morgan looked up at the blanket of clouds. "There was no sign earlier of an oncoming storm."

Rain drops splattered down.

"There is now," Cheech answered. "A big storm, dude."

Another bolt of lightning lit up the night. Thunder cracked like a bullwhip.

"Let's get this stuff inside," Morgan said. He closed the opened case, snapping it shut.

Rain pelted them.

Picking up two cases, he said, "Quick, before everything gets soaked." He turned, starting for the front door.

Behind, Cheech muttered, "We're so screwed."

Chapter Twenty-Six

Inside, an oncoming storm of another kind threatened. This storm walked the hallways, invisible. It lurked in the shadows, clandestine. It hid within the walls, in secrecy. It bided its time, spying. Patiently, it waited for the key to set it free.

Meanwhile, neither Cheech nor Morgan mentioned to anyone the experience with the ghost box. It gnawed at their brains like a vulture picking at a rotting carcass. Still, they spoke nothing about it with anyone or between themselves, either. It was as if voicing their concerns, as if discussing the event, made it somehow more real, more threatening. While ignoring it all made it more illusionary, almost dreamlike.

Instead, throughout the three floors of Fright House, they and the rest of the PSI team methodically set up infrared video cameras, EVP audio recorders, EMF detectors, ELF detectors, infrared motion detectors, vibration monitors, digital thermometers with sensing probes, full spectrum cameras, and thermal imaging cameras. Except for Isabel, they all were models of professionalism and efficiency as they ran wires and cables to Tech Central—a room on the top floor that had not currently been in use.

In that room, they had set up four computers, three four-channel digital video recorders, and three audio recorders, along with motion and vibration monitors. Three of the computers were hooked up for video. Their screens showed multiple shots of each floor from different angles. The fourth computer was programmed with *Audacity Audio Editor* to clean up EVP recordings and monitor audio levels. Gray wires and cables snaked their way everywhere along the floor.

Little did any of the ghost hunters know, that Fright House monitored *their* every move as Dead Time fast approached.

Chapter Twenty-Seven

The basement insulated Isabel from the turbulent storm outside. In the Cemetery Room, she sat in semi-darkness and quiet solitude among the glowing headstones, fashioning two voodoo dolls out of white linen.

The air conditioning clanked on without warning.

Startled, she let out a squeal. She stopped working, cocked her head, and listened.

The AC's steady hum broke her solitude, her concentration. The surrounding air currents planted unwanted cold kisses on her face, stroked her hair with what felt like cadaverous hands.

She was alone. She knew it. Still, she couldn't fight the weird feeling that someone watched her from afar.

Shivering, gooseflesh attacking the back of her neck, her scalp, her bare arms, she scanned her morbid surroundings.

No one was there. She was, after all, alone.

Still, her heart raced as if in the throes of passion, albeit cold, heartless passion rather than what she longed for—hot and heartfelt.

Taking a deep, frigid breath, she went back to her undertaking. She needed to concentrate if the spell was going to work.

The AC continued its cold-hearted attentions—kissing her face, stroking her hair, giving her goose bumps as if they were flowers.

With the white-linen voodoo dolls completed, she pulled the loose hairs she had taken from Morgan from her pocket. She folded the hairs into the cloth of one of the dolls. She then plucked a few hairs from her own head, folding them into the cloth of the other doll. With a length of blue silk thread, she bound the two voodoo dolls together.

As she did so, she chanted, "You, Morgan, are mine. I, Isabel, am yours. We are now bound together. We are now one."

A burst of chilly air slapped her across the face like a jealous lover.

She gasped, dropping the bound dolls. Shivering, hugging herself against the frosty air currents, she again scanned the Cemetery Room. The uneasy feeling of not being alone returned, yet she still saw no one in the bleakness of her surroundings.

Her imagination had surely taken control of her senses.

The air conditioning clanked off, its humming silenced, its unwanted cold advances done.

With a deep breath, she reached down and picked up the dolls. "It's done," she whispered. "He's mine."

Standing, she tiptoed to a fake tree. There, she hid the dolls within the branches. Now she only had to somehow maneuver Morgan into the Cemetery Room, as close to the dolls as possible, where the spell was at its most potent. That's when she'd make her move. There was no way he'd be able to resist her now.

She grinned. "He's mine," she whispered.

Turning away, she crept through the pretend graveyard, back through the entryway, into the torture room. From there, she made her way to the elevator for the ride back up to the top floor to rejoin her team.

No one the wiser.

Chapter Twenty-Eight

In the Cemetery Room, the AC clanked on. It hummed steadily. Frigid air blasted through the room, knocking the bound voodoo dolls from their secret perch. The blue silk thread that bound the dolls together unknotted. The dolls separated. A burst of swirling air freed the loose hairs from within the folds, sending them and the dolls scattering through the graveyard like dead leaves.

The spell was broken.

Chapter Twenty-Nine

Fright House's lobby glowed sickly yellow. Outside its barred windows, lightning flashed, thunder boomed, wind whistled an eerie tune, and rain pelted the glass.

Penny stood in the lobby at the foot of a stepladder. A set of tools lay at her feet. With little interest, she watched Tory at the top of the ladder as he installed a wireless video camera up by the ceiling. Her thoughts kept drifting to the old guy talking to Mister Peabody in the upstairs hallway.

Who was he? From where did he come? More importantly, what did he mean when he said if *they* remain there will be consequences, awful consequences? Was it a warning? Or was it a threat?

Lightning, thunder, wind, and rain answered those thoughts.

She shivered. Not from the furious storm outside. From the memory of the dark, cold look in the old guy's eyes when he had proclaimed the *awful consequences* if the ghost hunters remained. That look told her it was not just a warning. It was a threat.

A thought struck her. She didn't want the ghost hunters there. Maybe the warning or threat really came from her subconscious. Maybe the old guy hadn't been there at all. Maybe he was nothing more than a hallucination, a figment of her wild imagination that her mind created to lend voice to her own concerns. After all, Mister Peabody never truly acknowledged the man now that she thought on it.

As a lightning bolt cracked outside, another even more horrifying thought struck her. Maybe the old guy *was* really there. Maybe he was a ghost.

Crap...

Another hairline crack formed in her sanity, threatening to shatter it to pieces.

"Would you hand me that Phillips screwdriver?" Tory asked.

"Huh?" Penny muttered, the sound of the ghost hunter's

voice abruptly freeing her from her internal turmoil. She looked up, slightly confused. "Huh?" she repeated.

Tory smiled down at her. "The Phillips screwdriver...would you hand it to me, please?"

"Oh," Penny answered, "sure." Flustered, she stared down at the tools at her feet.

"The Phillips," Tory repeated.

Penny reached down, grabbed the screwdriver, and handed it to the ghost hunter. He still smiled at her as he took the tool, but it looked patronizing.

"Nice of you to volunteer to help out," Tory said as he went back to work installing the video camera.

Penny cleared her throat. "Seeing as you insisted on someone from Fright House management being present for this little *séance*, I didn't have much choice."

Tory chuckled. "You mean Peabody gave you no choice."

"That's right," Penny answered. "Did you think he was going to volunteer himself?"

"No, I expect not." Tory chuckled again. "Could be worse," he said. "You could be out in this storm."

"True," Penny acknowledged. In truth, however, she would have preferred taking her chances getting home in the downpour—lightning, thunder, and all—than remaining at Fright House for this ritualistic nonsense about to take place.

Tory stopped working as if just struck by a thought. He looked down the ladder at her. "You said that you'd been losing employees, right?"

Penny nodded. She wasn't sure she liked this sudden turn in the conversation, but she answered, "That's right."

Tory gave her a knowing look. He went back to work on the video camera. "Did anyone not show up for work tonight?"

"Well, let me think," Penny answered. She really did have to give it some thought. Was there anyone new missing? After a moment, she realized there was. "Actually, yes. Jake Brewer."

"Did he call?"

Penny shook her head. "No, just like the others." She then remembered Jake's antics in the hallway. "The funny thing is I saw him earlier in the day, too."

Tory continued working. "Did he seem okay?"

Penny laughed but without humor. "More than okay," she said. "Jake likes practical jokes. He played one on me today. Scared me half to death."

Tory stopped working. He looked back down the ladder. "If Jake was here earlier in the day, then why didn't he show up tonight for work?"

Penny shrugged. "I don't know," she mumbled. "He's unreliable like most college kids, I guess." Even as she repeated what had become Mister Peabody's mantra to explain everything, she didn't truly believe it. These so-called *kids* were in truth older than her and probably more reliable, too. Besides, why *would* Jake be practicing during the day just to not to show up that night for work? It didn't make sense.

"Here," Tory said.

"Huh?" Penny answered, flustered.

"I'm finished." Tory held the screwdriver out for her to take.

"Oh." Penny reached out for the tool. Her hand brushed Tory's. At that moment, something inexplicable happened, something that had never happened before. She saw something in her mind's eye that was as clear and as real as anything she had ever experienced or witnessed in the physical world.

* * * *

Except for the glow of a Darth Vader nightlight, darkness engulfed a small, cozy bedroom. Toys littered the floor. A little boy lay in bed, asleep.

A woman sat on the edge of the bed, next to the little boy, watching. With some apprehension, she reached out to touch the boy's forehead.

He startled awake. Gasping, he sat up. "Mom?" he whispered. He rubbed at his eyes. "Mom?"

The little boy's mom smiled. "Be a good boy, Tory," she whispered. "Always make me proud."

Before Tory could respond, the door to his bedroom opened. The light from the hallway washed over the small bedroom.

A man was framed in the doorway.

The woman looked over her shoulder at the man then back at her son. She smiled before whispering, "I love you."

She disappeared.

The man came into the bedroom, approaching the boy's bed.

Tory rubbed at his eyes, looked around, bewildered. "Mom? Mom?"

The man sat down right where Tory's mom had sat just a moment ago. When he spoke, his voice cracked. "Son, Mom's not..."

"Dad, where'd Mom go?" Tory asked.

Tory's dad choked back sobs. He pulled his son into his arms. He held on tight. "With God," he croaked.

The bedroom and its two occupants slowly faded away. In their place was another room—gloomy, the air thick with death. A woman swung from a rope, the noose tightly wound around her throat. Her eyes bulged. Her thick tongue protruded grotesquely from her open mouth. At her feet lay a knocked-over stool. Next to it rested a piece of paper with something written on it.

* * * *

"Miss Winters."

Someone was gently shaking her.

"Miss Winters? I mean, Penny."

Her eyes focused. It was Tory standing before her, the adult Tory, not the little boy from her vision. He was grasping her shoulders, gently shaking her, calling her name.

Dazed, Penny looked around. A flash of lightning at the windows, a boom of thunder, and rain pummeling the glass helped bring her around. She was back in Fright House's lobby, everything—including Tory's face—looking jaundiced.

"Penny," Tory said, "are you all right?"

Unable to stop herself for some inexplicable reason, Penny muttered, "You saw your mother, after she *hanged...*"

"What?" Tory's grasp tightened. His voice hardened. "What did you say?"

Penny stared into the ghost hunter's yellow face. What she saw there both saddened and frightened her at the same time.

Tory's grip constricted. "What did you say?" he hissed.

"Get off me," Penny demanded. The tone of the accusation reminded her of Tilly's not all that long ago. "Leave me alone." She shook herself free.

"What did you say about my *mother*?" Tory demanded, jaw clenched, hands fisted.

Penny shook her head. "Just leave me alone," she cried.

She turned away. She rushed from the lobby. Her feet moved as fast as her racing heart, through the open doorway and down the red-lit hallway, before she could even think of where she was heading.

Outside, the storm raged on.

Chapter Thirty

Penny made it to the elevator. She hit the glowing button. The doors swished open. Rushing on, she hit the button for the top floor. The doors swished closed. Before the elevator rose too far, she punched the emergency stop button. The elevator jerked to a stop, and the alarm rang. She didn't care. She just wanted to be alone, to get away from it all. The elevator offered insulation from the ongoing disturbance outside and from confrontation with Tory inside. The only turmoil it couldn't keep out was within herself.

She slid down the back wall and plopped onto the floor. There, she sat hugging her legs, knees pulled up under her chin. Hot tears streamed down her cheeks. Snot ran from her nose. Sobs choked her throat.

It was like school all over again. Tory's eyes held the same cold look. His voice had sounded just as incriminating as Tilly's had all those years ago. Even though he hadn't said it, she knew that he had thought the same thing her friends had accused her of being back then. What her high school classmates had posted on Facebook, on Twitter, in private texts. What her teachers surely believed. Her parents, too.

She was a *freak*.

It was why she ran away. She couldn't take the taunting at school anymore. She couldn't take the cyber bullying. Or the accusatory looks of her teachers, her parents.

She closed her tear-filled eyes. She sniffed snot back up her nose.

Tremors racked her entire body as she continued to cry uncontrollably.

Running away had accomplished nothing. She couldn't run from herself. She was still a *freak*.

She hugged her legs tighter, resting her forehead on top of her knees.

The fluorescent lights flickered. The alarm continued to sound.

It didn't matter. It didn't stop her befuddled thoughts

from beginning to wander down dark corridors better left unexplored.

Freak!

It didn't keep her mind focused on the reality of her own time, her own space.

Freak!

Soon, she no longer heard the alarm at all. Soon, her brain shut itself off to the sights and sounds of the physical world. Instead, her consciousness entered a hypnotic state that set her soul free to roam the world.

Chapter Thirty-One

Tony Scout sat on the floor of his living room in the lotus position—cross-legged, feet placed on opposing thighs. The medium's arms hung loose, hands resting palms up on his knees. This position encouraged him to breathe properly. It fostered physical stability during his daily meditation.

It helped set free his mind.

He closed his eyes even though the room was completely dark. His breathing became shallow. His heart rate slowed to a crawl as he allowed his consciousness to take him to wherever it chose. At first, his thoughts revisited the events of the day. They then stretched to random memories throughout his long life. Soon, however, his mind was empty, free to explore other possibilities, other streams of consciousness.

* * * *

He found himself standing in a long hallway, lit in red as if it were the path that led to the underworld. Instead of scorching heat as he imagined Hell to radiate, he shivered from the bone-chilling, bitter cold. His lungs felt as though they were going to freeze, as though he would never breathe again. What little breath he could muster came out in intermittent, frosty plumes. Gooseflesh tightened his scalp, ran amok along his spine. Frostbite threatened his already numbed extremities. Hugging himself against this biting cold, he turned in a circle to further examine his strange surroundings. Empty cells with iron bars lined the walls on both sides of him.

What kind of place was this? A prison? Why would his consciousness take him here?

Examining the cells closer, he thought he saw dark forms behind those iron bars. Shadows that shimmered and pulsed as they paced within the small confines of their prisons.

Evil lurked here, he was sure of it. He could feel it in the frigid air, see it in the red light, in the strangely moving shadows. Again, he asked himself why his mind would travel to such a place, why his mind would choose to show him such a thing.

That's when he heard it. Music. Faint at first, but growing in volume.

> *Every time it rains*
> *It rains pennies from heaven*
> *Don'tcha know each cloud contains*
> *Pennies from heaven?*
> *You'll find your fortune fallin' all over town*
> *Be sure that your umbrella*
> *Is upside down*

"*Pennies from Heaven* by Bing Crosby," he muttered, recognizing both the old song and the now-dead singer.

What could it mean? He wasn't sure. What he did notice was that the temperature rose with the volume of the song.

> *Trade them for a package of sunshine and*
> *flowers*
> *If you want the things you love*
> *You must have showers*
> *So when you hear it thunder*
> *Don't run under a tree*
> *There'll be pennies from heaven*
> *For you and me*

The temperature in the hallway continued to climb. A chime rang out above the music. At the far end of the hallway, doors swished open, revealing a heavenly white light in contrast to the surrounding lurid red. Out of that bright-white light stepped a beautiful angel. This angel had no wings, but still hovered above the floor. The song continued.

> *Every time it rains, it rains*
> *Pennies from heaven*
> *Don'tcha know each cloud contains*
> *Pennies from heaven?*
> *You'll find your fortune fallin'*
> *All over town*
> *Be sure that your umbrella*
> *Is upside down*

The climate in the hallway was now comfortable. He no longer shivered or hugged himself. He could feel his fingers and toes.

Bringing the white, heavenly light with her, the beautiful angel glided down the hallway toward him. As she did so, the pulsing, shimmering shadows no longer paced within their prisons. They apparently had either disappeared or remained hidden, fearful of the angel before them. It was as if the angel somehow beat back the evil, as if she were able to control everything around her, maybe with the song.

> *Trade them for a package of sunshine and flowers*
> *If you want the things you love you must have showers*

The angel stood before him. She looked young. Her pale skin radiated with the bright-white light. Her shoulder-length, brown hair fluttered as if caught in a soft, warm air current. Her deep-brown, penetrating eyes demanded full attention. She held out her hand. Within her palm, she held a key. She let go of it. The key floated in the air.

In that moment, she was gone. Only the key remained, floating there as the song ended.

> *So when you hear it thunder*
> *Don't run under a tree*
> *There'll be pennies from heaven*
> *For you and for me*

Tony reached for the key.

* * * *

His eyes shot open. He gasped for air as if he'd been deprived of it, held underwater. His heart rammed the inside of his ribcage. Sweat plastered thinning hair to scalp, shirt to body. He held his right hand in a tight fist, fingernails drawing blood.

"Holy Mother of God," he whispered, trying to catch his breath, slow his racing heart.

Slowly, painfully, he opened his fist and stared at his palm. Blood oozed from the cuts where his fingernails had dug into skin. Resting on his palm was a key made of copper.

"Pennies from heaven," he murmured.

His cell phone rang, startling him. Gulping down the lump in his throat, he pulled his cell from his shirt pocket.

The call was from Tory.

He looked from the picture of Tory's young, brooding face on the display of his cell to the copper key resting in his palm. He sang, "When you hear it thunder. Don't run under a tree. There'll be pennies from heaven. For you and for me."

Answering the phone, he whispered, "I knew you'd be calling."

Chapter Thirty-Two

Wind and rain attacked the windows. Lightning lit up the night outside. Thunder sounded, as if an omen of misfortune to come.

Tory stared after Penny, jaw clenched, hands fisted. His impulse was to go after the girl and demand an explanation.

He remained anchored. It was as if his legs were cement, immovable, like those of a statue.

Instead, he just glared in the direction Penny had fled. He stewed over what she had said, or at least at what she had almost said.

You saw your mother, after she hanged...

The girl hadn't finished her thought. She didn't need to.

Tory closed his eyes and rubbed his face with both hands. A headache, much like the one earlier that night, slammed him. Imagined mosquitoes again buzzed his ears. He began pacing in a circle, as agitated as Mother Nature outside.

There was no way Penny could know about his mother's suicide or that he had seen what he believed to be his mother's spirit afterward.

You saw your mother, after she hanged...

Penny did know. By all indications, she *did* know. That was impossible, though.

He continued to circle, rubbing the back of his achingly stiff neck as he did so. The buzzing intensified, the illusionary pests in his ears multiplying.

Nothing made sense.

He stopped circling. Pain slammed his head. His ears buzzed. Involuntarily, his head jerked, face twitched.

Glowering at the open doorway, he again thought of going after Penny, demanding she explain herself.

He made fists.

Or better yet, just smashing her pretty, little face.

That thought stopped him. How could he even consider such a violent thing?

Nothing made sense. Not the girl knowing all his dirty,

little secrets. Certainly not the way he felt. No matter what, he had never struck anyone before, especially a female.

His hands opened. He held them up, examining them as if they belonged to someone else.

How could he even have considered doing such a thing?

Perhaps the violent storm outside somehow fed his inner turbulence, altering his personal nature, for he was not a violent man.

"Be a good boy, Tory," his mother's spirit had whispered to him all those years ago while sitting on the edge of his bed. *"Always make me proud."*

At the time, as a little boy, he hadn't understood why or how his mother could've hanged herself. It wasn't until much later that he was allowed to read the note she'd left behind. That was when he discovered she had endured unimaginable pain from inoperable bone cancer. Still, even before that discovery, and especially after, he had always strived to be good, had always tried to make his mother proud, just as she had wanted.

The pain in his head subsided. The buzzing quieted. He let his arms drop to his sides, hands relaxed, open.

He would never hurt anyone. No matter what.

Besides, seeing his mother after death was the one defining moment in his life. That moment had motivated him to take the money from his substantial trust fund to establish *Paranormal Scene Investigations* and buy his way onto cable television. It's what started his quest to seek out proof of the spirit world, proof of paranormal activity. That's all he ever really wanted—validation of what he had experienced as a child, affirmation that his mother's spirit truly visited him, confirmation of life after death.

He took a deep breath. Slowly, he released it. His headache and the pesky buzzing completely vanished. The storm within him had passed.

His thoughts did turn back to Penny, though. There was still the mystery of how she knew the secrets he had worked so long and hard to hide. He no longer wanted to confront her. He no longer wanted to punch her. He only wanted answers. He felt relatively sure that this supposedly innocent girl had abilities maybe she wasn't even aware she possessed. Maybe those abilities were somehow responsible for what was happening at Fright House.

In full command of his faculties again, he placed a call to Tony Scout. The medium might be able to help him sort this out.

Answering the call, Tony whispered, "I knew you'd be calling."

Tory smirked. "You did, huh?"

"I did," came Tony's dead-serious response on the other end of the phone.

"Always the drama queen."

"You're calling me about a young girl, aren't you?" Tony asked.

Tory stiffened. The smirk on his face faded. "Yeah, how did you—"

"Her name is Penny, isn't it?"

A shiver shot up Tory's spine. It exploded onto his scalp. "Tony, you're scaring me."

Tony chuckled. "Who's the drama queen now, kid?"

Gathering himself, Tory asked. "How do you know about her?"

"From a dream."

Tory sighed. He had no interest in competing with Tony in a drama queen contest. He'd let the old medium win this one. "Okay," he said, taking a deep breath. He in turn, the *kid*, would get to business. "Look, Tony. I think this girl, Penny, has abilities or powers she doesn't understand, maybe even can't control."

"She's the key," Tony replied.

Tory's brow furrowed. "What do you mean?"

Lightning flashed, illuminating the entire lobby through the windows. Thunder exploded, rocking the building almost at its foundation.

Tony's response had been lost to the outside ruckus.

"Repeat that," Tory barked. To hear better, he pressed the phone hard to one ear while he held the other ear closed with a finger. "What do you mean?"

"Whatever's...going...on..."

Static interrupted Tony's response.

"Tony? Are you there?"

"...there...she's..."

Static.

"Tony?"

"...the..."

Static.

"...key..."

Static.

"Tony!"

Again, lightning flashed. Thunder boomed right outside the lobby's windows.

"Tony!"

The call was lost.

"Damn," Tory barked. He tried calling Tony back but only got voicemail. "Tony, when you get this," he began his message, "call me back. I couldn't hear you. I didn't understand what you were trying to tell me." He paused a second. Upon further reflection, he said, "Better yet, get to San Jose ASAP. I think you can help this girl somehow and, in turn, help our investigation." He hung up.

What had Tony meant? How was Penny the key? The key to what?

Tory winced, rubbing the back of his neck. Something in his ears buzzed.

Lightning pressed against the rain-soaked windows. Thunder exploded.

Chapter Thirty-Three

The elevator's loud alarm rang Penny back to life. She opened her eyes, the white fluorescent lights almost blinding her. They didn't flicker but instead remained steady, bright. The elevator felt warm, comfortable. She released the tight hold she had on her legs. Straightening them, she groaned as she worked out the cramps, and the blood flowed again. Sitting there, legs outstretched, she wiped away the dried-up tears on her face and the crusty snot under her nose.

The alarm continued.

She remembered what had brought her there—her desperate flight to get away from Tory, from his accusations; however, everything after that was a blank.

She did remember her vision of Tory as a little boy. She remembered his mother's supposedly spiritual, afterlife visitation, as well as the realization that the woman had committed suicide by hanging.

Penny took a deep, hitched breath. Slowly, she let it out.

What a horrible thing for a young boy to experience. The death of a parent by suicide. No wonder he had the hallucination of his mother's spirit coming to him afterward. No wonder he believed in the existence of ghosts. The shock of such an event could push anyone over the edge.

The alarm still blared.

Penny climbed to her feet. She wobbled a bit on unsteady legs, catching herself against the wall of the elevator.

She felt sorry for the would-be ghost hunter. At the same time, the guy scared her, too. She had seen before the accusatory look in his eyes as he demanded an explanation. He definitely thought her a *freak*, just as Tilly, just as so many others from her past. A past that still haunted her even as she ran from it.

An alarm, much like the one in the elevator, suddenly rang in her head as well.

How *had* she known about Tory's mother? She couldn't. Still, she had seen it all happen as if with her own eyes, as if she had been there. How was that possible?

Before she could give those disquieting thoughts much consideration, the alarm in the elevator abruptly stopped. The elevator started to ascend.

Gasping, she backed against the wall.

Who turned off the alarm? Who started the elevator? Not her.

The elevator passed the lobby, continuing on to the top floor. It jerked to a stop.

Reluctantly, and with much trepidation, Penny stepped off the elevator, into the hallway. A cold chill and flickering fluorescent lights greeted her. She also caught a fleeting glimpse of the old guy from earlier as he ducked into a nearby storage room.

There was no escape.

Her breath caught in her throat. Her heart thumped—loud and steady. Tremors attacked her hands, her arms. Her legs almost buckled under the strain.

She could no longer bury her head in the sand. She could no longer hide from the truth. Everyone was right.

She was, after all, a *freak*.

Outside, lightning and thunder punctuated that thought with a tumultuous exclamation point.

Chapter Thirty-Four

Rain trounced the roof, the windows. Wind rattled the glass. Lightning and thunder danced together in the night sky.

Morgan lugged empty equipment cases off the elevator, adding them to the stack already in the top-floor hallway. Next, he planned to find an empty room to temporarily store them. Before he could do that, Cheech found him, interrupting his work.

"Dude," Cheech said, "we gotta talk."

Morgan set down the cases in his hands. "What about, bro?"

"About what happened outside with the ghost box," Cheech whispered. "About this Penny chick."

Morgan shook his head. "What happened with the ghost box was a fluke. It just happened to get jostled and turned on."

"Tuned into a station when I myself converted it to automatically scan the air waves to produce nothing but white noise?"

Morgan shrugged. "A fluke," he insisted. "You screwed up. Wouldn't be the first time."

Cheech chewed on his lower lip and scanned the hallway. "What about the song it was playing?" he whispered. "*Penny's Song.* Was that a fluke, too?"

A flash of lightning followed closely by a boom of thunder answered.

Both ghost hunters startled.

"This storm gives me the creeps, dude," Cheech said. "Wish it would stop."

Morgan nodded in agreement. Mother Nature was only adding to their already growing disquiet.

Rain and wind attacked the surrounding windows.

"Back to the question at hand," Morgan said, determined not to let the uproar outside deter their mission within the walls of Fright House. "Yes," he insisted, "just a fluke."

"What about it turning itself off? A fluke, too?"

"Yes."

"Okay, let's say it was all just a big coincidence," Cheech conceded. "Which I don't believe exist, coincidences that is."

"I'm following, bro," Morgan said. "Get on with your thought."

Cheech scanned the hallway. "I did some checking on Miss Penny Winters," he whispered.

"Huh?" Now Morgan scanned the hallway. "You did a background check on her? Without her permission?"

Cheech whispered, "You got it."

"Dude, that's so uncool."

Lightning and thunder wholeheartedly agreed.

Cheech jumped as if struck by the bolt outside the window. Catching his breath, he admitted, "Maybe uncool, but I dug up some curious dirt. Want to hear?"

Morgan checked the hallway, again. "Really uncool," he repeated, "but, yeah. Hit me with it, bro."

Cheech chewed his lower lip to the point that it slightly bled. Fidgeting from foot to foot, he whispered, "First of all, the Penny Winters that we know doesn't exist."

Morgan shook his head. "Huh? What you babbling about, bro?"

"I couldn't find any records for her," Cheech whispered, looking up and down the hallway. "She doesn't exist."

The windows lit up, lightning pressing against the panes. Thunder cracked. Rain pelted glass.

"How's that possible?" Morgan wondered. "You screwed up."

"Uh-uh," Cheech protested. "I'm too good for that, and you know it."

"There's gotta be a reasonable explanation, bro."

Cheech again scanned the hall. "There is," he said. "When I couldn't find any records for her, I sneaked back into Peabody's office." He shrugged. "I found her purse."

"You rifled through her purse?" Morgan rolled his eyes. "Even more uncool, bro."

"Maybe," Cheech admitted, "but I found a *Pasadena High School* ID." He scanned the hall. "Dude, she's only seventeen."

Morgan could only stare at his friend in disbelief. He thought the girl looked younger than a *manager* of anything should look. Seventeen, though? No way.

"That's not all," Cheech whispered. "Penny Winters isn't her real name. That's why I couldn't find anything on her."

"Wait a minute," Morgan interrupted, "what's her real name?"

Cheech grinned. "Penelope Snow."

Morgan sighed. "*Penny Winters*," he mumbled. "Makes sense. The correlation between the two names makes the new one easy to remember. Less likely to slip up. Smart girl."

"Glad now that I have no ethics?" Cheech asked.

Rain pounded against the glass as if desperately wanting in.

Morgan nodded. "I guess someone has to do the dirty work." He thought for a moment. "Okay, she's an underage runaway, using a false identity, working under false pretenses. How does any of that have a bearing on what's going on in this place?"

"It gets better," Cheech said. He shrugged. "Or worse. Depending on how you look at it."

"Tell me."

"Dude, I'm dragging you down to my level."

"Yeah, yeah, gutter level. Just tell me, bro."

"With this new information, I ran another background check," Cheech said.

"Yeah?"

"Get this, bro." Cheech again checked for unwanted ears that might be listening before saying, "She's been institutionalized."

"What?"

"That's right," Cheech confirmed. "When she was about thirteen, she began seeing people who weren't there." He looked up then down the hallway. "Dead people."

"How do you know they were dead people? How do you know they weren't just imaginary people? You know, people her mind made up?"

"According to her records," Cheech began.

"Wait," Morgan interrupted, "you actually saw her medical records?"

Cheech grinned. "I told you I'm good. It's all online if you know where to look, how to hack in. There are no secrets anymore."

Morgan shook his head in awe. "You're inspiring," he said.

Pounding rain argued the point.

Undaunted, Cheech continued, "Anyway, her medical records stated that she saw and talked with people who were confirmed as real. One time alive, then dead. What do you think of that?"

Morgan didn't know what to think. This certainly was disturbing information, but he wasn't sure if Penny's unstable background had any more bearing on what was going on at Fright House than her being underage or her using a false identity. He certainly wasn't sure that the song playing on the converted radio had anything to do with the girl. It still seemed to him a fluke that the radio turned on and off, a coincidence that it was playing *Penny's Song*. In fact, he—and he felt certain the rest of the team too, maybe excluding his ponytailed friend here—wasn't sure anything out of the ordinary was even going on at Fright House.

Cheech wouldn't relent. "She spent a few years undergoing electric shock treatment, drug therapy, eventually even hypnosis. Dude, she's a looney tunes teenager."

"How did she get out?" Morgan asked.

"Apparently, the hypnosis therapy did the trick," Cheech explained. "She supposedly stopped seeing and talking with dead people. They pronounced her sane, releasing her into an unsuspecting world."

Morgan considered everything Cheech had told him. "If she was released, why would she run away? Why is she here, at Fright House, using a fake name, working as a manager rather than being back in So. Cal, going to high school with her friends?"

Cheech shrugged. "I say she's still looney tunes."

Morgan said, "Okay, for the sake of argument, let's say you're right. Penny's as crazy as the Mad Hatter. What, if anything, does that have to do with Fright House being haunted or not?"

Lightning and thunder put an exclamation on that point.

Cheech scratched thoughtfully at his beard. "I don't know," he conceded. "All I do know is that I don't like it. Any of it."

Morgan sighed. "Actually, I don't either."

"Do we tell Tory?"

Morgan considered it but said, "Not until after Dead Time." "Why?"

Morgan put an arm around Cheech's shoulder. "My intellectually nerdy but socially inept friend, because it would be just like Tory to impulsively confront the poor girl about her secrets, about her past. Something we might all regret, considering how you got the information illegally."

"She's a minor, dude," Cheech protested. "A mentally disturbed minor."

"A minor, yes," Morgan said. "Mentally disturbed, remains to be seen."

"But—"

Morgan put a hand up, interrupting. "Let's see what happens during Dead Time first. If nothing happens, if there's no measurable paranormal activity here, then there's no reason to embarrass the girl."

"But she's a minor."

"Nevertheless, she still has rights," Morgan insisted. "You *did* illegally and unethically snoop into her personal life." He shrugged. "Besides, maybe she had good reason to do what she's done. Who are we to judge or interfere?"

Cheech took a deep breath, slowly letting it out. "If something does happen during Dead Time, then what?"

"We tell Tory, confront Penny, and try to somehow connect her past with the possible haunting."

Cheech nodded in apparent appreciation. "Dude," he said, "and people say you're nothing but muscles."

Morgan frowned. "What people?"

Cheech chewed on his bloody lip, fidgeted from foot to foot. "Uh, not me." He shrugged. "Just, *people*."

"Uh-huh." Morgan gave his friend a hard stare. "Come on. Help me get these empty cases into a storage room." He picked up several and started down the hallway.

Cheech grabbed two. He quickly followed. "Bro," he insisted, "I'm just saying, *people*."

Outside, the deluge and the dance continued.

Chapter Thirty-Five

Tony had yet to call back, so Tory decided not to share with his team the conversation between himself and the medium. Mostly because he wasn't sure of the relevancy. The conversation had been cut short. Besides, he didn't understand what Tony had meant anyway.

How was Penny the key? The key to what?

A slight ache formed at the base of his neck.

He didn't see a need to build mistrust between his team and Penny Winters now. Possibly, it could prove detrimental to the proceedings at hand. He didn't want that. Tonight could prove to be important.

With an involuntary moan, he rubbed at his neck. His ears hummed with white noise.

No, for now, the rest of the ghost hunters didn't need to know about any misgivings concerning Penny. He would keep them to himself. In the meantime, he would keep a close watch on the girl.

He did wish that Tony would call back, though.

He placed another call to the medium. This time, Tony not only didn't answer, but neither did his voicemail.

Tory ended the call.

Why wouldn't the call at least go to voicemail? It didn't make sense. Now he couldn't even leave another message.

Frustrated, he rubbed at his neck and the side of his face.

He wished he could figure out what Tony had meant. Better yet, he wished the medium was here. Hopefully, Tony would get the earlier message and get himself to San Jose as requested.

Tory checked his watch. It was almost time. He'd better get to Tech Central. He took a step but abruptly stopped.

Something was different. Something had changed.

He rubbed at the base of his neck, cocked his head, and listened. All he could hear was the white noise softly humming in his ears. As he scanned the lobby, he looked out the windows.

Odd, he thought.

Without him realizing it, the storm outside Fright House had died.

He shrugged, giving it no further thought as he rushed off to conduct Dead Time.

Little did he know, a turbulent storm within the walls was coming fast.

Chapter Thirty-Six

Everyone met in the storage room the PSI team dubbed Tech Central. Cables and wires littered the floor. The room was full of techie equipment Penny couldn't readily identify. The one they called Cheech sat on a chair with rollers, manning the machines set up on top of tables and desks. The other team members gathered around Tory.

Penny stood off to one side, intently watching and listening. In truth, she felt more relaxed than in a long time. The storm outside had ended. The storm within her had calmed, as well. She no longer clung to her sanity like a drowning girl clutching a lifeline. She had always believed that a firm refusal of anything considered out of the norm equaled a healthy mind. Now, with everything that had happened since coming to this morbid place, she came to believe that questioning the so-called norm was judicious, levelheaded. What she used to think of as a curse, she now accepted as a gift. In fact, she not only unexpectedly accepted it, she suddenly embraced it. Somehow, the realization that she indeed knew things and saw things she couldn't possibly know or see freed her, strengthened her. Where this knowledge would take her and these ghost hunters, though, remained to be seen.

Maybe this *gift* could actually save them.

Standing among his team, Tory asked, "Cheech, we good to go?"

Cheech eyed Penny with a look of suspicion, of distrust. Gulping, he said, "All set, boss."

Tory didn't seem to notice Cheech's odd behavior. "Good," he said. "As you all know, Penny will be joining us for Dead Time."

Everyone glared at her, wariness in their collective stares. What had Tory told them? He hadn't broached the subject with her at all. Had he shared with them what happened in the hallway earlier? Probably. Each one of them glowered at her as if they had already decided she was a *freak*.

After all, she was. She accepted it. She relished it.

Squaring her shoulders, Penny asked, "Do you really have to call it that?"

Everyone scowled. No one answered.

Penny shrugged. "It sounds a bit overdramatic," she said. "Don't you think?"

Again, no one answered. They only scowled.

Tory ignored her as well. He rubbed the base of his neck. His right eye twitched slightly. "Cheech," he said, "you're in charge of Tech Central."

"Right," Cheech replied.

Tory continued, "The rest of us will split up into three groups of two. Morgan and Isabel will take the Cemetery Room."

Isabel giggled. "Awesome," she said.

Morgan rolled his eyes. "Great," he mumbled.

"Gabe and Liz will take the first floor," Tory commanded. "Penny and I will take the torture room."

Lizzie opened her mouth as if to protest but stopped short. Dejection shadowed her face, crept into her eyes.

Self-absorbed, heedless of Lizzie's obvious feelings, Tory ordered, "Gabe and Liz, find a way to prop open the iron door. That way, you'll be able to monitor both the hallway and the lobby at the same time."

Gabriel nodded.

Lizzie pushed her thick glasses in place and looked away.

Tory rubbed the back of his neck. His right eye twitched.

"Kid, you okay?" Morgan asked.

Tory shot the muscle-bound man an agitated look. "Yeah, fine." His head gave a sudden jerk as he continued, "Even though we have the entire place rigged to automatically record and monitor everything, I still want each team to take along standard equipment as backup. Just in case we experience technical problems."

Everyone except Penny nodded.

Turning toward Penny, Tory instructed, "That would be a Mel-8704 meter, which measures both electromagnetic fields and ambient temperatures, a digital voice recorder for possible Electronic Voice Phenomena, a 29 LED tricolor flashlight, a two-way radio to stay in constant contact, and a small bottle of Holy water."

Penny smirked. "Holy water? Really?"

"Don't ridicule what you choose not to believe," Gabriel

chided. "That Holy water might be the only thing standing between you and damnation."

"I'm sorry," Penny responded.

She meant it, too. The minister was right. Hadn't everyone for years ridiculed her because they didn't understand what she saw or chose not to accept it? Even those who hadn't ridiculed her, like Doctor Rosenthal, convinced her she was imagining things, just because they couldn't comprehend the possibility that she might be seeing something not of this world. Who was she to refute anything out of turn? Especially now.

Tory's right eye involuntarily twitched. "The idea of Dead Time," he continued, soldiering on in spite of obvious pain, "is to try to make contact with any spirits that might be haunting the place."

"Are you sure that's wise?" Penny asked.

Tory ignored the interruption. "We ask questions. We make requests. We hope to get some kind of response, such as a sound like a knock, or even better, an actual answer, a voice. Even if we can't hear that voice with our human ears, we might get an EVP recording."

"That's the Electronic Voice Phenomena that Tory mentioned earlier," Cheech said.

Tory nodded. "Right," he agreed. "If we're really lucky, we might record some visual phenomena that we can't see ourselves with the naked eye."

"On either the thermal cams," Cheech added, "or the full spectrum cams." He shrugged. "Maybe even the infrared video cams. That'd be cool."

"Very cool," Isabel agreed.

Tory continued, "Actual visual contact of a spirit with our own eyes would be—"

"Awesome," Isabel finished the sentence.

Tory rubbed at his neck. "Awesome," he agreed, "not to mention lucky."

"You've never actually seen a ghost?" Penny asked. She eyed the ghost hunter, waiting for his response.

Tory's eye twitched. His head gave an involuntary jerk. He scowled. "No," he answered emphatically.

"Oh," Penny said.

She now knew for certain that the others didn't know anything about what had happened between herself and Tory earlier in the lobby. Not only that, but she felt certain that the others knew nothing about Tory's mother and his experience as a young boy, either. He had kept it a secret even from his ghost-hunting team. Why? Besides that, if the others had no knowledge of her and Tory's experience, then why did they seem so suspect of her? They couldn't possibly know of her past. It didn't make sense.

Tory shook his head as if to clear it. "It's almost 3:00 a.m.," he announced. "Everyone ready to do this?"

Everyone except Penny nodded.

Tory turned to the minister. "Gabe?" he asked.

Gabriel bowed his head. He prayed, "May the power of God surround us. May the power of God enfold us. May the power of God protect us. Amen."

"Amen," Tory repeated. He looked up, his right eye twitching. "Let's do this."

Chapter Thirty-Seven

The '66 Ford Fairlane 500 sped down a lonely stretch of Highway 5, between LA and the Bay Area. The drab, green car with dull, rusty chrome drove like a tank—no power steering, no power brakes. It was a cyclops, with only one light cutting through the night, illuminating half the road ahead. It had over 150,000 miles. It shook and shimmied at high speeds. Still, with its eight cylinders, 390 motor, manual 4-speed transmission, and B&M shifter, this baby could still haul ass.

With Tony behind the vibrating steering wheel, it did just that—barreling along with no regard for the speed limit, engine roaring like a beast. He didn't care about the shakes, shimmies, or vibrations. Nothing was going to slow him down, not even the highway patrol, who most times didn't even bother to monitor this lonely stretch of highway anyway. This is where he planned on making up the time lost earlier in heavy LA traffic. He hoped the usual six-hour trip between Southern California and Northern California would only take him a little more than four.

All around, hidden in the dark, was barren land not worth seeing—a dust bowl created by economic bust and lack of water. With the antenna missing, the Fairlane's radio no longer worked. There was nothing to see, nothing to do, but watch the half-lit road ahead, think about the young girl in his vision, and about his conversation with Tory.

That and worry about what was going on at Fright House.

Somehow, he had known that Tory was going to call. It was that call which immediately put the inexplicable vision into context. The girl—the angel—in his vision had to be the same Penny that was at Fright House. The song *Pennies from Heaven* playing in the background when the girl appeared in the vision proved that beyond a doubt.

Besides, Tory had said, *I think this girl, Penny, has abilities or powers she doesn't understand, maybe even can't control.*

Tony held the vibrating steering wheel in a death grip as

he contemplated that statement. To him, it confirmed what he gleaned from the vision—Penny was the key to everything. He had the copper key that miraculously transcended the limits of the vision, physically hanging around his neck on a chain to prove it. Yes, beyond any doubt, this girl Penny was the key to everything.

What, though, was *everything*?

Tony pressed down on the accelerator. The old car rocketed with a thunderous bellow down the road.

With the call cut short, he wasn't really sure what was going on at the old Halloween attraction. Tory hadn't had the time to tell him. The chill in his bones, however, told him that nothing good was going on there, that evil lay in wait within its walls. If that evil had yet to make itself known, it soon would. When it did, he wanted—no needed—to be there.

There was Tory's voicemail, too.

Get to San Jose ASAP. I think you can help this girl somehow and in turn, help our investigation.

When he heard that message, he immediately packed a small bag, jumped into his Fairlane, and got on the road. He felt certain that he could indeed help this girl control whatever powers she possessed. He wasn't sure why, but he also believed that, if successful in doing so, they could beat back the evil lurking there within the shadows. At the very least, they could keep the devilry at bay.

With those thoughts flooding his mind, he felt an immediate urge to talk with Tory again. He worried about the kid, about all of them. He had tried calling back several times before leaving LA but with no luck. Determined to finally get through, he pressed the button on the Bluetooth device in his ear.

His Bluetooth voice said, "Please give a command."

"Call Tory," Tony ordered.

"Did you say call Tim?" the computerized female voice asked.

Tony grimaced. "No," he said. "Call Tory."

"Did you say call Amy?"

"No, call Tory."

"Did you say call Lori?"

Frustrated, Tony yelled, "No, dammit."

"Command not recognized. Please try again."

Tony took a deep, calming breath, through his nose,

releasing it out his mouth. Distinctly, enunciating each syllable, he said, "Call Tory."

"Did you say call Tory?"

With almost giggly excitement, Tony exclaimed, "Yes."

"Calling Tory. Mobile."

Tony listened to Tory's cell phone ring on the other end. While he waited for his friend to pick up, he muttered, "About time, you stupid piece of tech crap."

Tory's cell phone picked up.

"Tory?" Tony almost bellowed into the Bluetooth device.

Tory, however, hadn't answered. Instead, Tony heard, "You've reached Tory Jackson of Paranormal Scene Investigations. Leave a name and number. I'll get back to you."

Tony groaned. He said, "Kid, it's Tony. I've been trying to reach you again all night. I'm still an hour or two out, but *I am coming.*" He paused a moment. Chuckling, he added, "Tell Gabe that I'm bringing my balls with me. I'll—"

Before he could finish that statement, he saw someone in the road ahead. Illuminated within the cyclops headlight was a man, who oddly enough wore a straitjacket. He sat in the middle of Highway 5, legs crossed, rocking back and forth, screeching like a wild banshee.

"No," Tony screeched right back.

He jerked the steering wheel to the left, swerving to miss the crazy guy in the road. The back end of the Fairlane fishtailed as he lost control, careened off the road and crashed into a nearby tree.

With no air bags or seat belts in the old car, Tony's head slammed against the steering wheel, jerked backward, came forward again to forcefully rest against the car's horn. Blood oozed from an open wound on his forehead while he fought against losing consciousness.

The Fairlane hissed as steam and smoke rose into the air from the smashed-in front end. The horn blared into the night.

In the road, the crazy guy in the straitjacket slowly dissolved. His lingering screech, however, still played a haunting duet with the car's resounding horn.

Chapter Thirty-Eight

Penny and Tory stood within the eerie, blue-green glow of the large basement. A strong odor of mildew and mold clung to the chilly air. Drops of condensation from the over-head water pipes dripped to the floor. The darkened and life-less, Plexiglas torture chambers stood between them and the Cemetery Room where Morgan and Isabel were stationed. From where Penny and Tory stood by the elevator, they could see the archway and the sign that read *Fright House Cemetery* at the far end of the basement; however, beyond that, they could only make out the dim glow of fake headstones that dot-ted the cemetery's surrounding darkness. Their cohorts were nowhere in sight.

Penny shivered. She moved closer to Tory. "No good can come from this," she muttered.

Tory eyed her with suspect. "I'm not so sure," he said. "We might, at least, find out that Fright House isn't haunted, that there's no paranormal activity here."

"Do you really believe that?" Penny asked.

"We'll see," Tory said with a shrug. He hesitated, adding, "You apparently know all of my secrets. I'm hoping that to-night I'll find out some of yours."

Penny shivered again. She looked away. "I have no secrets."

"Don't you?" Tory asked.

"No," Penny insisted.

Tory gave a self-serving smile. "Well, then," he said, "you have nothing at all to worry about."

Penny shivered at the cold, hard stare the ghost hunter gave her. She took a step back, worried about an involuntary twitch in his right eye. What it meant, she wasn't sure. Maybe an insight into the guy's state of mind, an instability, a volatil-ity. Maybe it meant nothing at all. She doubted that, though.

"What do you think I'm hiding?" Penny asked, not really sure she wanted to know if the ghost hunter truly had any idea.

"Ghosts, Miss Winters," Tory whispered. "Ghosts."

Penny said nothing.

Tory apparently had no knowledge concerning her age or identity. Did he suspect that she could see ghosts? She didn't care. She now accepted her curse or gift. If asked, she'd readily admit to it. He never asked, though.

Still, she didn't like the accusatory tone to Tory's voice. She didn't like the look in his twitching eye.

She had the incomprehensible feeling that this guy's suspicions somehow went deeper than her just seeing ghosts or having visions. It was almost as if he had conjectured that she in some way might actually control the ghosts, that she was responsible for everything happening at Fright House.

Which was just crazy.

That didn't matter, though, because when push came to shove, she didn't completely trust Tory or his thought process. She thought him unpredictable, a loose cannon who always believed he was right, no matter how crazy the theory.

That scared the crap out of her.

Tory took out his two-way radio. Into it, he said, "Cheech, we set to go?"

Cheech's answer came through the two-way radio. He said, "There are cameras and recorders all around. I can hear and see all. So don't say or do anything *I* would say or do."

Without responding, Tory pocketed the radio. He checked his watch. "Right on time," he muttered. He found the nearest mounted camera. He looked directly into it. "It's 3:00 a.m.," he announced. "The PSI team is in place throughout Fright House. With me is the manager of Fright House, Penny Winters."

Penny looked away from the camera. She fidgeted from foot to foot. She had conveniently forgotten that this was a TV show. Someone from her past might eventually see the show, maybe recognize her. That wouldn't be good. Besides that, she had literally just admitted to *herself* that she was able to see ghosts, possibly more due to the spontaneous vision concerning Tory. Even though she didn't plan on hiding those facts anymore, that didn't mean she wanted the whole world to find out all at once on television. Her only consolation was that probably by the time this episode aired, she'd be long gone, using another name, working another job.

That's if they actually survived the night.

Tory continued, "We're going to attempt contact with any

spirits that might still be lingering here from when this place was Ludlum Insane Asylum."

He again took out the two-way radio. Into it, he said to his entire team, "Let's begin Dead Time."

Chapter Thirty-Nine

Gabriel and Lizzie stood in semi-darkness. The red lights in the hallway were off. Instead, along with the sickly yellow glow created by the lobby lights subtly washing through the open doorway and over the hall, they used their flashlights to brighten their surroundings.

Gabriel shined the beam of his flashlight along the empty cells. "Sorry you got stuck with me," he said.

Lizzie carried a flashlight in one hand and an EMF-TEMP meter in the other. The backlight illumination from the meter's display cast a strange glow across her frowning face and reflected oddly off the lenses of her glasses, creating the illusion that her eyes were like those of an animal's. "No worries, preacher man."

Gabriel knew better. Even in the poorly lit hallway, he could see the hurt written all over Lizzie's face. The Occult Specialist usually always paired up with Tory. After all, they'd been classmates and friends for years. Besides, Lizzie had a big-time crush on Tory. The *kid* knew it, too. In spite of that, this time, Tory chose another—a beautiful stranger at that.

"I think Tory just wants to keep an eye on Miss Winters," Gabriel said in an attempt to abort any jealousy on Lizzie's part. "I don't think he fully trusts her."

Lizzie ignored the minister. She continued to study the display before her. "Electromagnetic field is normal. Temp is seventy-two degrees. No cold spots."

Gabriel swept the beam of his flashlight across the empty cells a second time. "So, you don't want to talk about it, huh?"

"That's right." Lizzie studied the EMF-TEMP meter. "We've got a job to do. Let's do it, okay?"

Gabriel nodded. Lizzie was right. This was no time to meddle in relationships. It was time to get to work. He said, "Spirit or spirits occupying this place, make yourselves known." He paused, listening intently, never really expecting any otherworldly answer.

"No change in EMF or temp," Lizzie said.

Gabriel continued, "If you're here, make a noise. Knock. Give us some kind of sign."

As he expected. No response.

"We're not afraid of you," Gabriel announced. "Don't be afraid of us. We won't hurt you. We're here to help. Show yourselves."

Dead quiet.

"Anything on the meter?" Gabriel asked.

Lizzie studied the glowing display. She shook her head. "Nothing."

Gabriel sighed. "Either this whole gig is a scam—which I believe it is," he muttered, but in a loud voice finished, "or the spirits here are chickenshits."

Lizzie looked at Gabriel for the first time. "I wouldn't do that."

Heedless of the warning, even louder, Gabriel pushed on. "Did you hear me? I called you chickenshits. Now make yourselves known."

The iron door between the lobby and the hallway slammed shut.

Both ghost hunters whirled toward the sound.

Lizzie let out a yelp.

Gabriel gasped.

They stood in total darkness except for the dual beams from their flashlights.

"I told you not to—"

"The doorstop didn't hold," Gabriel interrupted. "That's all."

He felt sure that there was no way this place was haunted. No place they'd investigated yet proved beyond a doubt to be haunted. Ghosts didn't exist. Souls either went to heaven or hell. They didn't get stuck in between.

"Uh-huh," Lizzie said. She shivered. "It's a bit colder." She checked the meter. "Temp's down to sixty-five and dropping." She paused, intently staring at the display. "I've got an EMF burst."

Gabriel shivered, too. "AC must've kicked on."

"How do you explain the EMF burst?"

"I don't know," Gabriel muttered.

He couldn't readily explain it. Maybe the meter malfunctioned. Maybe the EMF burst was natural, due to a cell phone or an electrical spike in the old building's faulty wiring. There was no way this place was haunted. Still, he clutched at the Saint Michael medal hanging around his neck with one hand, while his other hand tightly gripped the flashlight, sweeping its beam up and down the hallway.

"Hello," Lizzie called. "Is anyone there?"

Screams and loud bangs suddenly echoed all around them.

Both investigators instinctively cried out. They moved closer together. They swept the beams of their flashlights up and down the hallway along the still empty cells.

Gabriel's heart felt lodged in his throat. "Where's it all coming from?"

"I don't know." Lizzie checked the meter again. "What I do know is EMF is off the charts. Temp's dropping fast, too."

Breathing hard, both investigators could see their breaths in the frosty air.

Gabriel shouted, "In God's name, show yourselves."

With that demand, the screams and bangs grew louder, more intense. The red lights in the hallway inexplicably turned on. Mental patients instantly occupied each cell, their faces masks of insanity as they rushed the iron bars. They reached through those bars, frantically grabbing for the two investigators in the middle of the hallway.

Gabriel froze, body and voice gripped by terror. He had been wrong after all. Ghosts truly existed. Here was the proof.

Lizzie screamed. Her flashlight and meter clanked to the floor as she stumbled backward in shock.

Crazies in the cells behind grabbed her and pulled her to the floor. There, they scratched and clawed at her face, hair, and body.

Lizzie's scream turned bloodcurdling.

Gabriel remained frozen in the middle of the hallway, just out of harm's way on both sides. "God help me," he pleaded. Letting go of the talisman around his neck, he reached for the small bottle of Holy water in his pocket. He held the flashlight in one hand, as he fumbled with the bottle in the other, trying to hold it and uncap it at the same time. He dropped the uncapped bottle and watched helplessly as the Holy water gurgled out onto the floor. "God help me," he pleaded again.

"Help me, Gabe," Lizzie cried.

Rather than making a move to help his struggling partner, Gabriel dropped to his knees. In a tight fist, he gripped the Saint Michael medal. He rocked back and forth as he prayed,

"Saint Michael the Archangel, defend us in battle. Be our safeguard against the wickedness and snares of the devil. May God rebuke him, we humbly pray; and you, O Prince of the heavenly host, by the power of God, cast into Hell Satan and all evil spirits who wander through the world seeking ruin. Amen."

Lizzie's scream took on new heights, new intensity.

The crazies pinned her to the floor. They clawed, scratched, and bit at her through the iron bars.

Lizzie fought back. Somehow, she broke free and rolled out of the crazies' reach. Bleeding, disheveled, basically blind without her glasses, she crawled to Gabriel.

With Lizzie's escape, the surrounding screams and bangs grew louder. The crazies threw themselves against the iron bars in fits of rage.

Gabriel pulled Lizzie to him. He held on tight. Loudly, he prayed, "Saint Michael the Archangel, defend us in battle. Be our safeguard against the wickedness and snares of the devil. May God rebuke him, we humbly pray; and you, O Prince of the heavenly host, by the power of God, cast into Hell Satan and all evil spirits who wander through the world seeking ruin. Amen."

All at once, the screams and bangs stopped. The crazies disappeared.

Gabriel continued to hold Lizzie in a protective embrace. "I did it," he exclaimed. "My prayers were answered." He breathed hard. Frosty plumes escaped with each breath.

Lizzie looked up at the minister. She too breathed hard, her warm breath visible in the chilly air. "I'm not so sure," she whispered.

The iron door to the lobby flew open, confirming Lizzie's fear. It clanged against the inner wall of the hallway but remained ajar. Sickly yellow light washed over the hall, mixing with the red in ghoulish fashion.

The two investigators jumped with renewed fright, holding each other tighter.

A curious sound followed the clanging of the iron door.

Gabriel groaned in disappointment, in confusion. He listened with growing disquiet to what sounded like a bouncing ball coming toward them.

From the lobby, out of the wash of yellow light, came a round object about the size of a volleyball. It bounced ominously down the hallway toward the two huddling investigators.

"What the—" Gabriel gasped.

The ball-like thing bounced slower and slower as it approached, until finally it only rolled, coming to a stop just a few feet away.

Lizzie yelped at the sight.

Gabriel proclaimed, "My God."

Before them rested the decapitated head of a little girl. Pigtails dangled to each side. The little girl opened her eyes. She stared at the two investigators. A wicked grin spread across her otherwise innocent face.

Gabriel choked on his scream.

Lizzie remained stone quiet.

Out of nowhere, the little girl's body loomed over the two. The girl reached down, picked up her head, and placed it back on her shoulders. The wicked grin still played across her face. In a sing-song voice, she said, "You're gonna die." Turning, the little girl skipped away, back toward the lobby. Over her shoulder, she repeated, "You're gonna die."

The little girl disappeared. The iron door clanged shut. The red lights turned off.

Left in darkness, neither Gabriel nor Lizzie could move.

Chapter Forty

The Cemetery Room was dark as night, except for the glowing headstones and Morgan and Isabel's dueling flashlights. There were no fake ghosts, no fog, no full moon or stars in the pretend sky. The mechanized vultures were turned off, as well.

The two investigators stood amongst the fake trees and headstones, almost exactly where Isabel had performed her ceremony, almost exactly where she had left the two voodoo dolls earlier.

Morgan swept the beam of his flashlight around the room. Seeing nothing out of the ordinary, he checked the EMF-Temp meter he held in his other hand. He said, "EMF is normal. Temp is a comfortable seventy-two degrees."

Isabel moved closer to her partner. Without warning, she jumped into Morgan's arms, wrapping her own arms around his neck.

Morgan struggled against the Goth chick's advances. "What're you doing?"

Isabel held on tight, pushing her body into Morgan. "You, Morgan, are mine," she proclaimed. "I, Isabel, am yours. We are bound together. We are now one."

Morgan pried the girl's arms from around his neck. He pushed her away. "Are you crazy, girl?"

Isabel stood back, a mixture of emotional pain and confusion on her face. "The spell should've worked."

"What are you talking about?" Morgan asked. "Spell? What spell?"

This chick was obviously crazier than he first had thought. What was she babbling about? A spell? A spell she had tried to put on *him*?

"It should've worked," Isabel insisted. Tears formed in her eyes. They mixed with her heavy, black mascara, and ran down her face like rivers of polluted water. "You should love me."

"Love you," Morgan repeated in bewilderment. "Love

you?" He shook his head. "I *might* have considered banging you if you weren't a minor, but I'll never love you."

Isabel burst into tears, her face marred with black streaks.

Morgan took a deep breath, releasing his anger and frustration with a slow exhale. He hadn't really meant to hurt Isabel's feelings. She was only seventeen, with a schoolgirl crush. It was just that she had made him so blasted mad with that crap about a spell. He sighed. "I'm sorry, but—"

A blast of frigid air interrupted, catching the two unaware. It swirled around them, knocking over fake trees and mechanized vultures.

Isabel dropped her flashlight. She stumbled backward as if pushed or pulled. "Morgan," she screamed.

Morgan reached forward. He tried to grab hold of one of Isabel's arms, but the swirling wind kept him off-balance.

The supernatural tempest lifted Isabel right off her feet. Hanging in midair, she again screamed.

Morgan held onto a fake boulder for dear life. He knew if he let go the furor could take him, as well. "Isabel," he cried.

The windstorm stole his voice, carried it away. He could no longer hear Isabel's screams either, even though her mouth remained opened wide.

That's when he saw it. An apparition. Faintly visible. Sputtering in and out of existence as if electrically charged by faulty wiring. It looked vaguely like a man.

"Isabel!"

While tightly gripping the boulder with one arm, he reached out with the other toward his cohort.

She, however, was captive within a spectral cyclone, well out of reach.

"Isabel!"

The sputtering apparition held onto Isabel from behind the girl. One hand gripped her throat. Its fingernails dug into skin, leaving behind puncture wounds, leaving behind blood. The other hand raked across the girl's tight, black top, shredding it. Deep, bloody gashes appeared on her midriff in wake of the attack.

"Isabel," Morgan cried.

Again, his cries died within the din of the whirlwind.

The apparition ripped into Isabel's top again. Bloody gashes exposed themselves across her breasts as her eyes bulged, as her body convulsed.

"No," Morgan begged.

Even he couldn't hear his own voice.

He had to do something. Without letting go of his lifeline, he reached as far as he could.

It was no use.

Isabel's body went limp. Her head flopped forward. She suddenly looked like a rag doll within the ghostly thing's grasp.

Without any more thought, Morgan released his grip on the boulder. He let the whirlwind take him. He had no other option. He had to risk it. Isabel's life depended on it.

The spectral cyclone whirled him toward Isabel and her attacker. With arms and legs flailing out of control, he plowed into the two. They broke apart. Isabel crash-landed to the floor with a thud. The sputtering apparition turned on Morgan. Ghostly hands wrapped around his throat, sharp fingernails digging in, puncturing skin. The sputtering apparition let loose with a hellish shrill before hefting the ghost hunter high overhead and throwing him across the room.

Morgan plunged headfirst to the floor. He skidded across it, smashing into fake trees and glowing headstones, until finally banging into the same boulder he had held onto just moments ago.

Having come to a stop, lying amongst the debris, he groaned, fighting to hang onto consciousness.

His head ached. His thoughts were a jumbled mess. His mind swirled much like the surrounding wind. Mental and physical paralysis beckoned him.

Nevertheless, he lifted his throbbing head. He groaned, struggling onto his hands and knees.

The windstorm had died.

He looked around. There was no sign of the apparition. All that was left as proof of its existence was the destruction left in its wake.

"Isabel," Morgan muttered.

His head still throbbed even while his mind began to clear. "Isabel..."

He scanned the wreckage.

Isabel lay face down just a few feet away. She didn't move.

Morgan crawled on hands and knees to the girl. He gently turned her over, sat down beside her, and pulled her into his lap, face up. He felt her throat for a pulse.

None.

"I'm so sorry, Isabel," he whispered. Tears welled in his eyes. "I didn't mean it. I didn't."

He rocked back and forth, holding the broken girl, wishing he could take it all back, everything he'd said. Long ago, he had failed his brother Shaun. Now, he failed Isabel, too. As with Shaun, grief and guilt proved a deadly combination.

He pulled Isabel up into his arms and held her there. "I'm so sorry," he whimpered, "I didn't mean it. I'm so sorry."

Chapter Forty-One

The beam of Penny's flashlight trembled as she shined the light along the walls of the basement, through the Plexiglas torture chambers, looking for anything *unusual.*

Tory announced, "Are there any spirits here with us?" Without any noticeable shaking, he too swept the beam of his flashlight along the walls, along the torture chambers. "If you're here with us, then give us a sign." He checked the display on the EMF-Temp meter in his other hand. "Temp's at seventy degrees," he said, softer, this information apparently only for Penny, not for any possible ghosts. "No unusual EMF readings, either." He sighed. "Everything's normal."

"You sound disappointed," Penny said. She kept one eye on Tory, the other on her surroundings. "To me, normal sounds good."

"Does it?" Tory asked, still checking the readings on the meter.

"Yes," Penny said emphatically.

Tory shrugged. "Hmmm," he said. He turned his attention away from the meter. He squinted at Penny. His head gave a slight, spasmodic jerk. His right eye twitched. "Well, let's see if we can stir things up a bit. It's what your boss is paying us for, after all."

Penny looked away. When she had first seen Tory, she thought he was cute, in a brooding, sulking sort of way. Now, she couldn't stand to look at the guy anymore. Something about him wasn't right. He looked to be in some sort of pain. Not terrible agony or anything, but just a painful annoyance of some kind.

Of course, she could be wrong. He could be fine. Maybe the poor lighting made him look *off.* Maybe it was the circumstances. After all, these were stressful times. Or maybe it was just her imagination. She didn't really know the guy well enough to know what his normal behavior was like, to truly compare.

Still, she couldn't deny that the behavior he exhibited

bothered her, worried her.

"We're here to help," Tory announced. "We're not here to hurt you. Don't be afraid."

Penny scowled. "You think *they're* afraid of *us*?" She swept her trembling flashlight beam around the large room.

Tory ignored her question. He continued, "You've been scaring away people who work here. So, you must want to make yourself known." He swept the flashlight beam across the basement. "Show yourself, *now*. Or go away and leave this place forever."

Penny startled. She squealed.

"What's the matter?" Tory asked.

"I felt something cold on my neck." Penny turned around, shining her light toward the elevator. "It was like someone or something touched me."

Tory checked his EMF-Temp meter. "Temp has dropped to sixty-five." He paused, checking the glowing display. "Continuing to drop. Fast. Sixty. Fifty-five. Forty."

Penny shivered. Her ragged breath blew out in front of her. She turned back to Tory to see his panting breath visible, as well. Erratically, she swept the beam of her flashlight all around the large room.

"EMF bursts are off the charts," Tory exclaimed. "I've never seen anything like it."

With that, the lights to all the torture chambers, but one, turned on. Electrical machinery and drills whined. Screams, screeches, and maniacal laughter echoed throughout the basement.

Penny and Tory spun in circles to see everywhere at once.

"Where's it coming from?" Penny cried. "Where?"

As if in answer, the occupants to the torture chambers inexplicably appeared. The sights and sounds were horrific as doctors did unspeakable things to their *patients*. The most horrific sight, though, was one man's bloody arm dangling from a manacle.

Penny dropped her flashlight. It clanked on impact and rolled across the hard floor. She screamed, loud and long.

Tory dropped the meter. It, too, clanked to the floor. Meanwhile, he fumbled for his two-way radio. "Cheech, you gettin' this?" he cried.

Only static answered.

"Cheech!"

Static!

"Morgan! Isabel!"

Static!

"Gabe! Liz!"

Static!

"Cheech! You gotta be there! Cheech!"

Static!

"Crap."

Tory threw the radio. It banged off one of the torture chamber's Plexiglas walls.

Penny continued screaming.

Without warning, the blue-green lights in the basement flicked off. The chambers all went dark. The horrible sounds accompanying the monstrous acts of torture, died.

Only Penny's scream remained. Slowly, it too died.

The flashlight in Tory's hand, the flashlight on the floor, and the backlight from the meter's display were all that lit the dark basement.

Penny and Tory stood side-by-side. Both breathed hard, their breath still visible in the frigid air. Tory reached over and took Penny's hand in his. Penny didn't pull away. Instead, to her surprise, she squeezed the ghost hunter's hand right back.

"It's okay," Tory whispered. "Dead Time is over. The spirits are gone."

Penny squeezed Tory's hand harder. She shook her head in disbelief. "You don't understand," she hissed. "Those weren't ghosts. At least, not all of them. The doctors and staff might have been, but not the ones having those *things* done to them."

Neither she nor Tory took their eyes off the room to look at each other.

"What do you mean?" Tory asked.

"I recognized some of them, most of them."

Tory gripped Penny's hand tighter. "I don't understand."

"They were the employees that never came back. Don't you get it? They never called. Never came back. Peabody thought, that is...*we* thought, that they had all quit."

"They were here all the time, though," Tory muttered. He released his hold on Penny's hand. "Are you sure?"

Penny gulped. Here it was happening again—doubt, an unwillingness to believe, questioning her sanity. Tory's question was the same as him calling her a freak. She answered anyway. "The man shackled to the wall, the one who chewed off his arm, that was Jake Brewer, the guy who didn't show up for work tonight."

"Jesus H—"

A curious buzzing noise cut Tory off. It grew louder with each passing second, as if the basement were filling up with flies.

"Tory, what's happening?"

The darkness around them began to shimmer and pulse. The walls, ceiling, and floor started to ripple.

Tory gave no response. He didn't move, as if frozen in time.

The buzzing grew deafening.

Penny struggled to move. The surrounding air seemed thick as mud. She felt trapped within it. Her eyes rolled back in her head.

All was lost.

Chapter Forty-Two

All hell had broken loose.

Within Tech Central, Cheech panicked. He felt helpless and didn't know what to do, as the monitors simultaneously revealed some crazy, whacked out stuff. He was forced to witness Lizzie and Gabriel's ordeal in the hallway with the crazies in the cells and the headless, little girl. He could only stare in disbelief as some sputtering spectral swept Isabel off her feet and Morgan aside as if they were nothing more than playthings. He couldn't stop the choke hold on his throat or the tears welling in his eyes as he wondered whether Isabel lived through the nightmare. On another monitor, there was Tory and Penny in the basement, the torture chambers coming to life with abhorrent activity, before all going dark. There were also the sounds coming through the speakers. Terrible sounds. Whining. Buzzing. Banging. Laughing. Crying. Yelling. Screaming.

He couldn't make it stop. Any of it.

He hurried to the door. He didn't know what he was going to do. All he knew was that one way or another, he had to try to rescue his team. Grabbing the door handle, he turned it hard and yanked. The door didn't open. He yanked again. It wouldn't budge. The door was locked. That couldn't be. He knew no one had locked it. He yanked again. Whether it was possible or not, the door *was* locked.

He pulled and kicked at the door, but to no avail. He pounded on the door. He yelled for help, which was a lesson in futility, because there was no one to hear. He had to face facts. There was no getting out. His friends were in trouble, and he couldn't help them.

Giving up, he left the door, returning to his equipment and monitors. Maybe there was some way to help his team from within Tech Central. There had to be. How?

He strained to think of a plan, checking the equipment for various possibilities, however unlikely or implausible. As he did this, the various feeds from multiple cameras suddenly and inexplicably connected to only one camera. Instead of each monitor revealing the horrible events befalling his team throughout Fright House, they all focused on the hallway right outside the door to Tech Central.

He stopped fussing with buttons and controls. Dumbfounded, he stared at the monitors. How had they changed? Only he was in control of the cameras and angles displayed on the monitors. No one else. It was impossible for the feed for all the monitors to switch to one camera without him doing it.

Before he could wrap his brain around that problem, however, another presented itself. Someone appeared in the hallway. Nurse Gillian, from the tour earlier that night, stood there, staring up at the camera. He could see her on all the monitors as plain and as clear as anything, looking hot as ever in her tight but archaic nurse's uniform.

Cheech scratched nervously at his beard. "What's going on?"

A noise came from behind. He whirled around, facing the door. Slowly, the door handle turned.

"What the—"

He backed up into the table of equipment and monitors. There was no place to go, no place to hide.

The door that had been inexplicably locked moments before was now just as inexplicably unlocked. Slowly, it squeaked open.

Nurse Gillian stood there, framed in the doorway.

Cheech gulped. Blood pounded in his ears. Tremors racked his extremities. He thought his knees might actually buckle. He braced himself with both hands on the tabletop behind him. "What do you want?" he croaked, mouth dry.

Gillian licked her luscious lips. She grinned. Her eyes glinted with evil as she stepped into the room, closing the door behind her.

Cheech shivered. His breath blew out in front of him. He hadn't even noticed the sudden, rapid drop in temperature until that moment. "What are you doing here?" he asked, his voice quivering.

Gillian's tongue again flicked out, licking her lips. "I work here. My name's Gillian."

"I know *who* you are." Mustering his courage, Cheech pushed away from the table. He stood without support on trembling legs. "You're not supposed to be here. What do you want?"

Gillian grinned. "I just want to talk." She slowly approached, hips swaying seductively within the tight confines of her uniform.

Frigid air swirled around them.

Cheech quaked almost violently from the cold. His lungs felt frozen, barely capable of taking a breath. Teeth chattering, he said, "I need to get to my friends."

Gillian stopped just inches away. "You're not going anywhere."

"Get out of my way." Cheech tried to move, tried to push past the hot but creepy nurse. He couldn't. Maybe the supernaturally arctic air within the room had actually frozen him in place, for he seemed to be nothing more than an ice sculpture.

"You're not going anywhere," Gillian repeated. Her voice was soft, sultry. Her gaze, however, was frosty, hard. She reached out, caressing Cheech's cheek, running her cold fingers through his beard. "You're not going anywhere."

Again, Cheech shivered. He struggled to move, to fend her off, but couldn't. It was as if he were under a black spell. "My friends need me."

Gillian moved closer, until their bodies touched. "*I* need you." She wrapped one arm around Cheech's back, the other around his neck.

Cheech shivered. Even the closeness of Gillian didn't warm him, as if the girl had no body temperature. In fact, her touching him only made him shiver more. "Leave me alone," he pleaded. His tears almost instantly froze as they left his eyes and began to stream down his cheeks.

Gillian didn't listen. She stood on tiptoes, face to face with the Tech Specialist. With their lips almost touching, she opened her mouth wide.

Still frozen, Cheech stared into the creepy nurse's icy gaze. His own mouth was agape in terror and shock as a single fly escaped from somewhere within Gillian. It landed on her bottom lip, rubbing its front arms together, twitching its wings in anticipation. It buzzed as it took flight.

Cheech jerked but otherwise still couldn't move as the fly landed on his own bottom lip. He wanted to scream. He wanted to reach out, grab Gillian by the throat, and throttle her. He wanted to at least swat the fly away or close his mouth or turn away and run.

He could do nothing as the fly took flight again, this time entering *his* mouth. It choked him as it made its way down his throat.

Still, he could do nothing but scream within his mind.

Another fly emerged from within Gillian. This one didn't even take the time to land, but instead flew straight into Cheech's mouth, down his throat. Behind that fly came another then another and another, until it seemed like hundreds of flies streamed from within the nurse. The buzzing became louder, deafening. The flies continued to transfer from Gillian's mouth to Cheech's. As more and more flies escaped from the girl's mouth, she herself transformed into a mass of buzzing flies. Soon, those flies followed the others, until nothing was left of the nurse, and every fly had taken refuge within their prey.

Choking, Cheech dropped to his knees. Rivers of blood streamed from his eyes, his nose. He swayed back and forth, fighting to keep hold of consciousness.

Behind him, the monitors all went dark. The audio equipment spat out only white noise.

Chapter Forty-Three

Penny and Tory stood in the basement, trancelike, not moving, staring into nothingness. The darkness around them still shimmered, pulsed. The walls, ceiling, and floor still rippled.

Not a sound existed.

Chapter Forty-Four

Tory's consciousness awoke to a dimly lit room. Dark shadows played across the floor, walls, and ceiling. The wallop of his heartbeat and the inhalation and exhalation of his ragged breath, were the only sounds he could hear.

He struggled to get his bearings, make some sense of where he was and what was happening. The last thing he remembered was being in the basement, conducting Dead Time with Penny.

Penny.

He quickly scanned the dimly lit room.

Where was Penny?

Nowhere to be seen.

The shadows around him shimmered and pulsed. They moved about, circling him as if they were alive.

"Where am I?" he croaked, throat scratchy and sore.

His mind forgot Penny. Instead, it focused on his dilemma at hand. Suddenly, he realized he couldn't move. Without his knowing it, he had been strapped into a large, wooden chair.

"What the—"

He struggled against the leather restraints across his wrists, ankles, and waist, but to no avail.

"What's going on? Where am I?"

He became aware of a cold, peculiar feeling on his head, right around his temples. It felt as if things were attached to him.

"What's going on?"

He shook his head in an attempt to dislodge whatever was stuck to his temples. They didn't come off, but he discovered that wires ran from those things to a nearby machine he hadn't noticed before.

That's when he remembered the tour earlier that night. The torture chamber that held the electric shock treatment machine.

His heart thrashed within him like a caged bird desperately seeking release. Ragged breath escaped from overworked lungs. Sweat plastered his hair, trickled down his back, soaked his shirt.

"Let me go."

He battled against his restraints.

"Let me go."

The leather straps held tight.

"Let me go."

The shimmering, pulsating shadows circled like vultures.

"Please."

What sounded like a thousand demonic voices spoke as one. "You can save them. You can save them all."

Tory stopped struggling. Bug-eyed, he scanned the room. There was no sign of anyone. Only the shimmering, pulsating shadows were visible. "Who are you?" he pleaded. "What do you want from me?"

The demonic voices answered, "You can save them. You can save them all."

Tory again fought his restraints. "Save who?" he screamed.

The click of a switch being thrown answered. Volts of electricity followed. Sparks flew. The air crackled, hissed.

Tory spasmed and convulsed as electricity fired into the electrodes attached to his temples.

The switch clicked again. The electricity stopped.

Tory slumped in the wooden chair, chin on chest. His breath came out shallow, slow. Spittle hung from his open mouth.

The shadows continued to circle.

"You can save them all," the demonic voices insisted. "You can save them all."

The switch again clicked. Sparks flew. The air crackled and hissed. Electricity fired into the electrodes.

Tory stiffened, convulsed. His head flew up, slamming into the back of the wooden chair. His hands clawed at the wooden armrests. His mouth opened wide into a silent scream.

The switch clicked off. The electricity died. The room went silent.

Tory slumped in the chair. His head dangled as if it were about to dislodge from his neck. His hands went slack. Spittle ran like strings to his chest.

"You can save them all."

Without raising his head, Tory mumbled, "Who?"

"All of them."

Tory struggled to raise his head. Through bleary eyes, he could see the shimmering, pulsating shadows move about him in a tighter circle. "How?" he croaked.

"Kill her."

Tory coughed, hacking up a glob of mucus. He spat it into his lap. Shaking his head in confusion, he asked, "Kill who?"

"Her. Kill her. She's the cause of everyone's pain, everyone's suffering. She's the reason for it all. You can save them. Kill her."

Tory spat again. "Why—"

The switch clicked. Sparks flew. Electricity fired.

Tory stiffened. His head slammed against the chair. His fingernails dug into wood. His silent scream could only be heard by the damned in Hell.

The switch clicked off. Singed flesh permeated the air.

Tory slumped, head lolling, only semiconscious.

The demonic voices resonated. "Kill her," they demanded. "Kill her. She's the cause of it all. Kill her. Kill her. Kill her."

Those were the last words Tory heard before losing consciousness.

Chapter Forty-Five

Unforeseen, Penny found herself in the lobby of Ludlum Insane Asylum. No one paid her any mind. Yet, all around her, visitors and docile patients sat in chairs and wheelchairs, staring up at an old, black-and-white television. She recognized the program as *I Love Lucy* from re-runs on cable. The patients were in hospital gowns and robes, the visitors in clothes right out of the 1950's. No one had a cell phone or a Notebook or an iPad. In fact, there were no hospital computers behind the registration counter, either. The only things on the counter were a black, rotary phone, paper forms, and three pens attached to the counter by small, metal chains. A young, blonde nurse stood behind the counter, dressed in a tight, white uniform. A doctor in a white lab coat stood on the opposite side of the counter, writing instructions on a clipboard. He looked to be a younger version of the old guy that had been talking to Mister Peabody in the upstairs hallway of Fright House.

Penny spun in a dizzying circle, taking it all in. She didn't understand how she had gotten there. She didn't understand how the young doctor could be the same man as the grandfatherly guy she'd seen earlier that night. Had she somehow been transported back in time?

No matter. All questions were suddenly unimportant. She stopped spinning when the front doors burst open, and wild shrieks echoed through the lobby. Two burly attendants dragged a little girl with pigtails through the doorway. The little girl wore a straitjacket, but still she fought as best she could, kicking and shrieking.

Penny let out a gasp. Had she fallen through the looking-glass? It was the same little girl from the nightmare, the same little girl who haunted Mister Peabody's office.

Behind the two attendants and the little girl marched a young couple—the man stoic, face set in stone, the woman red-eyed, crying hysterically. They stopped at the counter to talk to the doctor and fill out paperwork.

The burly attendants forced the little girl across the lobby to the iron door. A buzz rose above the girl's wails as the iron door opened. The attendants dragged the girl through the doorway.

"No," Penny screamed.

Quickly she followed, the iron door slamming shut behind her. She ran down the hallway, dodging staff and patients alike, chasing the two attendants who dragged the screeching, kicking girl toward the elevator.

The attendants and their *patient* arrived at the elevator. The attendants forced the screaming girl on. The doors swished closed behind them.

"No," Penny cried. She slammed into the elevator doors too late. She looked up at the lighted numbers above the elevator. It was going down, stopping at the basement.

Instead of waiting for the elevator to return, she found a stairwell. Throwing open the door, she frantically descended, her footsteps clanging against the metal steps. At the bottom, she burst through that door. She ran into an empty hallway, greeted by the whine of an electrical instrument that reminded her of a dentist's drill. Somewhere, the little girl's scream rose to a fevered pitch.

Where had they gone? How had they moved so fast? Where had they taken the girl?

There was no time to ask questions, no time to think. Working on pure adrenaline and instinct, she raced down the hallway toward an imposing iron door. She didn't know how, but she was sure the sounds came from there. As she reached the door, the electrical instrument whined on, but the girl's screams died.

"No," Penny shrieked.

She slammed into the iron door, surprised that it wasn't locked. Once inside, though, she wished that she hadn't gained access. Inside, a doctor held a rotating saw of some kind that whined, bloody blade spinning, cutting at the air. The headless body of the little girl was strapped to an operating table, blood spurting from her neck, her lifeless body still spasming as if it didn't know death had already come. The girl's head lay on the floor next to the table, and her pigtails flopped backward into an ever-growing pool of blood.

"No," Penny shrieked again. She shook her head in disbelief. She grabbed hands full of her own hair and pulled, as if she, too, was insane, as if she, too, should be institutionalized or maybe even beheaded like the little girl.

With that, as if being called back from the dead, the girl's eyes opened. A macabre smile crept across her blood-splashed face.

"Welcome," the little girl's detached head croaked. "We've been waiting for you."

Penny screamed.

Chapter Forty-Six

Penny woke, the scream still on her lips.

Alice had returned through the looking glass.

She stood in the basement of Fright House, in the exact spot she stood before the time transport. Her scream died a slow death as she recognized her surroundings, realizing the nightmare was over.

Was it, though?

Tory lay at her feet, collapsed, unconscious.

Had she just traded one nightmare for another?

Tears came to her eyes. A lump in her throat choked her.

Which world was Wonderland and which world was real? Did it matter? One was no better than the other.

She dropped to her knees, sobbing.

Would Dead Time ever truly be over?

Chapter Forty-Seven

Somewhere, a horn resounded, echoed, as if announcing the arrival of a heavenly being. There was a faraway hiss too, like demonic snakes gathering to battle with the coming deity. A celestial light radiated outward. At the same time, a dense blackness crept along the edges of that light, constantly pressing its rays back to its point of origin, effectively keeping the celestial light at bay.

Tony groaned. His head throbbed. He couldn't move.

A song played through his head.

> *Every time it rains*
> *It rains pennies from heaven*
> *Don'tcha know each cloud contains*
> *Pennies from heaven?*
> *You'll find your fortune fallin' all over town*
> *Be sure that your umbrella*
> *Is upside down*

Combating the song was a distant shriek. It echoed along the landscape of his mind, growing in volume, growing in pitch, attacking the song.

> *Trade them for a package of sunshine and flowers*
> *If you want the things you love*
> *You must have showers*
> *So when you hear it thunder*
> *Don't run under a tree*
> *There'll be pennies from heaven*
> *For you and me*

He felt sure, the blaring horn foretold the arrival of the angel—the girl—he had seen in his vision, which lifted his heart, along with the sweet song.

Every time it rains, it rains
Pennies from heaven
Don'tcha know each cloud contains
Pennies from heaven?
You'll find your fortune fallin'
All over town
Be sure that your umbrella
Is upside down

At the same time, the hissing snakes and the wild shriek gave him a sense of dread that all was not well.

Nevertheless, he could see the angel emerge from the center of the bright light. She was as beautiful, as magnificent, as he remembered. She came toward him, floating across the heaven of his mind like a puffy cloud. The sight of her calmed him, along with the song.

Trade them for a package of sunshine and
flowers
If you want the things you love you must
have showers
So when you hear it thunder
Don't run under a tree

Still, there were dark storm clouds too. Lurking around the edges. Threatening to desecrate the angel's hallowed appearance.

There'll be pennies from heaven
For you and for me

The horn went silent. The wild shriek began to drown out the lovely song. Not only that, but the angel halted her advance. She slowly began to fade. The storm clouds, the blackness, pushed the celestial light inward. Soon, he could hardly hear the song at all over the deafening shriek. The light became smaller, dimmer. The angel became just a faint outline. Before he knew it, the song ended, the angel disappeared altogether, and the light was completely swallowed. Only pitch black remained.

The dread he felt before turned to terror.

Gasping for air, Tony opened his eyes. The driver's door

stood open. He lay on the ground, crumpled into a ball. Struggling, he used the door to pull himself into a sitting position. He looked around at the night through double vision. His thoughts were nothing more than scrambled eggs. He could barely remember the lunatic in the road. The memory of the crash, for the most part, eluded him. How he had gotten out of the car after the crash he couldn't remember.

He did recollect the song, though, and the light, the angel. He recalled the snakes, the darkness, the wild shriek.

Groaning, he felt the golfball-sized lump protruding from his forehead. A sharp pain streaked up the back of his neck, too.

None of that mattered, though.

Maybe his memories of the events, leading up to and including the accident, were muddled, hazy. What was clear, though, was that the battle between good and evil was reaching out. No longer confined within the walls of Fright House.

Worse, evil was winning.

Chapter Forty-Eight

Penny and Tory sat on the floor of the gloomy, damp basement. The beams of their two fallen flashlights sliced through the surrounding darkness like surgeon's scalpels. Those beams of light pointed at nothing in particular, illuminating nothing of importance, if indeed anything of importance at all remained in the bleak room.

Penny choked back leftover sobs.

Tory groaned, rubbing at the back of his neck and head.

Neither of them spoke of their individual, anomalous experiences. Instead, they concentrated on their circumstances, on their current shared ordeal.

"Are you all right?" Penny whispered.

Tory groaned in response.

"Tory?"

"Yeah, I guess." Tory continued to rub his neck and head as if plagued by a horrendous headache.

"Are you sure?" Penny urged.

She wondered just how truthful the ghost hunter was being because he didn't look all right to her. Besides, she was not even close to being *all right*. The nightmare she'd endured haunted her soul. She couldn't help wondering if Tory had suffered through a similar experience. All she knew for sure was that her partner was unconscious when she came back to reality. She didn't know what had rendered him that way. She dared not ask, though, for fear of having to acknowledge her own horrid vision.

"I said I was, didn't I?" Tory snapped.

"Yes, just making sure."

Tory sighed. "Sorry."

Penny said nothing.

"What happened here?" Tory asked. "Did you see what I saw?"

"If you mean the torture chambers coming to life with horrendous acts, yes."

Tory shook his head in disbelief. "How is that possible?"

"I thought you were the one who believed in hauntings and ghosts."

Tory jerked his head. "You said something, right at the end. You said they weren't all ghosts. That the ones being tortured were missing employees. You even named one."

Penny nodded. "Jake Brewer."

"How can *that* be? Where have they been? Where did they go?"

"Good questions." Penny shook her head. "No answers."

Tory's head jerked again. It looked as though the involuntary twitch had returned to his right eye, too.

"It's over," Penny insisted, even though she knew it would never truly be over as long as they remained within the walls of this grim place.

Tory stared toward the Cemetery Room. "Is it?" He stiffened. His eyes bugged out.

Penny turned around. She followed the ghost hunter's troubled gaze.

Out of the gloom came a peculiar looking figure. Its stiff, faltering gait made it look like a creature out of an old-time monster movie. With each halting step came a clomp and a scrape.

Penny and Tory both scrambled on hands and knees for their flashlights. They grabbed their respective flashlights almost simultaneously, shining beams of light at the slowly emerging monster.

What they saw, however, wasn't a monster or a ghost or anything supernatural at all. Still, what they saw made them both gasp in horror.

It was Morgan who stumbled out of the shadows toward them. The big man himself looked as if he'd been on the losing end of a schoolyard brawl between himself and multiple bullies. Even worse, cradled in his muscular arms, Isabel looked like a broken doll. Her head flopped backward. Her arms dangled, swinging lifelessly with each of the big man's forced steps.

Penny gulped hard. She had no idea what to do, what to say. She looked to Tory, hoping he would react accordingly. He looked just as shaken, just as clueless as to how to proceed.

Morgan dropped to his knees. Tenderly, he laid Isabel on the floor. Tears marred his face. Snot dripped from his red nose. "She's dead," he croaked. He shook his head as if it couldn't possibly be, even though he had just acknowledged it. "Dead."

Penny looked away. She choked back sobs and wiped tears away from her face. This was no time to break down. She had to keep her head. She had to be strong.

"How?" Tory asked.

Morgan continued to shake his head. "I failed her."

Tory sat back on his haunches. The flashlight slipped from his hand. He stared hard into nothingness. His eye twitched. Head jerked. "How?" he demanded.

Morgan focused on the dead girl in front of him. "I failed her." He wiped away tears, sniffed snot back up his nose. "Just as I had Shaun."

Penny looked from Tory to Morgan. Tory looked distracted, agitated. Whereas Morgan appeared lost, grief-stricken, not to mention confused. Who was this Shaun he mentioned? What did this Shaun guy have to do with what happened to Isabel?

Not even daring to glance down at the dead girl, Penny eyed her cohorts, again. If she didn't keep her wits about her, apparently no one would. These two were definitely losing it. She had to find the courage and fortitude, to lead them away from their grief, their internal demons, back to the danger at hand for all of them. Unfortunately, there was no time to mourn the dead, for the living were still in mortal danger.

"I'm sorry about Isabel," Penny said. "I really am. But don't you think—"

"It's your fault," Tory muttered.

Penny gaped at the ghost hunter. She couldn't believe her ears. "What?"

Tory glared back at Penny. His face hardened. "It's your fault." Vengeance shone in his eyes, the right one habitually twitching. "All your fault." His entire body convulsed as if hit with an electrical jolt. "Your fault." Without warning, he lunged.

Penny fell backward. She tried to scream, but the hands around her throat choked all sound from her.

Tory's face loomed above, features twisted into a grotesque mask. His breath smelled sour, as if he'd just vomited. "Your fault," he hissed, spittle flying from his mouth.

Penny grabbed the maniac's wrists, digging in her fingernails.

Tory wouldn't let go.

Morgan jumped on top of Tory's back, struggling with his friend. "Let her go." The big man wrapped an arm around Tory's throat. He squeezed. "Let her go."

Reluctantly, Tory slowly released his death grip.

Morgan ripped Tory away.

Penny sat up, grabbing her throat, gasping for air.

Tory rested backward in Morgan's arms, breathing hard, the fight gone out of him.

Morgan held his friend in a bear hug. "It wasn't her fault." He too breathed hard. "*I* failed Isabel. Me. No one else."

Tory caught his breath. Vengeance disappeared from his eyes. No twitch or spasmodic jerk was visible. Although physically and emotionally spent, he seemed himself again.

Penny caressed her throat. Catching her breath, as well, she said, "You're crazy."

Tory swallowed hard. "I'm sorry, Penny." Tears dribbled down his cheeks. "Truly sorry. I don't know what came over me. Please forgive me." He relaxed in Morgan's firm grip.

"You should be sorry, Tory," Morgan said. "We already have one dead. We don't need another." He paused, catching his breath. "What came over you?"

"I don't know," Tory answered.

Penny coughed, her throat sore. She eyed the broken guy before her, knowing full well she should feel spiteful for what he had tried to do. Instead, she could only feel pity.

Tory got a faraway look in his eyes. "I'll try to be good," he muttered. "I promise."

At that, Penny shivered.

To whom had Tory been talking?

That question somewhat dampened her pity for the man, replacing it with renewed wariness. She didn't trust Tory at all. His grasp on reality seemed more tenuous than hers ever had been, even on her worse days at the institution.

Still, she needed him. She needed all of them.

"Forget it," Penny said. "All's forgiven."

Forgiven, maybe. Not forgotten. Not by her. She'd keep a sharp eye on this guy.

Morgan released his hold on Tory. He stretched his arms, then rubbed at his face as if wiping away all grief.

Tory sat up, scooting away from Morgan, stretching his own muscles, wiping at his own face.

Penny looked from one to the other. She desperately needed to say what she'd meant to say after her condolences concerning Isabel and before the attack by Tory. Without wasting any more time, she voiced her concern. "We've got to get out of here."

Tory cocked his head but didn't respond.

Morgan nodded, his gaze meeting Penny's. "*Penelope's* right," he said.

Penny strangled on her own breath.

Morgan knew who she was. Somehow, he knew.

Tory, though, didn't notice, didn't pay Morgan's subtle proclamation any mind. Thank goodness.

Morgan continued staring at Penny. He spoke to Tory, though. "Let's collect the others, find a way out of here. Tonight." His gaze broke away from Penny and drifted down to Isabel. "I'm not leaving her behind."

Tory struggled to his feet. "Bring her along then."

Eyeing Morgan, Penny stood on wobbly legs. She couldn't figure out how Morgan had learned of her true identity. More importantly, she couldn't understand why Morgan was keeping quiet about it. It didn't matter, though. She didn't really trust the guy to stay quiet. Sooner or later, he'd spill the beans.

"Let's collect the others," Tory said.

Penny eyed Tory. She still didn't fully trust the guy, even though he took command again. She'd let him lead as long as he acted himself, as long as he acted sane.

"We're going then?" Penny asked.

"Let's collect the others," Tory repeated in way of a noncommittal answer.

"Then we'll go?" Penny pressed.

Tory turned away. Over his shoulder, he said to Morgan, "Bring Isabel."

Morgan picked up Isabel. In his arms, he cradled the girl's broken body, following Tory toward the elevator.

Penny followed. She wasn't sure what Tory had in mind. The ghost hunter had given the impression that they would all leave once together. In actuality, however, he really hadn't committed to going. That in itself worried her.

Once at the elevator, Tory pushed the button. Nothing happened. The elevator appeared to be out of commission.

"I guess we take the stairs," Tory said.

Using their flashlights, they found the stairwell. Tory led

them up the metal steps, the beam of his flashlight illuminating the way. Morgan followed, carrying Isabel in his arms. Penny brought up the rear, shining the beam of her light periodically behind, watching their backs.

When they reached the first floor hallway, Tory turned to the others. "Let's find Liz and Gabe."

"You don't think they made it back to Tech Central?" Morgan asked.

"There's no way to know for sure," Tory said. "We've lost communication with Cheech."

"Besides," Penny added, "we can check the iron door to the lobby while we're there. You told Lizzie and Gabriel to prop it open. If it's still open then we can get into the lobby. Hopefully from there we can get outside. That is if the front door isn't locked."

Tory nodded in agreement, but he said, "First, let's find Liz and Gabe." He opened the stairwell door, stepped into the hallway, and held the door open for Morgan and Penny to follow.

Once in the dark hallway, it didn't take long to find their cohorts. Lizzie and Gabriel stumbled toward them, flashlight beams quivering along the way.

"Tory," Lizzie cried.

"Thank God," Gabriel added.

As they got closer, their quivering lights settled on Morgan and Isabel.

Lizzie rushed toward Morgan. "Is she...is she..."

Morgan solemnly nodded.

Lizzie openly cried.

Gabriel stood at her side. "May God take her soul," he prayed.

Penny shined her light on the two.

Lizzie looked as though she'd been mauled. Red gouges and scratches scarred her face, blood still oozing but beginning to dry. Her hair was a tangled mess. Her glasses looked bent, cockeyed on her face, with one lens cracked.

In contrast, Gabriel looked shaken but otherwise suspiciously unscathed.

"What happened to you two?" Penny asked.

Gabriel looked away, embarrassed.

"Don't ask," Lizzie said. In a forgiving gesture, she put a hand on Gabriel's shoulder. "The important thing is we're alive," she added.

"Thank God," Gabriel said.

Reluctantly accepting Lizzie's request not to pursue the matter, Penny said, "We're looking for a way out."

Gabriel shook his head. "The iron door to the lobby slammed shut, locked."

"The elevators aren't working either," Lizzie said.

"That means Peabody's private outside elevator isn't operable," Penny muttered.

Morgan shifted from foot to foot, the strain of carrying Isabel showing more. "There's no way out?"

"What about fire exits?" Gabriel asked.

Penny shook her head. "This place is old. It was a locked-down, mental hospital. There aren't any."

"How can that be?" Lizzie asked. "It should've been brought up to code at some point, when it became a Halloween attraction, at least, if not before."

"Shoulda, woulda, coulda..." Morgan mumbled.

Gabriel sighed. "It's a deathtrap."

"Our deathtrap," Lizzie added.

"What about the windows?" Gabriel asked.

"Iron bars on all of them," Penny replied. "Probably original too. Which means rusted in place."

"Deathtrap," Gabriel repeated.

"I'm sorry," Penny whispered. She scanned the ghost hunters' faces. Only Tory looked unfazed. The rest wore worried scowls on their features, scowls that looked as though they blamed her for there being no way out.

"What are we going to do?" Morgan asked. He shifted Isabel in his arms, straining from carrying the dead weight for so long.

"Wait a minute," Gabriel said. He took out his cell phone. "We can call out. Get help from the outside."

"Who are you going to call?" Morgan asked.

Everyone looked uneasy. No one answered.

Morgan cringed. "Yeah, that's where Cheech would've said, *Ghostbusters.*"

"We need to get back to Tech Central," Tory suggested. "Find out what's going on with Cheech and the equipment. Regroup."

"Wait up," Penny argued. "Gabriel had a great idea. Let's try calling for help first." She took out her own cell. "I'll call Mister Peabody."

Everyone looked hopeful.

Penny checked her cell. Her heart sank. "No signal," she whispered.

Gabriel checked his cell. "No signal."

Lizzie checked hers. "Same."

"You guys ready to listen to me," Tory admonished. His head gave a slight jerk to one side. His right eye twitched. "We go back to Tech Central. Find Cheech. Regroup. No more arguments."

"We're not arguing," Penny said. "We're just trying to come up with solutions."

Tory stared hard, eye twitching.

"I'm with Tory," Lizzie interrupted. "We go back to Tech Central. We need to find out what, if anything, happened with Cheech during Dead Time anyway."

"Yeah," Morgan agreed. "Let's regroup."

Gabriel nodded his consent.

Tory looked triumphant, albeit agitated and anxious.

Before Penny could agree or disagree, the red lights in the hallway blinked on.

Everyone startled.

"What in God's name now?" Gabriel asked.

Faraway cries and wails answered. They came from all around, as if the walls themselves were alive, grief-stricken.

"I suggest we move fast," Tory urged.

The red lights flickered in agreement.

"Move," Tory ordered. "Back to the stairwell. I'll watch your backs."

The team of ghost hunters followed orders—Lizzie leading the way, Morgan behind her with Isabel's broken body still cradled in his muscular arms, and Gabriel behind him.

Reluctantly, Penny fell into formation, maneuvering through the doorway as Tory held the door open and shined his light up and down the hallway. Whether she liked it or not, they were heading back to Tech Central on the upper floor. She had no better plan to offer anyway. She hated to admit it, but Tory was right. They needed to find Cheech and regroup. Besides, there really was no place else to go. No better option or plan to follow.

Cries and wails hastened her along as she hurried up the stairs behind the others.

At least for now.

The lights in the stairwell flicked on. Dim. Like during a brownout.

That didn't mean she had to like it.

The door behind her slammed shut. Tory's footfalls slapped against the metal steps at her back. She didn't like having Tory behind her, either. She resisted the urge to look back, though. Instead, she kept moving forward, up the stairway, toward Tech Central. Like the others, blindly following her destiny.

Chapter Forty-Nine

The lights in Tech Central dimmed, flickered, dimmed. White noise hummed from the surrounding speakers. The monitors wired to the video cameras only displayed *snow*, as if reception was interrupted or the cables disconnected. The monitors hooked up to computers were dark, lifeless.

Fidgeting from foot to foot, Cheech stood behind the tables and desks laden with computers and equipment, staring down at it all as if there were actually something to see, something to monitor. He opened his mouth to speak, but no words came out. Instead, only a fly emerged. It buzzed around his face a few seconds before landing on his lower lip and crawling back inside its new home. Closing his mouth, he wiped tears of blood from his eyes and dribbles of blood from his nose.

He couldn't remember what happened, He didn't know what he was supposed to be doing. His mind was lost in a labyrinth of hazy thoughts, bleary memories.

He didn't feel well, either. The thought of food nauseated him.

His gaze landed on a half-eaten Twinkie and an opened can of Mountain Dew that he had left, forgotten, next to a computer keyboard.

The sight gagged him. He'd never eat again.

As his stomach roiled, and vomiting felt imminent, his attention pulled away from the discarded food.

The lights in the room brightened, remaining that way. The speakers no longer spat out white noise.

Both of those events interrupted his obsession over the food, somewhat settling his stomach.

Next, a computer monitor that had displayed only fuzzy white stuff a moment ago showed the hallway outside Tech Central. On that monitor, he saw people emerge from a stairwell doorway.

Fully focusing on these people helped to further quell his nausea. They were not strangers to him. He recognized them, understood that he knew them, but couldn't remember the circumstances of his relationship to them. He couldn't even remember their names.

Whoever they were, however he knew them, didn't feel all that important, though. What felt important was that they were heading right toward the room in which he stood.

Why that was important, he wasn't sure.

All the monitors suddenly came back to life. The ones wired to video cams displayed different rooms, some at more than one angle at a time. The ones hooked up to computers displayed software programs again, as if the computers had just booted up.

What did it all mean?

The monitor with the people on it revealed them right outside the door. Their voices drifted through the speakers, argumentative but indecipherable.

Absentmindedly, Cheech sat down in a chair, studying the people on the monitor, listening to their scrambled but heated debate.

He wiped blood from his eyes, sniffed the red mucus back up his nose. His head buzzed as if flies filled his skull.

Instinctively, he reached out to touch a keyboard, but the sight of open sores on his hands and forearms stopped him cold, took his attention away from the people on the screen, made him forget—if he ever really knew—what he had intended to do or achieve. Instead, he studied the sores, the infectious, yellowish-brown gunk that oozed from them, with dismay and dread.

What was happening?

He held up his other arm, examining it, as well. Both arms trembled as he scrutinized the decaying flesh.

His heart drubbed. His head buzzed.

On one of the monitors the face of a man appeared. He was older, face creased, hair white.

Cheech gulped at the sight. Not only did his arms and hands tremble, but his entire being convulsed.

Who was this old fart whose face loomed on the screen? What did he want?

A lurid grin played across the old guy's face.

"Consequences." His voice crackled over the speakers. "I said there'd be consequences."

Cheech shivered.

What did that mean?

He opened his mouth, but no words spewed forth. Instead, several flies emerged, taking flight around the room. A few landed on different walls while others perched on various equipment. All seemed to be waiting, watching.

The voice again crackled through the speakers. "Consequences." The leering face slowly faded from the monitor, replaced by a shot of the vacant basement.

The buzzing within Cheech's head heightened in volume, in pitch. He clamped his hands over his ears. That only made the unnerving noise worse. For the buzzing didn't come from without, but from within.

Abruptly, he got to his feet, sending the rolling chair crashing backward into the wall. He couldn't stand up straight, though. Instead, he doubled over in pain, his insides feeling as though they were being slowly, but voraciously, eaten.

His eyes, ears, and nose shed rivers of blood as he forced himself to straighten. Lifting his shirt, he examined his torso, riddled with sores that oozed foul-smelling gunk and blood.

"What's happening?" he cried.

"Consequences," a disembodied voice answered. "Consequences."

Cheech screeched.

Chapter Fifty

The cries and wails had stopped. The lights in the upstairs hallway still flickered. Cold spots, like those when swimming in deep water, were felt here and there as Penny and the ghost hunters crept toward Tech Central.

Penny followed Lizzie, Gabriel, and Morgan—who still carried Isabel's corpse. Tory brought up the rear. She could hear his footfalls. She could feel his presence. Paranoia perched on her shoulder, whispered in her ear not to trust the guy at her back, but she dared not look behind for fear of how he might take it or what he might do. He seemed himself again, for the most part. Still, he'd proven that he was at best irrational and unstable, and at worst delirious and violent.

The irony that she didn't call into question her own sanity but that of another wasn't lost on her. Within her mind, the tables had turned. In the past, she had always doubted her own rationality, had always called into question her own tenuous grasp on reality. Now, it was her resolve alone, her sensibility alone, that she solely depended on for survival.

Lizzie opened the door to Tech Central just as Cheech's bloodcurdling screech reverberated throughout the room. Penny and the others pushed in around her in time to see the Tech Specialist turn toward them, revealing nothing but a dark shadow of the nerdy, fun-loving hippy they'd come to know.

"Cheech," Lizzie cried, but she made no move to help.

The other ghost hunters froze as well, apparently unable to react to their friend's plight.

Penny proved just as useless. She could only gasp, not believing her eyes. At first, she thought maybe Cheech was already dead, that this was his ghost. Everyone, however, saw him, not just her. He had to still be alive. Looking at him, though, she couldn't help wondering how.

Yes, Cheech was standing, but his pallor was that of a corpse. His eyes bulged as if he had died with them open. From them, he cried blood. Red crept out of his ears, dribbled from his nose. His voice had gone silent, his mouth agape. The flesh on his arms and face had already started to degrade, as if having rotted in the bright sun for two days. Flies buzzed around him, attracted by the stench of death, landing in open sores, feeding on oozing gunk.

"Cheech?" Tory mumbled. He then yelled, "Cheech." Still the ghost hunter made no move.

No one did.

Cheech dropped to his knees. He raised his arms as if being crucified. Throwing his head back, he looked at the ceiling or somewhere beyond, maybe to the heavens in prayer. Tremors racked his body as strange, gurgling noises came from deep inside his throat. Blood spurted from his mouth like a geyser while he fell backward, knees bent, thighs against calves, head banging onto the floor, arms still out in crucifixion.

Everyone except Morgan rushed to him *en masse*, as if whatever death grip that held them released all of them at once.

Tory and Lizzie knelt beside their cohort. Neither of them looked capable of taking further action, as if afraid to touch what they didn't understand.

The others, along with Penny, remained standing, huddling around the three on the floor but at a safe distance. Having placed Isabel's body safely in a corner, Morgan joined the rest in their vigil.

"Mother of God," Gabriel exclaimed. "Turn him over. He's choking on his own blood."

That must've shook Tory and Lizzie from fear's grasp because they did as Gabriel said, turning Cheech onto his side, away from them.

Once on his side, Cheech stopped gurgling, stopped choking, the blood flowing freely onto the floor.

"There's so much blood," Lizzie blurted. "How do we stop it?"

Everyone looked at one another, clueless.

Flies continued to buzz around them, some landing in the ever-growing pool of blood as if taking a swim.

"He's going to bleed out," Gabriel worried.

"Dude, not you too," Morgan pleaded with his fallen friend. "Don't you die on me, too."

Tory stood. "Gabe and Morgan, clear some of that equipment off one of those tables."

The two did as they were told.

"Good," Tory said. "Help me get Cheech onto it."

The three men lifted Cheech from the floor, carried him to the table, and gently placed him on his side.

Penny wasn't sure what they had achieved. At least, though, Tory seemed himself, seemed in command again. At least they had done something, whatever good it would do.

Everyone stood around the table, staring at Cheech as if he were a freak in a sideshow.

"I think the bleeding stopped," Lizzie announced, "at least from his mouth."

"I think you're right," Morgan agreed. "There's nowhere near the amount of blood as when he was on the floor."

Penny hesitated to ask, but someone had to, because she certainly couldn't tell. "Are we sure he hasn't already bled out? Are we sure he's not dead?"

Everyone turned their heads as one, staring hard at her, as if just by her asking the question it might be true.

Penny stepped forward. She held her breath, hesitantly touched Cheech's withered, sore-riddled neck, feeling for a pulse. "He's alive." She let her held breath out slowly. "His pulse is slow, weak."

Flies—even more now—buzzed all around.

Penny swatted at the things, wondering for the first time where the foul, little things came from. They never had a fly problem. In fact, she couldn't remember ever before seeing a fly inside the building.

"We should cover him," Lizzie suggested. "He might be in shock."

"Good idea," Tory agreed.

"There's a blanket in Mister Peabody's office," Penny said.

"I'll get it," Lizzie offered. She was off, out of the room and down the hallway before anyone could argue.

"What the hell happened to him?" Morgan asked. "He looks like a..."

"Like a corpse," Tory finished. "A corpse several days dead."

"That's impossible," Morgan insisted.

Penny stared at Cheech. She peered underneath the man's shirt.

The sight of his torso was just as ghastly, if not more so, than the rest of him. The guy's flesh was degrading right before their eyes. How could that be?

Penny pulled the shirt back down and stepped back. She had seen a lot of bizarre, inexplicable things over the last few years that made her, and everyone who knew her, question her sanity. This, however, was beyond anything she'd ever seen or experienced. Morgan was right. This was impossible.

Lizzie returned with the blanket. She went directly to Cheech. Gently, she covered him. "His eyes are closed," she whispered. "At least he's resting comfortably."

Morgan scanned the floor. "How much blood do you think he lost?"

Everyone was careful not to step in the gory mess.

Tory wiped blood from his hands onto his pants. Spatter already flecked his clothes, his shoes. Looking around, he said, "I don't know, but by the looks of things, too much."

Lizzie's hands and clothes also had red spatter on them, but she didn't notice or care. She hovered over Cheech like a mother over a sick child. "He's doing better." She looked up, staring at each one of them from behind her thick glasses. "There's hope."

Gabriel nodded. "There's always hope," he agreed. "God, hear me," he prayed. "Show mercy on this poor soul. Guard him against evil. Save him from Satan's grasp. Keep him in thine protective light. Watch over him. Keep him safe. Amen."

Except for Penny, everyone—including Lizzie—repeated, "Amen."

Everyone continued to stare at Cheech.

"I still don't understand," Morgan said. "How can this be happening?"

"It's Satan's work," Gabriel responded. "Good and evil are battling for his soul."

"From the looks of things," Tory said, "evil's winning." His eye twitched ever so slightly.

Penny couldn't argue the point.

She looked at Tory. His right eye again twitched.

Not just Cheech's, but all of their souls were in jeopardy. Evil was indeed winning.

Chapter Fifty-One

The lights within Tech Central dimmed, as if in a brownout. All of the computer monitors went completely black. Screams, shrieks, and wails drifted through the outside hallways and from deep within the bowels of the place, a constant background noise that rattled everyone's already frazzled nerves. To make matters worse, the stench of death hung over the room.

Cheech still lay on the table. A blanket covered him for comfort, to guard against shock, and to hide the unnerving sight of his decomposing body. He barely clung to life.

Lizzie hovered over her patient. She covered her mouth and nose with a handkerchief given to her by Tory. To all appearances, she was unwilling to accept Cheech's apparent, imminent demise.

Morgan and Gabriel had their cell phones out, both apparently unwilling to accept that there was no signal.

Penny stood in the corner of the room, a faraway look in her eyes. She used her hand to cover her mouth and nose against death's stink.

Tory stared at his dejected, grief-stricken, beaten group of ghost hunters. The ones still alive, anyway. Isabel was dead. Cheech might as well have been. How had it come to this?

His gaze drifted to Penny. It lingered on her, studied her, as if she were a lab experiment gone wrong.

A stabbing pain struck his right temple like a sudden lightning strike. In response, his head flinched, right eye twitched.

In his ear, a strange, disembodied voice whispered, "She's the cause of it all."

Lightning struck his temple, again. His head flinched. His eye twitched. The smell of burnt flesh beat back the odorous stench already in the room.

The disembodied voice whispered, "She's the cause of everyone's pain, everyone's suffering. She's the reason for it all."

He blinked, eyes hot and burning.

Three shimmering, pulsating silhouettes appeared around

Penny. They circled her, embraced her, like lovers come to call.

"She's the cause of it all," the disembodied voice whispered. "Everyone's pain, everyone's suffering."

This time, when the lightning bolt of pain struck, his vision went dark. Burnt flesh vanquished all other smells. The sound wind makes when blowing through the eaves of an old house whistled relentlessly through his ears. What he saw next was but a remnant of a nightmare.

A nightmare best forgotten.

* * * *

A dimly lit room. Dark shadows playing across the floor, walls, and ceiling.

The wallop of his heartbeat and the inhalation and exhalation of his ragged breath were the only sounds he could hear.

He struggled to get his bearings, make some sense of where he was, what was happening. The last thing he remembered was being in Tech Central.

He quickly scanned the dark room.

This wasn't Tech Central. None of his companions were to be seen.

The shadows around him shimmered and pulsed, much like those three silhouettes had. Unlike those dark shapes, however, these shadows overlapped, as if they were one large entity rather than separate. Still, they—or it—circled him as if alive.

"Where am I?" he croaked, throat scratchy and sore.

This all seemed eerily familiar.

He couldn't move, strapped down to a large, wooden chair. There were *things* attached to his temples and wires that ran from them to a nearby machine.

"Damn," he hissed.

Suddenly, he remembered: the torture chambers, the electric shock machine, the hallucination.

He struggled against the leather restraints across his wrists, ankles, and waist.

"Damn."

Had it been a hallucination?

His heartbeat continued to wallop. Ragged breath squeezed out of his lungs. Sweat plastered his hair, trickled down his back, and soaked his shirt.

"Let me go!"

He battled against his restraints.

The leather straps held tight.

"Let me go!"

The shimmering, pulsating shadows circled. What sounded like a thousand demonic voices spoke as one. "You can save them. You can save them all."

"Who are you? What do you want from me?"

The demonic voices answered, "You can save them all."

A switch clicked. Volts of electricity followed. Sparks flew. The air crackled, hissed. The switch clicked, again.

Tory slumped in the wooden chair. His labored breath came out shallow, slow. Spittle hung from his open mouth.

"You can save them all," the demonic voices insisted.

"How?" Tory croaked.

"Kill her."

The switch clicked. Sparks flew. Electricity fired.

Tory stiffened. His head slammed against the chair. His fingernails dug into wood. His silent scream could only be heard by the damned in Hell.

The demonic voices resonated. "Kill her," they demanded. "Kill her. She's the cause of it all. Kill her."

* * * *

Tory blinked. Hot tears ran down his face. His vision, although blurred, focused again on Tech Central, his team of ghost hunters, and *Penny*.

"Kill her," the disembodied voice whispered in his ear.

From the corner of his tear-filled eyes, Tory glimpsed the three silhouettes moving around Penny. One stopped next to the girl, coalescing into a faintly visible, sputtering apparition. The apparition looked like a doctor, wearing bloody surgical scrubs. The doctor held up a cranium saw as he leered with evil intent.

The disembodied voiced whispered, "Kill her."

Tory scrunched his eyes, shutting out the apparitions. Hot, searing pain slammed into his skull. A white, blinding light flashed behind his eyelids.

With a gasp, he opened his eyes in time to see another of the silhouettes coalesce into yet a different, faintly visible doctor. This doctor too wore bloody surgical scrubs as well as an evil glint in his eyes. Rather than a cranium saw, he held up some sort of large drill.

Next to him, the last silhouette turned into an apparition, only this one was a woman dressed in a hospital gown as if she were a patient. A maniacal look masked her face. Insanity sparked in her eyes as she sneaked up on Penny, hands ready to strangle the unsuspecting girl.

"Kill her. Kill her. Kill her."

Tory again clamped his eyelids shut, praying to a God he didn't necessarily believe in that the hot, searing pain wouldn't return, that the flash of white light wouldn't force his eyes open as before.

"Kill her. Kill her. Kill her."

Despite the aching pain, Tory shook his head. In his mind, he screamed, *No.*

"Kill her!"

No!

Whoever they were, he wouldn't do their dirty work for them. Never would he do such a thing as they demanded. No matter what.

Desperately, he tried to conjure images of his dead mother. Soon, she appeared within his mind's eye, instantly calming his frayed nerves, his fractured psyche. The gentle sound of her voice soothed him.

"Be a good boy, Tory," his mother said. "Always make me proud."

With a deep, hitched breath, Tory opened his eyes. His vision cleared. The searing pain in his skull was nothing more than a dull ache. To his relief, the evil apparitions around Penny had disappeared, too. Not even the shimmering, pulsating silhouettes remained.

All that remained was the echo of his mother's voice telling him to be a good boy.

"I will," Tory muttered. "I'll always try."

"Did you say something, Tory?" Penny asked.

Chapter Fifty-Two

Penny eyed Tory with wariness.

The man looked shaken, pale, a slightly haunted look to his eyes.

Or was it just her overactive imagination? Could well be.

Under the circumstances, she certainly was stressed to the max. She worried about Morgan, what he knew, what he might divulge to the rest. Strangely enough, Morgan knowing her true identity was really the least of her problems, the least of her fears at the moment. Her nerves were truly frayed by the relentless attacks of screams, shrieks, and wails that resounded from the walls of the horrid place. Isabel's corpse lying nearby also added to her disquiet, her anxiety. Mostly, it was the sight of Cheech's blood on the floor and the sight of Cheech himself decomposing before her eyes—not to mention the disgusting odor that reeked throughout the room—that truly shook her to her core. She couldn't help worrying that they might all end up the same as Cheech—living yet decomposing, breathing yet, for all intents and purposes, dead. The thought sickened her, terrified her.

Considering everything, she imagined that she fared no better than Tory in how she looked. A lot of the same worries and fears had to be plaguing the ghost hunter's mind. The guy had every right to look shaken, pale, haunted. She'd have to give Tory a break, the benefit of the doubt.

Still, Tory ignored her, hadn't answered her question. Was he evading her on purpose or just lost in his own fears?

Deciding it didn't matter, Penny repeated, "Tory, did you say something?"

Tory blinked at her and wiped away tears. His right eye still twitched a bit. The good news was no spasmodic jerks animated his head or extremities. Still, there was no doubt he looked *disturbed*.

Besides, he still hadn't answered.

"Tory?" Penny prompted.

Tory cleared his throat. "I said that I don't understand any of this."

Penny again eyed the ghost hunter with wariness. That wasn't what he had said, she was sure. She decided to let it pass. "I don't understand what's going on, either."

Gabriel stopped fussing with his phone. "I understand something," he said, his voice a tremor of fear. "We're trapped."

"We're screwed," Morgan muttered.

Lizzie left her patient's side. "Cheech is getting worse, Tory," she said, taking the handkerchief away from her face. "He's barely alive. I don't know how much more time he has."

"We need to get him to a doctor," Gabriel added.

Lizzie glanced at Cheech lying on the table. Turning back to the others, she said, "Agreed."

Gabriel *humphed*. "How? We can't get out. Every door's locked. We checked them all. The windows are barred."

Tory ran a hand across his face. "Everyone settle down," he pleaded.

"Kid, you don't get it," Gabriel continued. "There's no way out. There's no cell signal to call out. We're trapped."

Tory stiffened. A look of pure rage passed over his face like a lunar eclipse. Penny thought he was going to attack Gabriel. Just as quickly, the rage was gone, replaced by something almost as disturbing—misery, torment.

What was happening to this guy?

Penny watched, waited.

Tory righted himself, regaining control. His voice was soft-spoken when he said, "Gabriel, I understand better than you think. I know a lot's at stake here. That's why I propose we do what we came here to do."

Gabriel looked confused.

In fact, as Penny scanned the faces around her, everyone looked confused. She finally asked, "What do you mean, Tory? Do what you came here to do?"

Tory turned on Penny. Some sort of schizophrenic battle between good and evil waged behind his mask of normalcy.

Penny took an involuntary step backward.

Instead, Tory calmly explained, "Our job, Miss Winters. No matter what's happened, we're here to do a job. I, for one, intend on doing it."

Penny opened her mouth to respond. Before she could say anything, Morgan lost it, throwing his phone, smashing it against the nearest wall.

"Do a job?" Morgan yelled. He stood with fists at his side,

face red, breathing hard. "I'm sorry," he hissed through clenched teeth, "but Isabel's dead, and my best friend's turning into a freaking zombie. Screw the job. The job's over."

Tory took one step toward the raging man. "Our job may be the only way out of this mess. The only way to save Cheech. Can't you see that? Can't any of you see that?"

"What I see is if we stay, we're as good as dead," Morgan insisted.

"You don't see it." Fists clenched, Tory advanced another step toward his adversary.

Penny quickly stepped between the two. "Stop it. Both of you. This isn't helping."

Both men reluctantly backed down.

Gabriel cleared his throat before speaking, "Why don't we just sit tight, wait? Sooner or later, Peabody will try to open the place. If he can't get in, then he'll call the police." He gave Penny a hopeful look. "Right? I mean, it's Halloween. Tonight's the big money night. Right?"

Penny shook her head. Gabriel's argument was sound, maybe even logical. Nothing about Mister Peabody's attitude toward the cops approached logic, however. "Halloween or not, I'm not sure Mister Peabody would call the cops. I mean, he might. Then again, he might not," she said.

Lizzie interrupted, "Besides that, I don't think Cheech can wait. He needs help soon." She looked to Tory. "Tell us what to do. Whatever you say, I'm with you."

Gabriel *humphed* again. "Of course you are, little miss lovelorn."

"There's no time for this childish bickering," Penny scolded. She shot daggers at Gabriel and Morgan, all the while wondering how, in a group of adults, she ended up as the mature voice of reason.

Gabriel looked chagrined. "I apologize, Lizzie."

Lizzie adjusted her broken glasses. "Apology accepted, preacher man."

Gabriel pursed his lips. He nodded.

Morgan cast his gaze at the floor. His entire demeanor relaxed. "I'm sorry too, everyone," he said with a shrug. "I'm worried about Cheech is all."

"That's better," Penny said.

Morgan looked up, scrutiny in his eyes. He opened his mouth to speak, but no words came forth.

Was he thinking of revealing her secrets to the others?

Penny didn't give him a chance. She turned to Tory. "Tell us what you're thinking?" She still didn't trust the head ghost hunter, but maybe he had a viable plan of some kind. Which was more than anyone else had. Besides, her question threw attention back on Tory, away from her.

A half-smile of self-satisfaction played across Tory's lips. He said, "I'm thinking to hell with Peabody. We can't count on him. Even if he does go to the police, we can't count on them being able to get inside any better than we're able to get out. The way I see it, we can only count on ourselves to get us out of this mess. We can only count on what we do best."

Penny frowned. "Which is?"

"Doing our job, Miss Winters."

"You said that." Penny took a deep breath. "What are you suggesting?"

"That we do a cleansing," Tory answered.

As if in protest, the lights within the room flickered, then dimmed even more. The faraway screams, shrieks, and wails resonated louder, more insistent.

Tory suddenly grimaced, rocked back on his heels as if in tremendous pain.

Morgan, Lizzie, and Gabriel rushed forward to catch him. The three of them held him upright, steady on his feet.

Penny stood back, watching in alarm.

"Tory," Lizzie exclaimed, "what's wrong?"

Wild-eyed, breathing hard, Tory croaked, "A cleansing. It's the only way."

Chapter Fifty-Three

The Halloween attraction had gone dead quiet. The lights, although dim, remained steady within the room. Cheech neither moved nor uttered a sound.

Penny wasn't sure if these were good signs or bad.

As she watched Morgan ready his video equipment and Tory prepare himself for an on-camera declaration, she imagined Fright House readying itself for what was to come. She imagined the place as laughing at their pitiful, little plans to cleanse it of its wicked ways, to rid it of its ghosts.

It seemed laughable even to her. Fright House had too much history. There were too many repressed ghosts haunting the place. There had been too many horrible events that had taken place within its walls, too many people had suffered. It was too damn strong.

"I'm ready," Morgan announced.

Tory had cleaned himself up the best he could in the restroom down the hall. He was as presentable for the camera as could be expected. "You're using the Sony XDCAM, right? Not the smaller camcorder?"

"Yeah," Morgan answered. He held up the video camera for Tory to see. "The battery's not fully charged, but we're good for an hour or more."

Tory nodded. "That's more than enough time. I've got the feeling that we need to get this cleansing done ASAP." He paused and took a deep breath. "Or we're as good as dead," he muttered.

Penny stiffened. She didn't like the finality, the resignation of Tory's last statement. It was as if this was their only shot, and if it didn't work, all hope was lost. She couldn't let herself think that way. She had just come to terms with her haunted past, with her curse or gift or whatever it was. She had just found some peace within herself. She wasn't ready to give it up—not yet. A new determination for survival had planted its seed within her. For the first time in a long time, she really wanted to live—not just exist, but to live. No damn haunted asylum was going to take that away, not without a fight.

"Okay," Tory said, "roll 'em."

Morgan turned on the LED NightShot function, aimed the camera at Tory, and gave his boss the thumbs up.

Everyone else stood back. They remained as quiet as possible.

Tory looked into the camera, his face and body language a reflection of calm and self-assuredness not warranted by the circumstances at hand.

Penny watched carefully. She knew it was all an act. How had the guy gotten himself under such control? There was no hint of a twitch or a spasmodic jerk of any kind. There was no hint of torment, misery, pain, or grief that had been so apparent in his demeanor as of late. Tory was either a true professional or a total schizo.

Or both.

Tory cleared his throat. "Welcome back," he said to the camera, to future viewers. "In this episode of *Paranormal Scene Investigations*, we've proven beyond doubt that Fright House is under the control of a dark, demonic power, unlike anything we've ever encountered."

Tory's voice was as rock steady as his bearing.

"This demonic power not only haunts this place but possesses an unknown amount of people, holding their bodies, minds, and souls captive. This demonic power forces them to do unspeakable acts of violence and mayhem. Even as we mourn Isabel's death and Cheech's unstable condition, we can't run from our duty. These people, these poor possessed souls, as well as this place itself, will be lost to darkness forever unless we perform a successful cleansing."

Tory gave a dramatic pause.

"It's our job as paranormal investigators to free these victims, to free this place from demonic possession," he continued. "It's our job to send these demons back to Hell. That's just what we're going to do."

Tory motioned for everyone except Morgan to join him in front of the camera. Lizzie and Gabriel did.

Penny remained back in the shadows, hidden from the camera's eye. She preferred not to appear on camera anymore than she absolutely had to. Besides, she wasn't an official team member anyway. She wanted to keep it that way. Let *PSI* take the fight to Fright House in front of the camera. She'd remain in the background, doing her bit for survival behind the scenes.

Tory shot Penny a look of annoyance but continued, "Gabriel, lead us in prayer as we go out to fight the good fight against evil."

Gabriel bowed his head. "May the power of God surround us. May the power of God enfold us. May the power of God protect us. Amen."

"Amen," Tory repeated. Looking directly into the eye of the camera, he said, "Let's do this."

Chapter Fifty-Four

The screams, shrieks, and wails within Fright House were back. They sounded faraway, as if they resonated from some otherworldly plane. The lights in the room sputtered.

With his video camera, Morgan recorded everything.

Gabriel began the cleansing ritual by mounting a crucifix on a wall. He sprinkled Holy water in all four directions—north, south, east, and west. He said, "I command you, demons, to leave this room, this place. In the name of the Father, of the Son, and of the Holy Spirit."

When Gabriel finished, Lizzie lit frankincense within a glass bowl. As perfumed smoke wafted into the foul air, she said, "The elements of life—earth, wind, water, and fire—command you, demons, to leave this room, this place. Never to return." She placed selected crystals about the room.

"That takes care of this room," Tory announced.

Morgan continued to record anyway.

Penny remained skeptical about the whole affair. "Do you really think this ritual will rid the place of its demons and get us out of here?"

"Not without faith," Gabriel answered. "We must have faith."

The lights flickered off.

The room went completely dark.

Everyone gasped.

"I'm not sure about this," Penny said.

The lights turned back on, bright, blinding. Whirring sounds and beeps filled the room as the computers booted up, as the electronic equipment turned back on.

The faraway cries silenced.

"Yay," Lizzie squealed.

From behind his camera, Morgan even wore an encouraged look on his once somber face.

Gabriel grinned. "See, Penny? Have a little faith."

Penny gave the preacher a half-smile back. She nodded. Maybe there was hope after all. Maybe the religious ritual would somehow silence the demons, save everyone. "I'll try," she muttered.

Tory's gaze shot death rays at her. "See that you do, Miss Winters."

"I'll try," Penny repeated more firmly.

She meant it, too. The slightly irrational look in Tory's eyes, however, didn't boost either her faith or her morale. It also wasn't lost on her that Tory had become formal again as of late, calling her *Miss Winters*. It was as if he were distancing himself from her, for whatever reason.

Doubt crept back in.

Maybe the performed religious ritual had nothing to do with the lights, computers, or electronics turning on again. Maybe it hadn't silenced the cries, either. Maybe the evil place was just toying with them.

While Penny was deep in thought, Gabriel came up alongside her. The minister put a hand on her shoulder. "Have faith, Penny," he said.

Penny gazed into the preacher's face. His smile, his look of reassurance, calmed her. Maybe Gabriel was right. Maybe all they needed was faith.

She smiled back. "Faith," she whispered.

Chapter Fifty-Five

Everyone, including Penny, gathered at the door to Tech Central.

"We do this together," Tory ordered. "No one straggles off on their own."

Penny protested. "Wouldn't it be quicker if we split up into teams?"

Tory again shot her a death-ray look. "Quicker? Maybe. More dangerous? For certain."

Penny sighed. The guy had a point. Dammit. That, however, didn't mean she had to like it.

"We stay together," Tory insisted. "We go floor by floor, performing the ritual, completing the entire process in the basement. With any luck, we'll be able to get out of here in an hour or two."

With any luck?

This time, Penny stifled her sigh.

They hadn't had any luck except bad so far.

Faith, she reminded herself. *Have faith.*

"What about Cheech?" Lizzie asked, staring back at her patient.

Cheech lay on the table—curled into a fetal position, his back to them, as still as Isabel's corpse.

"Maybe we shouldn't leave him alone," Lizzie continued.

"The room's protected," Tory insisted. "That means he's protected. Besides, there's not much else we can do for him. The important thing is to cleanse this place, so we can get him out of here, so we can get him to a doctor."

"You're right, of course," Lizzie said in acceptance of Tory's logical argument.

Tory opened the door. "You ready, Morgan?" he asked.

Morgan turned on the video camera. He started shooting.

"Good," Tory said. "Let's do this."

He stepped out into the hallway. The others followed without question or hesitation.

Penny brought up the rear, halting in the doorway. An

eerie feeling crept across her mind, raising gooseflesh on her scalp, on her skin. She looked back at Cheech as if it were the last time she would ever see the Tech Specialist.

The last time she'd see him alive, anyway.

She shook that negative thought from her mind. "Have faith," she reminded herself.

Taking one last look at Cheech, she stepped out into the hallway, closing the door behind her.

Chapter Fifty-Six

With Morgan filming, the group made their way through the remaining rooms of the top floor, performing the cleansing ritual—all without incident. They made their way down the stairwell to the main floor where they performed the ritual in the cell-lined hallway. The iron door to the lobby remained locked, so they couldn't perform the ceremony there. Other than that, they saw and heard nothing out of the ordinary.

In fact, everything was way too normal to suit Penny.

The lights were on throughout the place. No cries or wails issued forth from anywhere. All was quiet except for the sounds made by the ghost hunters themselves.

It was unsettling to say the least.

By the time they made it down the stairwell to the damp, green-lit basement, Penny was completely unnerved. The others were in visibly better spirits, visibly more confident in their ability to rid Fright House of its demons. More confident in saving themselves from further danger.

Maybe overconfident.

Penny scanned the Plexiglas torture chambers. They remained dark, lifeless. She gazed past them, studying the archway to the *Fright House Cemetery*. She saw nothing out of the ordinary, if that word could describe anything about the place.

Faith, she reminded herself. She needed to have faith.

Maybe the others had every right to feel confident. Everything was going as planned. Everything was still, quiet, normal. Maybe the ghosts were gone. Maybe the curse had been lifted. After all, if anything paranormal remained, wouldn't she see it, sense it? Of course she would. The same curse that plagued her throughout her teen years wouldn't abandon her now when she needed it most.

She saw and sensed nothing.

Still, old habits die hard, so she couldn't relax. Instead, she remained watchful, skeptical—with a pinch of hope, along with faith thrown in for good measure.

"Let's finish up," Tory said. "Once the basement is cleansed, we should be able to get out of here."

Morgan positioned himself toward the back of the basement, the cemetery's archway behind him, and the expanse of torture chambers in front of him. "Ready," he announced. He started recording, again.

"I want crucifixes there, there, and there," Tory said, pointing to three separate spots on three separate walls.

Gabriel, Lizzie, and Penny all complied, each hanging a crucifix in one of Tory's specified spots.

When that was done, Gabriel and Lizzie performed the ritual.

Tory nodded in approval. "That only leaves the fake cemetery. After that, we're done and out of here." He grinned. "I feel better all ready."

Penny eyed the ghost hunter. He did look better, more in control, calm, torment free. In fact, he looked almost as he had when they'd first met.

Even she started to truly relax. Maybe everything *was* going to be okay.

Chapter Fifty-Seven

Morgan continued recording the proceedings.

Throughout, however, he struggled with his ongoing guilt concerning Isabel's death. It nagged at him, ate away at his soul.

Much the same as his brother's death so many years ago had done. In fact, it still did.

In both instances, logically, he knew that he wasn't truly to blame. At the time of his brother's death, he was only a kid. There was only so much he could do to keep his autistic brother under control, safe. He came to realize later that his parents never should've left him solely in charge of Shaun's welfare. At the time of Isabel's death, he had done everything possible to save her, even putting his own life at risk.

Still, logic and reason seldom won out over grief and guilt. Somehow, he still felt accountable for both deaths. Whether a kid or not, he was responsible for his brother's safety and wellbeing that day. There was no getting around that. Isabel herself was no more than a kid. In her case, unlike with his brother, he wasn't a kid anymore. He couldn't fall back on that excuse. He was supposedly the mature one, the one in charge when the apparition struck and took the girl's life. He should've done more.

Somehow.

To make matters worse, right before the attack, Isabel had offered him her heart. What had he done? He stomped on it. The heartbreak of unrequited love was the last human emotion the teenager had experienced before death took her. He was accountable for that, too.

Yeah, no matter what logic and reason told him, no matter how he shook it out, it still came down to this: Shaun had depended on him. Isabel had depended on him. In the end, he had failed them both.

Grief and guilt really did prove a deadly combination.

Having the cemetery room where Isabel died at his back totally creeped him out. Maybe because it felt like he had returned to the scene of the crime. Maybe because there was the distinct possibility the apparition that killed Isabel, the apparition he had tussled with, was still there, lurking amongst the fake headstones. Invisible.

He couldn't shake the dreaded feeling that someone watched him, stalked him, from somewhere behind. Maybe the same apparition that had taken Isabel's life.

Somehow, he fought the overwhelming urge to turn around, to take a look. Instead, he told himself it was just his overactive imagination brought on by his overabundance of guilt and grief. He told himself no one or nothing was really there.

The feeling of dread, however, wouldn't relent.

In spite of all that, he continued to film the ritual in front of him, continued to ignore the possible dangers behind.

At least, until he heard scuffling somewhere back by the archway. He whirled around to face the unknown fear that clung to him. Strangling on his own breath, he scanned the area in front of the cemetery room. *Fright House Cemetery* in big letters on the archway loomed just a few feet away. Otherwise, he didn't see anything at first. On closer look, though, he noticed a shimmering blackness under the archway, just at the entrance to the cemetery room. He definitely heard a scuffling noise, too.

Instead of taking a step backward, as his brain told him he should, he foolishly took a few steps forward, peering harder at the archway, at the shimmering blackness beneath it. The scuffling noise became more prominent. Out of the blackness appeared a single silhouette.

Was he seeing things? Or was someone really there?

He stared harder, concentrating, squinting. Still, all he could make out was the form of what looked like a person.

"Morgan..."

He gasped. Had he actually heard a voice call him or was it in his head? He couldn't be sure.

"Morgan..."

It was a girl's voice.

"Can I call you *Morg*?"

His heart stopped. He gulped, swallowing what felt like dust, his mouth was so parched. "Isabel?" he croaked.

The figure shifted slightly. "It has such a ring of death to it."

"Isabel?" Morgan whispered.

How could he be so stupid? He remembered the video camera with the LED NightShot in his hand. All he had to do was illuminate the silhouette to know for sure if it was Isabel.

Which it couldn't possibly be. Isabel was dead.

"Morg, could you ever love me?"

He gulped again, his throat raw, aching from lack of moisture.

It sure sounded like Isabel. No one else had ever called him *Morg*.

The video camera in his hand rattled from the tremors racking his extremities. He wasn't totally sure that he wanted to know whether it was Isabel or not. Maybe he should just turn away. Maybe he should just run, never looking back.

"Could you love me, Morg?"

He couldn't run away. He had to know.

Slowly, arm trembling, he raised the video camera, shining the light at the archway, illuminating the figure standing there.

"Isabel?"

The figure was definitely a woman, but she wore some kind of cloak. She had her back turned toward him, as well.

"Isabel?"

The woman's head turned slightly, revealing her profile in the light.

"Isabel?" Morgan muttered. "It can't be. You're dead."

Without moving her lips, Isabel again asked, "Could you love me, Morg?"

Morgan gulped, again swallowing dust. At the sight of Isabel, guilt and grief built within him until he thought he would burst. He had to tell her what she wanted to hear. "Sure," he muttered, "I *could* love you, Isabel."

Isabel turned her profile away. She stepped into the shimmering blackness within the cemetery room.

"Come to me, Morg."

Isabel's voice was somewhere inside his head. It called to him. He had to listen. He had no choice. He was accountable.

"Come to me, Morg."

As if under a spell, Morgan stepped toward the cemetery room, under the archway, into the shimmering blackness.

Chapter Fifty-Eight

Tech Central remained well-lit. All of the computers and electronic equipment remained on, humming with electromagnetic energy. The speakers spat out static, white noise.

Cheech still lay on the table, curled into a fetal position, covered by a blanket. He groaned in exorbitant pain as his mind crawled out of a black abyss toward consciousness.

On one of the computer monitors, the old guy appeared. A lurid grin played across that otherwise kind-looking face.

A voice crackled over the speakers. "Consequences," it said. "I said there'd be consequences."

Cheech groaned. He continued to stir, consciousness beckoning him back to cold reality. The pain within him, as if something was eating away at his insides, rudely shook him awake.

"Consequences," the voice over the speakers crackled.

Cheech threw the blanket aside and rolled onto his back. Forcing his blood-encrusted eyelids open, he stared at the white-paneled ceiling.

"Oh, God. Help me," he cried, in horrible pain.

In response, laughter crackled over the speakers.

Cheech clutched at his gut as if his insides would spill out. His mouth opened, but this time, no words spewed forth. Something marched through his innards, devouring him from the inside out. It was ravenous, unrelenting in its hunger. The agony of its gluttony was paralyzing, crushing.

"Oh, God," Cheech managed to croak.

The speakers again responded with resounding laughter.

"Oh, God."

The torment didn't stop in his gut. The unbearable pain spread to his back, his arms, his legs, up to his head. A feverish sweat beaded his brow and soaked into his clothes. His entire being quaked with chills. All the while, a relentless buzzing filled his ears, his head, driving him mad.

"Help me, God," Cheech again pleaded. "Help me."

The speakers crackled with laughter.

A voice answered Cheech's plea. "God can't help you," it said.

Cheech forced himself up, struggling against all odds into a sitting position. Flies buzzed all around him, some landing onto open sores, feeding on infectious gunk. He hadn't the strength or the resolve to swat them away. It had taken every ounce of energy and willpower just to sit up.

"God can't help you," the voice over the speakers repeated.

Through blurred vision, Cheech noticed the old guy's face on the computer screen before him. He had seen that face before but couldn't remember where or when. The torturous pain ate away at him, clouding his memory, stealing his ability to reason, to think.

"Consequences," the voice crackled over the speakers. "I said there'd be consequences."

From the monitor, the old guy's face leered.

Cheech shivered at the sight. He wiped at his eyes to clear his vision of what he thought was nothing more than a mixture of sweat and tears, but his trembling hand came away smeared with blood.

"No," he croaked.

Flies continued to buzz all around. They landed in his hair, in his beard, on his face, all over his arms. Somehow, he found the energy to swipe some away from around his head. As he did so, clumps of hair fell onto his shoulders, his lap, on the table he sat upon.

"No."

Panic swelled within him as he desperately ran both of his trembling hands across his scalp and face, coming away with hunks of blood-soaked hair.

With renewed energy, he swatted flies away from his bare arms. That was the first time he truly saw them. Within seconds, though, the flies were back on him, covering the open sores, rotting flesh, exposed bones.

He opened his mouth to scream, but only a raw, choking sound burst forth.

Laughter crackled from the speakers.

Cheech ripped open his T-shirt, only to reveal even more ruin, even more decomposition than was on his arms. Hundreds of flies immediately attacked, burrowing into his decaying flesh, exposed ribcage, and rotting organs.

More self-satisfying, wicked laughter crackled through the speakers.

Cheech twisted and contorted his face from the pain as he fought against the insanity pounding on the door to his brain.

On the computer monitor, the old guy continued to leer.

"Consequences," the all too familiar voice repeated, "I told you there'd be consequences."

Tears of blood ran down Cheech's deteriorating face. Uncontrollable spasms charged through his putrefying body.

Was there nothing he could do? No way to save himself?

"You're already dead," the voice over the speakers said. "Save yourself the agony."

Cheech choked back sobs. Through blood-soaked eyes, he stared hard at the leering face on the monitor.

The speakers crackled. White noise spat at him as if he were scum.

"What?" he croaked.

The voice over the speakers repeated, "Save yourself the agony."

Cheech gasped. Out of nowhere, a hangman's noose appeared, dangling before him.

Where had it come from? It hadn't been there before.

Wiping blood-stained tears away, he stared at the thing in disbelief. One white panel of the drop-down ceiling had been pushed up, shoved aside. Behind the panel was a ventilation duct and rusty, lead pipes. Secured to one of those pipes was the other end of the rope. The noose hung almost directly in front of him.

"No." Cheech sobbed. "No, no, no..." Disbelief was slowly giving way to hysteria. "...no, no, no..."

The speakers crackled. "Save yourself the agony," the voice urged.

"...no, no, no..." Cheech continued to sob, choking on the words.

"Do it," the voice instructed.

"No," Cheech cried. "I won't."

Buzzing filled his ears. Breath caught in his throat. Tremors shook him to his core.

"No!"

The eating away of his insides continued at a rapid, excruciating pace. Thousands of flies covered him, ravaging him from the outside, as well.

"Save yourself. Do it."

No matter how bad the pain. No matter how desperate the

situation. No matter how dismal his chances were for survival. He would never take his own life. He would never let this horrid place win that way.

"No!"

He wanted to live.

"No!"

"You're already dead."

Cheech shook his head. Bloody tears streamed from his quickly eroding eyes. "No!"

"Save yourself the agony."

"No!"

Laughter crackled from the speakers.

Flies buzzed all around. They crawled across his face, migrating into his nose, his ears, even his eyes. They consumed him from the outside, while whatever unknown organism devoured him from the inside.

"You're dead already."

The speakers crackled with morbid laughter.

"Save yourself the agony. Do it."

Maybe there was no other road to salvation. Maybe he was, as the disembodied voice said, dead already, decomposing quicker than a zombie roaming aimlessly under a hot desert sun. Nevertheless, he still wanted to live. He refused to give up.

What felt like hands gripped him under his arms.

"No," Cheech cried.

In a panic, Cheech looked around. No one was there.

Still, the strong hands gripped tighter. They lifted him up.

The buzzing in his ears was deafening. His own breath choked in his throat. Tremors harassed every inch of his being.

"Save yourself the agony. You're dead already."

Cheech struggled to break free, but he was too weak, too far gone.

The invisible death grip hoisted Cheech onto his feet. Held him there so that he couldn't move.

"No," Cheech wailed.

Bloody tears blinded him. Incessant buzzing deafened him. Agonizing pain ate at him. Still, he wanted nothing more than to live, even if only for a short time longer.

That couldn't be allowed. The noose magically slipped over Cheech's head. Tightened around his neck.

"Save yourself the agony. You're dead already."

Laughter crackled.

"God, help me," Cheech croaked.

The invisible hands pushed hard. Cheech flew from the tabletop. The rope went taut. His neck didn't snap.

Laughter crackled.

Choking noises wriggled from Cheech's gaping mouth. His hands clawed frantically at the rope around his neck. His legs and feet kicked at the air as the noose strangled the last bit of breath from him.

Laughter crackled.

The disembodied voice said, "I told you there'd be consequences."

With that proclamation, the old man's face slowly dissolved from the computer monitor. The speakers spat out only static. Flies buzzed all around.

Cheech was dead.

.

Chapter Fifty-Nine

The eerily green-lit basement remained quiet. The remaining *PSI* team, along with Penny, had completed the cleansing ritual throughout Fright House.

Except for the cemetery room.

The archway to the faux cemetery loomed just up ahead. A dense blackness shimmered at the entryway.

Penny, Tory, Lizzie, and Gabriel stood together. The Plexiglas torture chambers that flanked them were lifeless, dark.

"How do we know if it worked?" Penny asked. She was feeling much better about the possibility of success but remained somewhat skeptical.

"It just feels better," Lizzie said. She adjusted her broken glasses. She eyed the still macabre surroundings. "Cleaner, somehow."

Tory took a deep breath. In spite of the damp, musty air, he grinned. "I agree. *I* feel better, too. I don't mind telling you that this place was getting to me."

"No kidding." Gabriel chuckled. "Would've never known."

"Like you were immune, preacher man," Tory razzed back.

Ignoring the two, Penny looked around. "All well and good," she said, "but how do we know it *really* worked?"

Tory sighed. "Well, I think the fact that all the lights have remained on is a good sign. Wouldn't you say?"

"Agreed," Gabriel confirmed.

"It's quiet too," Tory continued. "Another good sign. Don't you think, Gabe?"

Gabriel nodded. "Quiet's good," he agreed.

"I'm sorry, but I won't feel better until we're walking out of here," Penny said, still not completely convinced they stood a chance of escaping the place so easily.

"Let's go up to the main floor, try the iron door," Lizzie urged. "Maybe we can get into the lobby."

"Sounds good to me," Penny agreed.

"Wait," Tory said. "We haven't completed the task."

"What do you mean?" Gabriel asked.

"We haven't cleansed the cemetery room yet," Tory explained.

"Is that really necessary?" Penny asked. She'd just as soon try to get out while the going was good.

"Yeah," Tory insisted. "We're not going to leave anything to chance. We're finishing this job, making sure every inch of this place is purified before we go."

"I want to get out of here as much as anyone, but I have to agree," Gabriel said.

Tory looked around, his face suddenly haunted by a worried expression. "Hey, anybody see Morgan?"

Everyone scanned their surroundings. Morgan was nowhere in sight.

Penny held her breath. She knew it had been too easy, that everything had gone too by the book. She had been chiding herself for being negative, for always looking for the other shoe to drop. After all, she hadn't seen or sensed anything out of the ordinary. Here it was, though. Apparently, she had every right to be skeptical because now all of her worst fears were beginning to come true. She felt it in her psychic bones.

"Where's Morgan?" Tory asked no one in particular.

"Who last saw him?" Lizzie added.

No one had answers. Only questions.

The other shoe dropped, as Penny had feared.

The basement went completely dark, green lights extinguished. Faraway cries and wails once again resonated all around. The temperature plummeted.

"Good Lord," Gabriel exclaimed, "it didn't work."

Everyone huddled closer together, shivering.

"I don't understand," Tory muttered. "I just don't understand."

Penny stared hard at Tory. She wished she could see his face, see how these new events were affecting his fragile psyche. She couldn't make out anything in the dark, though, not even as close as they were to each other.

Again, the irony of worrying about someone else's fragile psyche was not lost on her. Just hours ago, she would've been more worried about her own resolve, her own mental and emotional stability. Now, she felt as if she were the strong one.

The surrounding cries and wails grew louder.

Lizzie hugged herself against the cold. "Tory," she cried, "what are we going to do?"

Before Tory could answer, one of the torture chambers lit up. The sudden brightness in the midst of blackness was blinding.

Everyone gasped as one. They crowded even closer, turning toward the glassed-off room.

Lizzie screamed, her warm breath blasting into frosty plumes with the sound.

"Sweet Jesus," Gabriel hissed.

"Morgan?" Tory muttered.

Penny bit her tongue, tasting the coppery tang of blood in her mouth. She hadn't been able to rid herself of that nagging feeling that something would eventually go wrong, that the place was just toying with them, but she had no idea what to expect. She had no clue this would be the horror to come.

Morgan was being held prisoner within the well-lit torture chamber, strapped to an autopsy table by his wrists, ankles, waist, and head. His eyes were wide with terror. Cries of panic escaped his lips. All the while, he struggled desperately against the leather restraints.

Everyone, including Penny, froze in place, unable to react to the terror before them. All they could do was watch in horror at what looked like a freakish sideshow, but it was all too real.

A nurse dressed all in white stood next to a shiny, metal instrument tray. A surgical mask covered her face. Behind the autopsy table, a doctor dressed in surgical scrubs and a mask examined Morgan's head. With a black marker, he drew a line across Morgan's forehead, just above the leather restraint. Afterward, the nurse grabbed a heavy-looking object from the tray. She handed it to the doctor. The doctor held it up for all to see.

"It's a cranium saw," Tory exclaimed.

The cranium saw whined to life. The lights within the Plexiglas room flickered and dimmed at the surge of power. The round, rotating blade of the saw spun like a blur of razor-sharp teeth.

Lizzie screamed again. Bloodcurdling, long. Echoing over Morgan's cries for help and the faraway wails of Fright House's other victims.

"No," Tory yelled.

As if shot with adrenalin, he rushed the torture chamber and pounded frantically against the Plexiglas.

Still screaming, Lizzie followed suit.

Gabriel, too, advanced on the horrible room.

All three pounded and kicked at the Plexiglas between them and their friend, all the while screaming, yelling, and cursing at the doctor who was about to open Morgan's skull.

Lizzie began throwing herself against the chamber, her entire body slamming into the Plexiglas wall.

Except for a slight vibration, the wall held. Not even a scratch was visible.

Meanwhile, fright and revulsion had not released Penny. She remained silent, rooted, watching the proceedings behind the Plexiglas in trance-like dismay.

Under the dim, flickering lights, the doctor advanced on Morgan with the whining saw—blade rotating, ready to bite.

That was when Penny barely uttered, "Stop."

Her voice sounded small and frail underneath the cries, shouts, and screams that reverberated all around.

"Stop," she murmured again.

The saw spat its piercing whine. The blade spun like a blur. Its teeth, though, only cut the air as the doctor halted his advance on Morgan's skull. Instead, he looked up, eyes squinting, brow furrowing, as if suddenly confused.

Lizzie no longer screamed, no longer slammed herself against the chamber wall. Exhausted in her efforts, she slid down the Plexiglas, landing in a crumpled heap, whimpering like a frightened, confused dog.

Tory and Gabriel kept up their efforts, encouraged by the doctor's sudden pause.

It wasn't, however, their efforts that put a stop to the grim proceedings.

As if still in a trance, Penny tiptoed toward the chamber. She pressed both of her palms against the Plexiglas. "Stop," she said, this time louder, with more conviction.

The doctor squinted at Penny through the Plexiglas, studying her as if unsure of who or what the girl was, as if unsure whether she should be obeyed.

"Stop," Penny urged, palms still pressed against the Plexiglas wall.

The saw in the doctor's hands continued to whine. The blade spun harmlessly. Indecision held the doctor hostage, his ghastly, ruthless work grinding to a merciful halt.

Even so, Morgan continued to yell for mercy, struggling against his leather restraints.

The doctor ignored his victim and concentrated on Penny.

Tory and Gabriel both interrupted their efforts to save Morgan. Instead, like the evil doctor, they gazed at Penny with bewilderment.

Lizzie stopped whimpering. Although she remained in a heap on the floor, propped up against the Plexiglas wall, she, too, stared at Penny in bewildered awe.

Penny continued to press her palms against the wall. She also pressed her lips against it. The Plexiglas fogged with her warm breath as she whispered, "Stop."

Within the glassed-off torture chamber, the doctor slowly, methodically shook his head, as if saying no to Penny's request. His eyebrows knitted closer together. Despite the nip in the air, his face glistened with sweat. Slowly, deliberately, he lowered the cranium saw toward Morgan's forehead.

"Stop," Penny commanded, her warm breath fogging the glass.

The lights within the torture chamber flickered, dimmed, flickered. The cranium saw whined in protest. The rotating circular blade bit at the air.

The doctor *did* stop. Scrutinized Penny. Struggled to complete his task. He couldn't. An invisible force field kept the cranium saw at bay.

The nurse within the chamber disappeared. The faraway cries silenced. The temperature within the basement warmed. The green lights brightened.

"It's working," Gabriel muttered. "Dear Lord, it's working."

The doctor was frozen in time. Unable to back away, unable to stop.

The temperature was almost back to normal, no one's panting breath visible any longer. The green lights continued brightening.

Lizzie wiped away tears from behind her glasses but otherwise didn't move.

"Tell him again," Tory urged.

Penny didn't respond. Didn't speak. She, too, remained frozen in time. Hands and lips pressed against the Plexiglas wall. Her gaze locked onto the doctor's.

Good and evil stood at a standstill. Both struggling to force the other into submission. Neither willing to budge or give in.

Glowering at Penny, Tory's right eye twitched. His hands fisted at his sides. His body stiffened. Seizure-like tremors quaked through him. "Tell him again," he exploded. "Tell him again, dammit."

The spell broke. Evil had won.

Penny startled out of her trance. A gasp escaped her lips. Her palms squeaked against the Plexiglas as her hands slipped away. She backed off from the torture chamber and broke eye contact with the doctor. She glared at Tory.

"Tell him again," Tory shouted, red-faced, spittle flying. "Tell him again."

Penny could only gape at the madman before her. It felt as if she had just woken from a long sleep. Confusion cluttered her mind like cobwebs in an attic.

"Tell him again," Tory screeched, frosty breath exploding along with the spittle this time.

The temperature dropped again. The green lights in the basement dimmed. Faraway cries echoed.

"Tory, stop," Lizzie begged. She struggled to her feet, ran to Tory, and threw her arms around him. "You're ruining everything. Stop."

The piercing, high-shrill whine of the cranium saw brought everyone's attention back to the glassed-off room.

The lights within the torture chamber flickered and dimmed. Morgan continued his futile struggle to free himself. Renewed, evil determination replaced the doctor's once confused state.

Penny choked on her own breath. Morgan's look of terror and his cries for mercy both heightened. She was almost certain she could see a wicked grin beneath the doctor's surgical mask.

"Stop," Penny shrieked.

This time, the doctor paid her no heed.

Penny, Tory, Lizzie, and Gabriel all screamed.

The doctor lowered the cranium saw. The whine grew even more shrill as the rotating blade hit the skin. Blood spattered the inside wall of Plexiglas. When the blade hit skull, the whine deepened, struggling through the bone.

Morgan screeched. Agonizing. Rising to a fevered pitch. His eyes bulged. Body convulsed. His fingers clawed at the table. His legs and feet stiffened under the restraints.

Tory, Lizzie, and Gabriel continued to scream.

Penny cried, "Stop."

The doctor did. The saw went quiet, the blade still.

Morgan had gone silent, too. His face slack. His fingers and feet still flinched, but only involuntarily, as if death hadn't reached them yet. The top of his head fell away and hit the hard floor with a thud. Thick fluid and brain matter spilled out with a slurp, plopping onto the floor, splashing into a pool of blood.

Faraway cries resonated like a funeral dirge.

Lizzie clutched at Tory, wailing uncontrollably.

Gabriel shut his eyes, murmuring prayers.

Tory gawked at the grisly scene. His right eye twitched. Twitched. Twitched.

Penny rushed the torture chamber. She slapped at the Plexiglas with her open hands, blubbering incoherently.

Inside the glassed-off room, the doctor held up the cranium saw for all to see. Blood, tissue, and chunks of brain clung to the teeth of the stalled circular blade. Pulling down his surgical mask, the doctor cackled wildly.

The torture chamber went dark. The faraway cries sounded closer, louder. The temperature dropped. The green lights went out, plummeting everything into blackness.

Within that blackness, Tory hissed, "She's the reason. It's all her fault."

Chapter Sixty

Blackness engulfed them. The surrounding cries and wails no longer sounded far away at all. They were definitely getting closer.

Penny let the Plexiglas wall hold her up as she leaned heavily against it. Her body felt limp. She shivered. Despite the cold, she was soaked in sweat. Her breath shuddered with each inhale and exhale. Her heart throbbed out of rhythm, almost stopping altogether. Shock, fear, and grief gripped her, holding her mind, body, and soul hostage.

No one else moved or made a sound. Only their ragged breathing could be heard.

The surrounding cries and wails turned to shrieks and screams. Close. Getting closer.

"What now?" Lizzie asked as she sobbed.

Penny pushed away from the Plexiglas wall, standing on her own. Shivering, she took a deep breath. She fought to regain her composure, her courage, her strength of mind and spirit.

A bizarre sound accompanied the shrieks and screams, sounding like fish out of water. Lots of them. Flopping and slapping against a hard surface as they struggled to breathe.

It all sounded much too close for comfort.

Penny reached for her flashlight. The cold air numbed her fingers. She fumbled with it for a few seconds before freeing it from the clip on her belt. Pointing it in the direction of the oncoming noise, she illuminated the cemetery archway.

Tory had the same idea, because he shone the beam of his flashlight in the same direction. "What is that?" he muttered.

Penny cocked her head. She concentrated. That's when it hit her. "Feet," she suggested. "Bare feet, I think. A lot of them."

The shrieks and screams grew louder. The slap of oncoming feet got closer.

"Crap," Tory exclaimed.

Just beyond the archway, from out of the shimmering

blackness, came an onrush of mental patients. Illuminated within the flashlight beams, they ran with frantic single-mindedness, hospital gowns flapping around their exposed legs, bare feet slapping against the hard floor. Their shrieks and screams intensified as they neared the archway and passed underneath it, sounding like marauding Huns on the warpath.

Gabriel declared, "Dear God. They're possessed."

"Run," Tory shouted.

Everybody turned as one, running in the opposite direction of the oncoming horde of possessed raiders.

Tory and Penny's flashlights lit the way. Shrieks and screams echoed all around. Slapping footsteps bore down on them. Everyone kept moving, Tory in the lead.

With the others right behind her, Penny reluctantly followed a man she hardly trusted. Under the dire circumstances, though, she hadn't much choice.

"The stairwell," Tory shouted above the din of attacking lunatics. "Get to the stairwell."

The flashlight beams swept the area ahead. Crisscrossed. Uncrossed. Erratically jumped from wall to floor to ceiling. Crisscrossed again. Searching for the stairwell door.

Were they running in circles? Where was the damn door?

"There," Penny yelled. The beam of her light finally settled on the door, revealing it not far ahead.

Everyone rushed to it, the possessed hot on their heels.

Tory got there first. Grabbed the door. Held it open. "Get through. Quick."

Penny went through first, with her flashlight lighting the way. Gabriel and Lizzie quickly followed.

"Tory," Lizzie called.

"Right behind you."

The door slammed shut.

Penny dared not look behind. Huffing and puffing, her lungs felt frozen. Still, she kept moving, the beam of her light illuminating the narrow, grim passageway that wound its way to the upper floors. The others' heavy breathing, along with their pounding footsteps on the metal stairs, chased her ever upward.

Soon, she heard the door below fly open and slam against the back wall. The possessed shrieked wildly as they rushed into the stairwell, bare feet slapping against metal steps, not far behind.

Penny neared the first floor door.

"Keep going," Tory yelled from behind, voice echoing through the stairwell over all other noise. "We need to get to the top floor, to Tech Central. That's where we'll make our stand."

Reluctantly, Penny rounded the corner. She passed the door leading to the main floor. She thought briefly about pushing through it, trying for the iron door to the lobby. If that door opened, maybe the door to the outside world would, too. They'd be free. If the iron door didn't open, though, if it remained inexplicably locked as it had been, she and the others would be trapped. There was no reason to assume that anything had changed with the iron door. There was no reason to assume it didn't remain locked. Still, for a split second, she thought of going for it. In the end, however, she did as Tory ordered. Kept moving upward. Figuring being barricaded in a room with four walls and a door they could defend was better than being caught with their backs against a locked iron door, a cement wall, with nowhere to go. At least she hoped it would be better.

The beam of her light exposed the door ahead. For good or for bad, not too many more stairs to their destination.

She could feel the others behind her. Hear their heavy breathing, their pounding footsteps.

She could hear the screams and the slapping feet of the oncoming horde, too. They weren't that far behind.

She dared not slow to glance back. Instead, she kept moving, finally reaching the door. She hit the metal bar-handle, rushing through.

At the top, she held the door, waiting for the others. Lizzie followed almost immediately. Gabriel was right behind. Tory, though, wasn't anywhere in sight.

Penny, Lizzie, and Gabriel gathered in the hallway, just at the top of the stairs. All three breathed hard, their combined warm breaths creating plumes of eerie wisps within Penny's flashlight beam.

Panicked, gasping for air, Lizzie cried, "Where's Tory?" She made a move for the open doorway as if she were going back for her friend.

Gabriel grabbed her. "Whoa," he said, sucking air. "Give him time."

"Gabriel's right," Penny said, still breathing hard, ghostly wisps from her mouth taking flight. "He's coming."

Even as she said it, even as she shone her light down the stairwell in search of Tory, she wasn't so sure.

The flashlight beam found the ghost hunter as he rounded the corner and ascended the last flight of steps to the upper hallway. The trouble was the flashlight beam also found the possessed gaining ground, shrieking as they reached and clawed at his back.

"Hurry, Tory," Lizzie cried. "They're right behind you."

"Don't wait," Tory yelled back, wisps escaping his mouth, too. "Get to Tech Central."

That's when one of the possessed grabbed Tory's ankle from behind.

Tory yelled as he went down hard. Face first. Arms out. Hands bracing his fall.

"Tory," Lizzie cried. She struggled against Gabriel's embrace. The preacher held tight.

The possessed were on Tory like hyenas on a dead carcass. Ripping at his clothes. Clawing at his face. Teeth gnashing in their attempts to bite their downed prey.

"Tory." Lizzie's piercing cry was glass-shattering. She continued struggling to free herself from Gabriel's grip, but to no avail.

It was Penny who scrambled back down the metal steps to rescue their fallen cohort. The frenzied assailants were too busy with Tory to notice her oncoming descent. When she reached the entangled skirmish, she used her flashlight like a club, clobbering heads, one by one.

As the assailants began falling away, Tory was able to push up, shed the remaining *hyenas*, freeing himself from their clutches. Scratched and bloodied, with clothes torn, he fought to his feet.

"Let's move," Penny shouted. She grabbed Tory's arm, helping him ascend as fast as his injured body would allow.

"Tory," Lizzie cried.

"Hurry," Gabriel urged, still holding Lizzie back. "They're right behind."

The possessed had regrouped. They were advancing again upon their prey. Shrieks and screams echoed through the stairwell. Bare feet slapped against metal steps.

Penny and Tory kept moving upward, as if ascending to salvation. What salvation really existed on the second floor was anyone's guess. Maybe none. Maybe their destination would only prolong the inevitable. Still, it was better than what rushed them from behind.

Releasing Lizzie, Gabriel waited at the top of the stairs, holding onto the door. As Penny and Tory hurried through into the hallway, Gabriel slammed the door.

Within seconds, the assailants crashed into the other side, propelling it outward. It was only by pure chance, pure luck, that Gabriel still held fast to the door and put enough weight behind it to temporarily shut it again, effectively defending the hallway from attack.

"Some help here," Gabriel shouted, bracing the door with his full weight.

Penny, Tory, and Lizzie quickly responded, throwing their combined weight into the door before the horde on the other side was able to regroup and batter the door with their own combined effort.

When the possessed did wallop the other side, their force pushed the door at least a quarter of the way open before the ghost hunters could slam it shut again.

Tory had lost his flashlight on the stairs while fighting off the assailants.

Somehow, Penny had managed to keep a hold of hers. The only trouble was, by holding the door, she could only point the beam at the ceiling. It was of no discernible use at the time. She thought of tossing it to better brace the door but decided it may come in handy later, either as a light or maybe again as a club.

"Brace yourselves," Tory commanded.

Everyone did, putting all their weight and strength into holding the door.

Screeching wildly, the possessed again rammed the other side.

It opened slightly. Everyone's concerted effort slammed it shut again.

Sucking air, Tory said, "We're holding."

"For how long?" Gabriel asked breathlessly. "God help us. For how long?"

The possessed pounded against the other side of the door.

The door cracked open. Slammed shut.

"Gabriel's right," Tory said. "We can't hold them back forever."

"What do you suggest?" Penny asked. She herself had no ideas, no plan. She was open to almost anything.

The possessed pushed, prodded, pounded at the door.

The group held.

Tory gulped hard. "You and Lizzie get to Tech Central. Me and Gabriel will hold the door until you get there. Once you're there, we'll let go and run like hell."

Gabriel loudly gulped down a lump. "Bad plan."

"We're not leaving you," Lizzie said, shaking her head.

Shrieks and screams echoed from the other side of the door. A concerted force from the possessed pressed the door open before the ghost hunters slammed it shut again.

"If we're going to do this, it's gotta be now," Penny said.

"No," Lizzie again protested.

"It's gotta be this way," Tory continued. "When you get to Tech Central, hold the door open. Get ready to slam it closed behind us as soon as we make it there."

Lizzie shook her head. "No."

The possessed hit the other side of the door. The group managed to hold back the onslaught.

"Do this for me, Lizzie," Tory pleaded. "It's the only way. I'm depending on you."

"I don't like it," Lizzie said.

"I don't much like it, either," Gabriel protested.

"Penny and Lizzie, make your move right after they hit the door again," Tory commanded. "Move fast. Don't stop until you get there. I doubt that me and Gabe can hold them back for long."

Penny nodded. "Be ready, Lizzie," she urged.

The possessed shrieked. The door jolted. Opened a crack or two. Slammed shut.

"Now," Tory shouted.

Penny and Lizzie pushed away from the door. The beam of Penny's flashlight led them as they raced down the hallway.

Behind them came a pounding noise. Tory shouted, "Hold 'em back, Gabe."

Neither Penny nor Lizzie stopped or looked behind until they made it to Tech Central. Once at the door, even as Penny opened it, they both turned back to see.

Penny shone the beam of her flashlight back down the hallway just in time to see Gabriel lose his nerve. Releasing his grip on the door, he made a run for it before Tory was ready.

"Gabe," Tory shouted.

Simultaneously, the possessed hit the other side of the door, sending it and Tory crashing inward.

"Tory," Lizzie shrieked.

Tory flew backward across the hallway. He crashed into the opposite wall, the back of his head making a sickening thud on impact. He collapsed onto the floor, looking like a discarded, trampled scarecrow.

Gabriel continued his cowardice flight toward Penny, Lizzie, and the relative safety of Tech Central.

"Tory," Lizzie cried again as she took off back toward the stairwell door, back toward her fallen friend.

Penny took off after her. Ghostly wisps took flight with each heavy breath. The erratic beam of her flashlight spotlighted the macabre scene playing out down the hallway as she ran.

Shrieking wildly, the possessed were on Tory before he could come to his senses or react. Two grabbed him by the ankles, started pulling him toward the doorway. The others crowded around, ready to partake in the long-awaited meal.

Tory made no move to defend himself or halt his being taken. He let them drag him away on his back without a fight. As if at least semi-conscious, he did manage to weakly call, "Gabe."

Penny and Lizzie kept running.

"Gabe," Lizzie cried, "they got Tory."

With that, Gabriel skidded to a stop. He turned back around and stared. At first, though, he didn't move.

Penny and Lizzie continued their charge.

Penny yelled, "Gabriel, help Tory."

Gabriel hesitated.

"Help Tory," Penny yelled.

Gabriel hesitated only a moment longer before finally reversing his course. Somehow, he must have dug deep, summoned the nerve needed to throw himself back into the fray. "Tory, hold on."

Penny and Lizzie had almost gotten to Gabriel before he turned back to help Tory. Now, though, the preacher picked up speed, leaving the others behind.

"God, help me," Gabriel cried. He turned that loud prayer into the shriek of a crazed banshee as he caught the possessed absconding with his friend. Without regard, still shrieking, he plowed into the horde. Knocking them over like a bowling ball hitting a strike.

Everybody, including Gabriel, went down hard.

Tory rolled onto his stomach. Slowly, deliberately, he began slithering away.

Penny and Lizzie charged forward.

The possessed untangled themselves. They climbed to their feet. With Gabriel in their clutches, they began dragging the preacher off.

Unlike Tory, Gabriel fought back. Arms flailing. Legs kicking.

The possessed couldn't get a good hold.

That's when Penny and Lizzie waded in. Lizzie jumped onto the back of one assailant, scratching and clawing at his eyes. Penny used her flashlight like a club again, swinging wildly, clobbering assailants in the head, face, torso—wherever she could land a blow.

Meanwhile, four of the possessed succeeded in subduing Gabriel. Amidst his horrifying cries for help, he was dragged off. He clawed at the floor, trying to slow his assailants down, but to no avail. When they reached the doorway and began pulling him through, he clutched at the door frame, dug in his fingernails until they bled. He cried for mercy. He prayed to God for salvation. In the end, his bloody grip on the door frame slipped. He was pulled through. His bloodcurdling scream echoed through the stairwell with the steady thump of his head on metal as he was dragged down into the bowels of Fright House.

Penny couldn't save Gabriel, but she was determined not to let anyone else, including herself, be taken. She swung her flashlight, striking out at anything that moved. Loud thuds, along with yelps of pain, surrounded her. She saw an assailant make a move for Tory who lay helplessly to one side. Advancing on her quarry, she swung her makeshift club. The blow landed upside the assailant's head, dropping him to the floor.

She saw Lizzie taken just before something hit her in the back of the head. The hallway spun. Her vision blurred. Black spots floated before her. Her ears drubbed with the beat of a bass drum. She fell. Just to her knees, as if in prayer.

Then, everything went completely black.

Chapter Sixty-One

Dusk advanced on Fright House. Wind whistled through the parking lot and ripped at the surrounding foliage and strands of lifeless lights that once twinkled eerily all around the parking lot, all along the silhouette of the building. Searchlights were dark and motionless. The sign, with its mass of blinking, rotating lights and maniacal, screaming faces, was dead.

The old Ford Fairlane clunked into the parking lot, limping on one flat tire in the front. No headlight lit the way. The chrome grill looked like fragmented braces on demolished teeth. The drab-green hood resembled a pup tent over the hissing, steaming engine. The car backfired and coughed as it inched toward the front of the building. Suddenly, without further warning, the other three tires burst. The car crashed down onto its wheel rims. A hubcap was thrown clear, rolling across the parking lot in its escape. The engine shot off one last round of gunfire before it expired in a cloud of black smoke.

Tony groaned as he fought with the driver's door. The door was winning until he scooted away from the door, raised his leg, and planted a firm kick with the flat of his foot against the damn thing. When the door flew open, he spilled out, not in much better shape than his dead car.

Groaning again, he wiped blood away that dribbled into his eyes from the gash across his forehead. Apparently, it had again opened during the clash with the door and the effort of getting out of the car. He struggled to his feet, withstanding the onrush of wind as it tore at his clothes and disheveled his thinning hair. Straightening, he stretched his sore muscles and aching joints.

That's when he saw Fright House for the first time. Really saw it.

Blackness hung over the place like demonic fog. Shimmering. Rippling. He swore he could see the place breathe, walls expanding outward, retreating inward in a steady, rhythmic motion. From somewhere came the ceaseless beat of a single heart.

"My God," Tony muttered, "it's alive."

Not wasting any more time, he limped toward the front doors. When he saw a figure come into view through the shimmering blackness, he stopped cold.

The silhouette of a man stood outside Fright House. He fumbled with a set of keys. Pounded on the iron doors. Pulled on the door handles. Yelled for someone to answer. Most of the noise he made was lost to the wind or muffled under the beat of the heart.

"Hello," Tony shouted. "Who's there?"

The figure ended his dispute with the doors. Turning around, he asked, "Who's that?"

Tony swallowed hard. He felt reasonably sure the figure before him was just a man, not an evil ghost or demon. Still, he hesitated to answer.

"Who's that?" the figure repeated.

Tony braced himself against the wind, as well as against the unknown. "My name's Tony Scout," he answered.

"Tony Scout?" The figure moved out of shadows, the keys on his key ring clinking together like chimes in Hell. "Tony Scout, the medium?"

Tony took a hesitant step forward. "That's right. Do you know me?"

"I know *of* you," the man said. "I saw you on TV, with the ghost hunters."

The two men stood just a few feet apart.

"I'm Cyrus Peabody."

Tony nodded. "The owner of this place."

Peabody's sunken eyes looked crestfallen. He swiped a hand across his ashen face and ran trembling fingers through wind-whipped, gray hair. "That's right," he muttered.

"Where are they?" Tony asked.

"I'm not sure. They might all still be inside."

"Penny, too?"

Peabody arched his eyebrows. "What do you know of Miss Winters?"

"I know we need to get her out of there to end this."

Peabody cleared his throat. "End what?"

"Whatever evil's going on inside this place," Tony answered. "She's the key."

Peabody shook his head. "The key to what? I don't understand."

Tony stared past Peabody.

Fright House breathed. The heart beat louder, steadier. The iron doors taunted him.

When Tony looked back at Peabody, he realized that the owner of Fright House couldn't truly see the place or its heinous intent. "I think this place wants her," he explained. "Needs her psychic energy to survive. To that end, it'll do anything."

Peabody continued to shake his head. "You're talking crazy."

"We need to get inside," Tony insisted, "now."

Peabody held up his set of keys. He cleared his throat. "We-We c-can't," he stuttered. "I-I have misplaced my k-key."

"Misplaced it? Or it doesn't work anymore?"

Peabody again looked crestfallen. "I-It must be misplaced."

Tony shook his head. "I saw you pounding on the doors. Pulling at the door handles. Yelling." He paused, staring hard at Peabody. "You don't believe that anymore than I do."

Peabody didn't respond.

Tony pulled out his cell phone.

"What are you doing?" Peabody asked in a panic.

"Calling 9-1-1."

"No," Peabody insisted, "not the police."

"We need help getting inside."

Peabody fussed with his key ring. "I'm sure I have the key here. Somewhere. I can get us in. We don't need the police. It's Halloween. Cars will be streaming into this place soon. In an hour, people will be lining up to get inside. The police will blockade the place. Shut it down. I'll lose thousands of dollars." The keys clinked together as he checked each one.

"Everyone inside might be dying or already dead," Tony hissed. "All you care about is money?"

Peabody stopped fussing, looked up from his keys. "You have no reason to believe, no proof, that anyone inside is dying or dead or even in danger. You're letting your imagination run wild." He chewed on his lower lip until it bled. "It's all in good fun."

Tony dialed 9-1-1. He said, "Fun's over."

Chapter Sixty-Two

Penny groaned. She lay on the hard, cold floor, face down in a semiconscious state. Her head throbbed. Blood pounded in her ears. Her eyes fluttered open, but all she could see were black dots floating before her.

Where was she?

She attempted to lift her head, but it weighed a ton. Another groan.

What happened?

She lay there longer, desperately trying to get her bearings.

It was all just a blur.

"Penny…"

Someone called her name. The voice sounded faraway, though, barely audible.

"Penny…Penny…"

The blood pounding in her ears and the ache throbbing in her head drowned out the voice. The black spots in her field of vision, however, started to break up, clear away. Between the black spots, she could see flashes of light.

"Penny…"

Someone or something touched her shoulder and shook her. She couldn't react, though, no matter the rising fear of who or what loomed above.

"Penny, wake up."

She again felt the light touch on her shoulder, felt the shake of her body.

The pounding in her ears quieted. The throbbing in her head dulled.

"Penny, wake up."

It was Tory. She recognized his voice.

"Penny."

She groaned in response. Endeavored to lift her head.

"Here, let me help," Tory offered. Gently, he took her by the shoulders and lifted her off the floor into a sitting position.

Penny groaned, again. The effort of sitting up, even with help, exhausted her. Not to mention the throbbing in her head and the aches in her joints and muscles that accompanied the sudden movement. She felt as though a horde of out of control shoppers at a half-off shoe sale had trampled her, and she somehow survived.

Tory knelt next to her. "Better?" he asked.

Penny coughed and hacked up a glob but hesitated to expel it.

"Spit it out," Tory suggested. "Under the circumstance, I think it's okay."

Penny turned her head. She spat the glob onto the floor.

"Better?"

Penny coughed again, but this time, nothing came up. "Not much," she croaked.

Both her vision and her hearing were almost completely clear, so maybe she was doing better than she'd first thought. She could see the fluorescent lights in the hallway flickering. She could hear the accompanying sporadic sputter of the electrical current.

"Power's back on," she mumbled.

Tory looked around. "Such as it is."

The lights flashed like lightning. The spit and sputter of electrical current followed like thunder shot from a gun with a silencer.

"Temperature's normal, too," Penny added.

Tory nodded. "What happened?" he asked.

Penny shook her head, trying to clear away the cobwebs. That just made the throbbing worse. Instead, she sat motionless, struggling to clear her thoughts, struggling to remember.

"My memory's not too clear," she whispered. "I was going to ask you the same thing."

Overhead, the lights flashed and sputtered, the hallway seemingly in the midst of an ongoing preternatural electrical storm.

"Penny," Tory said, "where are the others?"

"The others?" Penny answered the question with a question of her own.

"Lizzie and Gabe? Where are they?"

Penny eyed the man kneeling before her, but she didn't answer.

Tory's right eye spasmodically twitched. "When I came to, you were unconscious. They were gone. So were those lunatics that chased us."

Penny looked away and squeezed her eyes shut. "Lunatics? Lizzie? Gabe?"

She reached back into her muddled memory in the hopes of recalling a fragment of what occurred. All she could see, however, was Tory's terrifying face, his twitching eye. Everything else before awakening was lost.

"Where are they?" Tory asked again, voice rising. He grabbed Penny by the shoulders and gave her a shake.

Penny's eyes shot open. Her breath caught in her throat at the sight of Tory's face looming before her. His right eye twitched. His head jerked. Just as in her mind's eye.

All around, the fluorescent lights flashed and flickered. Electrical current sputtered.

"Where are Lizzie and Gabe?" Spittle flew from Tory's mouth.

Penny dared not wipe at the wetness on her face. In fact, she dared not speak, either. Fearful of Tory's reaction. She saw him as on the precipice of sanity, teetering on the edge, primed for the plunge into the abyss of madness.

"They're gone, aren't they?" Tory squeezed Penny's shoulders. He gave the girl another shake. "Lizzie and Gabe are gone."

Penny gaped at the ghost hunter. The guy's wild-looking eyes resembled those of the possessed that had given chase.

"Gone," Tory hissed. He gave Penny's shoulders one last hard squeeze before releasing his grip. His body suddenly relaxed, all the fight had gone out of him. He sat back on his haunches, arms hanging at his sides, head bowed as if in prayer. "Gone," he muttered. "Forever gone." Covering his face with both hands, he sobbed.

Penny reached out, placing a gentle hand on Tory's shoulder. Despite her fear, she couldn't help feeling sorry for the guy.

"I try to be a good boy," Tory muttered into his hands. "I try to keep my promise."

"It's going to be okay," Penny whispered, not really believing it herself.

It was this place. It had to be. Tory wasn't responsible for his actions. This place was messing with him. It made him say and do things he normally wouldn't say or do.

"I try to be a good boy. I try to make you proud."

"It's going to be okay," Penny repeated.

Tory uncovered his face. He looked up, tears streaming down his cheeks. "No, it's not," he said. The twitch returned to his right eye. "Nothing's ever going to be okay, again."

The hallway's preternatural electrical storm continued to rage.

Penny gave Tory's shoulder a reassuring squeeze.

"I try to be a good boy," Tory said. "This place won't let me."

A teardrop fell from Tory's chin and splashed onto the back of Penny's hand.

In that instant, in a visual flash, she saw Tory's psychic struggle.

* * * *

A dimly lit room. Dark shadows playing across the floor, walls, ceiling. The wallop of a heartbeat. The inhalation and exhalation of ragged breath.

Tory sat in a large, wooden chair. Leather restraints were strapped across his waist, wrists, and ankles. Electrodes were attached to his forehead. Wires ran from the electrodes to a nearby electric shock treatment machine.

Tory scanned the dark room, confused by both his surroundings and by the predicament in which he found himself.

"Where am I?" he croaked.

The overlapping shadows that surrounded him shimmered and pulsed as they circled like starving vultures.

Suddenly, Tory struggled against the leather restraints, as if he'd just noticed them for the first time.

"What the—"

His struggles were to no avail.

"What's going on? Where am I?"

He shook his head in an attempt to dislodge the electrodes stuck to his temples. That was to no avail, either.

"What's going on?"

The dark room filled with the sounds of Tory's thrashing heart, his ragged breath.

"Let me go."

Sweat beaded his brow and plastered his hair to his forehead as he battled against the restraints.

"Let me go."

The leather straps held tight.

"Let me go!"

The shimmering, pulsating shadows circled.

"Please!"

What sounded like a thousand demonic voices spoke as one. "You can save them. You can save them all."

Tory stopped struggling. Bug-eyed, he scanned the room.

There was no sign of anyone else being there. Only the shimmering, pulsating shadows were visible.

"Who are you?" Tory pleaded. "What do you want from me?"

The demonic voices answered, "You can save them. You can save them all."

Tory again fought his restraints. "Save who?" he screamed.

The click of a switch being thrown answered. Volts of electricity followed. Sparks flew. The air crackled, hissed.

Tory spasmed and convulsed as electricity fired into the electrodes attached to his temples.

The switch clicked, again. The electricity stopped.

Tory slumped in the wooden chair, chin on chest. His labored breath came out shallow, slow. Spittle hung from his open mouth.

The shadows continued to circle.

"You can save them all," the demonic voices insisted. "You can save them all."

The switch again clicked. Sparks flew. The air crackled and hissed. Electricity fired into the electrodes.

Tory stiffened, convulsed. His head slammed into the back of the wooden chair. His hands clawed at the wooden arm rests. His mouth opened wide into a silent scream.

The switch clicked off. The electricity died. The room went silent.

Tory slumped in the chair. His head dangled as if it were about to dislodge from his neck. His hands went slack. Spittle clung to his open mouth, ran like strings to his chest.

"You can save them all."

Without raising his head, Tory mumbled, "Who?"

"All of them."

Tory struggled to raise his head.

The shimmering, pulsating shadows moved about him in a tighter circle.

"How?" Tory croaked.

"Kill her."

Tory coughed, hacking up a glob of mucus. He spat it into his lap. Shaking his head, he asked, "Kill who?"

"Her. Kill her. She's the cause of everyone's pain, everyone's suffering. She's the reason for it all. You can save them. Kill her."

Tory spat again. "Why—"

The switch clicked. Sparks flew. Electricity fired.

Tory stiffened. His head slammed against the chair. His fingernails dug into wood. He gave a silent scream.

The switch clicked off. Singed flesh permeated the air.

Tory slumped, head lolling, as if he were only semiconscious.

The demonic voices resonated. "Kill her," they demanded. "Kill her. She's the cause of it all. Kill her. Kill her. Kill her."

* * * *

Penny woke from the vision with a gasp. She jerked away from Tory, frantically wiping the teardrop from the back of her hand.

"I try to be a good boy," Tory continued. Tears streamed down his cheeks. His breath hitched with each inhale, each exhale. "I try to make you proud."

Penny scooted farther away. She now understood. This place wanted her dead. Wanted her to become a permanent resident. It was conditioning Tory, torturing his mind, in an attempt to force him to do its bidding, force him to kill.

"Nothing's ever going to be okay again," Tory sobbed, his right eye twitching.

Penny scooted toward Tory. "Yes it will," she insisted, reaching out, placing her hand back on the ghost hunter's shoulder. "Yes it will."

She couldn't allow this horrid place to win. She needed to save them both. The only way to do that was to get her and Tory out of there.

"Come on," Penny said.

She stood, grabbed Tory by the arm, and hauled him to his feet.

"What are we doing?" Tory asked, wiping tears from his face.

"We're getting out of here," Penny insisted. "First, though, we're getting Cheech."

Tory took a deep breath. He nodded. "Let's go."

The two hurried down the hallway to Tech Central. Above them, the fluorescent lights flashed. All around, electrical current sputtered.

"You can't have me," Penny whispered. "Somehow, we're getting out of here. You can't have me."

They made it back to Tech Central without incident. Penny opened the door. They crossed the threshold from one horrible level of Hell into a worse one.

Cheech swung from a rope by his neck. His ravaged body still swayed slightly back and forth as if the dirty deed had just completed. The stench of death permeated the air. Hundreds of flies buzzed about the room. They landed in Cheech's open sores and decaying flesh. His face was a frozen reflection of the insanity that must have overwhelmed him in his last moments before his demise.

Turning away, Penny screamed. She threw herself into Tory's arms and buried her face against his chest. "You can't have me," she cried, overcome with grief, guilt, and fear. "You can't have me."

Chapter Sixty-Three

The electrical storm from the hallway continued in Tech Central; however, unlike in the hallway, the temperature plummeted as soon as they crossed the threshold. Frosty plumes escaped with each of their panted breaths.

Tory held Penny without much comfort or emotion in his embrace. He couldn't tear his gaze away from the horrible sight of his dead friend. He couldn't stop his thoughts from traveling back to his mother's suicide. The similarities between her and Cheech's deaths sucker punched him.

I try to be good. I try to do the right thing.

Where had being good, doing the right thing ever gotten him? Nowhere. His mother had been ravaged by cancer. She hanged herself when he was a child, when he most needed her. His friends and colleagues were all surely dead. Cheech, ravaged by some sort of aberrant disease, apparently hanged himself, too.

For what? Why? Who was to blame?

Cheech opened his eyes. Empty blackness stared out at the horrid world. A lurid grin spread across his rotted face.

Tory choked on his own breath. Tumultuous tremors began at his core, spread outward throughout his body. He held Penny tighter as he gaped at his dead friend coming back to life before his eyes.

"She's the reason, bro," Cheech croaked. No frosty plumes escaped his mouth as he spoke. "She's to blame. It's her fault we're all dead."

Tory held the girl in his arms even tighter as the tremors within surfaced—arms and hands trembling, knees feeling as though they'd buckle.

He couldn't believe his eyes. He couldn't believe his ears. Still, there Cheech was, hanging in death, yet somehow still alive, speaking the truth.

"Save yourself, bro," Cheech continued, that lurid grin still on his death mask. "Give her to Fright House. Kill her."

With that, Tory yowled. He threw Penny aside like a broken

doll, sending her across the room, crashing into chairs and equipment. Finally, the girl came to rest in a heap of broken computers and tangled wires.

Penny moaned. She whimpered as she struggled to get up but couldn't.

With growing hatred, Tory stared hard at the girl.

In his mind's eye, though, he saw himself strapped to a wooden chair. The leather restraints bit into his wrists, ankles, and waist. He felt the cold electrodes attached to his temples. In his head, the switch to the EST machine clicked on. The air crackled, hissed. His body convulsed as volts of electricity fired into his brain. The acrid odor of burnt flesh filled his nostrils. He could feel his fingernails dig into the arms of the wooden chair.

From somewhere, demonic voices commanded, "Kill her. Kill her now."

The switch clicked off. The electric current to his brain ceased.

Tory breathed hard, frosty breath blowing outward. Sweat soaked his clothes. Tremors racked his extremities. Nausea churned his stomach. His legs almost buckled again, but somehow, he kept his feet.

Penny moaned. She scuffled in the debris.

With his right eye twitching, and his head jerking, Tory watched her.

She wasn't going anywhere.

Hatred for the girl boiled over within him.

Meanwhile, old friends came to call.

Isabel appeared in the room. Her clothes torn to shreds. Bloody claw marks scarred her face, portions of exposed flesh. She stood over Penny, watching the girl strive to get up. She turned to Tory. "She's the reason I'm dead. It's her fault. All her fault," she said.

Gabriel suddenly appeared alongside Isabel. His clothes also looked ripped apart. Bloody bite marks and deep, red gouges marred him. "Fright House wants her," he announced. "Give her to it."

Lizzie and Morgan joined the obscene party, both appearing alongside Isabel and Gabriel. All four stood around Cheech's dangling feet. One of Lizzie's eyeballs hung from its socket. Bite marks and wounds scarred her face, her arms. Morgan was missing the top of his head. Blood and brain fluid stained his open skull, streaked down his ravaged face.

"Give her to Fright House," Lizzie insisted. "It wants her."

Morgan added, "It needs her. It's you or her, dude."

"I told you, bro," Cheech continued. "She's the reason. Kill her."

All four chanted, "Kill her. Kill her. Kill her."

Tory heard the click of a switch. The air crackled, hissed. Electric shock charged through his body. His eyes bugged. Burnt flesh permeated the air. Drool ran from his gaping mouth. He convulsed violently as if possessed by an angry demon.

"Kill her. Kill her. Kill her."

Tory answered the chants of his dead friends with a cruel-sounding, animalistic yowl. Frosty breath exploded with that yowl as he quickly advanced on Penny, who was just getting herself untangled from the broken debris she'd been hurled amongst. He grabbed Penny and pushed her backward until she hit the wall, the impact of the girl's head making a sickening thud. Baring teeth like a rabid wolf, he throttled Penny with both hands, squeezing hard, wringing the life out of her.

"You're the reason they're all dead," Tory hissed, leaning close. "Fright House wants you. It needs you. I'm going to give you to it."

Chapter Sixty-Four

Penny choked and gagged. A death rattle played a funeral dirge within her. She drew blood clawing at Tory's hands, trying to yank them away from her throat.

Tory was too strong, too crazed.

Darkness pressed against the edges of her vision. All sounds were muffled, almost to the point of complete deafness. Her mind spun in a dizzying circle. Her thoughts were lost within a barren wasteland. The only thing driving her was the instinctual need to survive. She was losing the battle.

Tory leaned close. He hissed, "You're the reason they're all dead. Fright House wants you. It needs you. I'm going to give you to it."

Penny found her opening and took it. Reaching up with both hands, she raked her fingernails across Tory's eyes, digging them into the crazy man's eyeballs, drawing blood.

Tory screeched. Simultaneously, he released his death grip on Penny's throat. His hands covered his bleeding, stinging eyes. Blindly, he staggered about the room, cursing as he banged into tables, tripped over debris.

Sucking air, throat burning, Penny stumbled away. Her legs wobbled underneath her. Somehow, she gathered herself and remained on her feet. Soon, both her vision and hearing began to clear. Her mind stopped spinning. Her thoughts crystallized from just survival instinct to a logical plan. Grabbing a computer keyboard, she swung it with all her might, cracking Tory over the head.

Tory screeched again. He dropped to his knees, blindly swiping his arms around him in futile defense.

Again, Penny reared back with the keyboard, bringing it down hard over Tory's head.

This time, Tory went down face first with a loud thud. This time, he didn't move.

Hacking, catching her breath, Penny dropped the keyboard at Tory's feet. She lurched for the doorway in desperation. At the threshold, she halted her escape. She turned and glared at her fallen foe. Giving it further thought, she decided to go back. She picked up the keyboard. For good measure, she gave Tory another whack across the head.

"Screw you." Penny flung the keyboard across the room. "Screw this place. You can't have me." Tears streamed down her face. "You can't have me," she muttered, wiping away the tears, choking back her sobs.

The overhead lights brightened and remained steady. The computers not already busted up, turned back on. White noise spat out of the speakers. Far off, the shrieks and cries of the possessed resonated, calling for her to join them.

"You can't have me," Penny said again.

She turned away. This time, she kept on going. Out the door. Down the hallway. The overhead lights in the hallway had brightened and remained steady, as well.

Maybe that meant the power was fully restored. Maybe that meant the elevators were working again.

She hoped so. She really didn't want to go back down the stairs. That was where the possessed lunatics had taken Gabriel and Lizzie.

She limped and stumbled as fast as she could toward the elevator, glancing periodically over her shoulder as she went.

No sign or sound of Tory following. No one else either, for that matter.

Still, the far-off shrieks and cries spurred her forward. She needed to get down to the main floor, hopefully out of the place as quickly as possible.

She made it to the elevators without incident. The far-off cries still reminded her that danger lurked around every corner, hid in every shadow. Frantically, over and over, she pushed the elevator button.

Nothing happened.

She scanned the hallway behind her, continuing to hit the damn button. Hoping against hope that the elevator would arrive. That she could descend to the main floor without having to chance taking the horrid stairwell and possibly coming face-to-face with the possessed.

Still nothing happened.

Putting her back against the elevator doors, she glared at the stairwell door. Just the sight of it looked foreboding, ominous.

Tory, however, wouldn't remain unconscious forever. He'd

be coming for her soon. The choice was to stay and face him or take her chances that the possessed were no longer loitering in the stairwell. That wasn't really much of a choice. Her only chance of survival was to get downstairs and somehow make it to the iron door. If it opened, she could barricade herself inside the lobby. Maybe she could even get to the outside world. That is, if the front doors opened, too.

That was a lot of ifs. Still, those ifs were her only chance.

Without further thought, she lunged across the hallway to the door. She didn't readily open it, though. Instead, she stopped with her hand on the door handle. She put her ear to the door to listen.

She heard nothing from the other side. No indication that anyone waited there to do her harm.

"Please, no one be there."

She pulled the door handle and yanked. The door opened. No one jumped out at her.

Still, she didn't cross the threshold and begin her descent. Rather, she stared down the stairwell, squinting, trying to discern if anyone was hiding within the gloom.

That's when she heard a noise over the far-off cries. The noise didn't come from the stairwell ahead, though. It came from the hallway behind.

"Tory," she hissed, glancing back toward Tech Central.

Without further mental debate, she plunged across the threshold, into the gloomy stairwell, into the unknown.

The door slammed behind her.

Chapter Sixty-Five

Tory moaned.

Consciousness slowly came knocking.

He pushed himself into a sitting position.

Or was it a remnant from getting repeatedly smacked in the head that knocked against his brain? Either way, his senses were returning.

After rubbing the back of his head, his hand came away bloody. Again, a moan escaped his lips.

His vision was blurry. Spots floated before him. Still, he could somewhat see his surroundings. His ears whistled like a windstorm. In spite of that, he could hear the growing cries and wails of his kindred spirits echo from somewhere deep within Fright House.

He glared at his bloody hand.

Thoughts, although still scrambled, were forming. Just snippets at first. Soon, though, full-fledged introspection.

Penny had tried to kill him. Just like she had killed the others.

The temperature in the room grew cold. He shivered. Gooseflesh formed on his arms, his scalp. Short hairs stood on end. He could see his breath.

His bloody hand trembled.

Penny had killed them all.

Suddenly, apparitions appeared before him.

Cheech stood not far away, the noose still around his neck, but the end of the rope dangling down to where it looked like it had been cut. Isabel, Gabriel, Morgan, and Lizzie were all with the dead Tech Specialist. Each of them tattered and torn, clawed and bloody, a body part or two either hanging loose or missing, flesh decaying.

Penny had killed them all. She was the reason for everything.

Groaning, Tory struggled to his feet. He swayed back and forth as if he were a landlubber on the deck of a ship navigating a stormy sea. Still, the black spots in his field of vision were fewer. The whistle in his ears had quieted to a slight hum.

Steadying himself, he looked fixedly at his group of dead, silent friends.

How could he have let this happen? Penny had killed them all.

He shivered and watched his breath float from him in ghostly wisps.

He noticed someone else standing with his friends. It was the pigtailed, little girl he'd seen in the Cemetery Room during the tour, the one with the severed head. Hiding her hands behind her back, she stepped out front of the group, grinning mischievously.

"Who are you?" Tory whispered. "What do you want?"

The little girl stepped closer. Her grin widened. "We want Penny," she said.

The little girl revealed her hands from behind her back. In them she held a nasty-looking drill. The drill's long, pointy bit was already caked with dry blood.

"Give her to us."

Tory's right eye twitched. His head jerked. Breathlessly, frosty plumes escaping from his lips, he asked, "Why can't you just take her? Why do you need me?"

The little girl frowned. "She's too strong. Her powers are too great." The little girl cocked her severed head in thoughtful repose. She continued, "At the same time, that's the exact reason we need her."

Tory shook his aching head. "You're just using me."

The little girl giggled. "Oh, no," she insisted. "We *want* you."

"You do?"

"You too have strength," the little girl said. "That's why we chose you to help us."

"You chose me?"

When the little girl nodded affirmation, her head almost slipped from her shoulders. "Oh, yes. We chose you. We want you, too." The little girl paused. Her face became hard. When she spoke again, her voice was low, guttural. "But we *need* her," she declared.

Tory rubbed the back of his head. His hand came away with fresh blood.

"She's the reason," the little girl said, her voice sounding like gravel crunching underfoot.

"She's the reason for it all," Tory muttered.

"Without her," the little girl rasped, "none of this would exist. Your friends would be gone. Gone forever." She held the drill out and beseeched Tory. "We want you to join us. First, you must help us. First you must give us Penny."

"I don't want to fade into nonexistence," Cheech implored. "Save me. Save us all, and kill her."

The others took up the chorus. "Kill her. Kill her."

Tory's eye twitched. "No," he sobbed. "I don't want to." Tears rolled down his cheeks. "I promised to be good. To always make my mother proud."

Somewhere in Tory's brain, a switch clicked. His head jerked. His body contorted with a seizure induced by electrical shock. The odor of burnt flesh stung his nostrils. Drool ran from his mouth, down his chin. The switch in his brain clicked, again. He was barely able to stand. Barely able to think.

"Kill her."

The little girl stretched out her arms as far as they would go. She extended the drill in her small hands. "Save everyone," the little girl commanded in her deep, gravelly voice. "Save yourself."

Tory shuffled forward. With trembling hands, he reluctantly took the drill from the little girl.

"Give us Penny."

Cheech, Lizzie, Morgan, Gabriel, and Isabel continued their chant.

Tory's head jerked. His right eye twitched. He held the drill like a gun, pulled the trigger. The drill hummed to life. He pressed the trigger harder. The motor squealed in response. The blood-caked drill bit churned.

Tory growled, deep and low. Suddenly, he felt as alive as the drill. Alive and powerful. He turned on his heels, running from the room in hot pursuit of Penny.

Fright House would have its prey. Everything and everyone else be damned.

Chapter Sixty-Six

Outside Fright House, the windstorm continued its assault. Dusk had given way to night. The sign, with its maniacal faces and blinking lights, again came to life. The strands of lights again glowed with jaundice. Spotlights shot beams into the surrounding darkness.

What's more, red and blue lights from parked police cars and other emergency vehicles swept across the parking lot, across the front of the building. The road leading to the Halloween attraction had been blocked off by police, leaving a line of cars backed up for blocks, headlights cutting into the night, horns blasting, impatient drivers and their passengers wanting to get their Halloween thrills. Little did these people know that the thrills waiting for them within the walls of Fright House were all too real.

Tony stood outside the iron doors, wind ripping at his clothes, his hair. "We need to get inside," he said.

Only he seemed to realize just how real the *thrills* were inside and outside. He still saw the demonic black fog that hung over the place. He still saw the walls inhale and exhale, still heard the beating heart, as if the place were alive or, at the very least, undead. If things were this bad outside, he figured inside had to be Hell.

Cyrus Peabody stood there too, still fumbling with his keys, unsuccessfully trying to unlock the doors. Apparently, he was oblivious to the evil surrounding him.

Two policemen, Sergeant Kline and Officer Gibbons, watched over Peabody's shoulders, the sergeant with growing impatience, the young officer with questioning fascination.

All the while, other policemen, paramedics, and firemen stood uselessly about the parking lot, waiting for someone to tell them what to do next, none of them apparently aware of the impending doom the Halloween attraction represented any more than the sergeant, or Peabody for that matter.

In fact, Sergeant Kline turned toward Tony with a look of disdain. He said, "You know, not being able to unlock a Halloween attraction isn't exactly an emergency."

"We need to get inside," Tony repeated for the umpteenth time since emergency crews responded to his 9-1-1 call.

"You've said that before," Sergeant Kline responded.

"I'd listen to him, Sarge," Officer Gibbons said. "It's just a feeling, but I think something's not right here."

Tony eyed Officer Gibbons, recognizing that the young officer was a bit sensitive to otherworldly activity, whether he knew it or not.

Sergeant Kline ignored his partner. Still talking to Tony, he said, "You know that calling in a false 9-1-1 call is a punishable offense."

Whereas, the sergeant showed no signs of sensitivity.

"We need to get inside," Tony repeated. "Isn't there a way to break down the door?"

"You said there was a fire," Sergeant Kline said, ignoring Tony's question. "There's no sign of a fire."

Tony sighed with resignation. Yes, he had called in the emergency as a fire. At the time, it was the only way he could think of to get help out there quickly. What was he supposed to do? Calling it in as a ghostly emergency wouldn't have gotten any action at all. Except maybe one police car sent to arrest him for being crazy.

"I'm sure I saw smoke coming from the roof," Tony lied. "There *are* people in there that can't get out. If there is a fire, they're trapped. Isn't that an emergency?"

Officer Gibbons rubbed at his gut. "Listen to him, Sarge."

Sergeant Kline still didn't look convinced.

The car horns of irate, impatient party-goers continued to blast into the night. Headlights blinked to bright, back to normal, and back to bright, like some kind of ticked off SOS.

"I have a good mind to pull everyone out of here," Sergeant Kline threatened.

Officer Gibbons scanned the line of cars backed up for what looked like a mile or two. He said, "Gonna take some time, Sarge."

Peabody silently continued his failed attempts at opening the doors.

"Don't I know it," Sergeant Kline said, finally responding to something the young officer said.

Frustrated, Tony swiped a hand across his face. How could he make this bungler realize just how desperate the situation probably was in there? He knew if he mentioned one word about evil spirits or premonitions, the sergeant would think him insane and haul him away. It didn't matter. He had to convince the sergeant that there was a life and death emergency, just not a paranormal one.

"Look, Sergeant," Tony said, "fire or not, this is a matter of life and death. There are people in there whose lives are in danger."

"What do you mean, fire or not?" Sergeant Kline asked. "Did you see smoke or not?"

"There's no fire or proof of anyone being in there," Peabody said over his shoulder as he continued to work with the keys. "There's no proof of any danger at all."

"Peabody, you know my friends and Miss Winters are in there," Tony insisted. "You know there's something dangerous going on."

Officer Gibbons continued to rub at his gut.

Sergeant Kline asked, "If there's no fire, just what kind of danger are you alluding to?"

Tony ignored the question. "Sergeant, can't you just break the door down? Use a battering ram or something?"

The sergeant glared at Tony. "Legally, there's only three ways that can happen," he said. "One: I attain a court-ordered search warrant. Two: I have probable cause that either a crime is in the process of being committed or that there's an actual danger to people's lives. Three: I have the permission of the owner."

"That's not going to happen," Peabody said.

Sergeant Kline shook his head. "It's time to pull out. Gibbons, take down the roadblock. Let those cars into the parking lot. Afterward, we can clear the emergency vehicles out of here."

"Sarge," Officer Gibbons said, "I really do think there's something wrong here."

"This isn't a debate, Gibbons," the sergeant barked. "Do it."

Tony couldn't let this happen. He began to plead, "Sergeant—"

Sergeant Kline interrupted with a hand on Tony's shoulder. "I'm sorry," he said. "There's no reason to continue this."

"There's a bomb," Tony blurted in desperation.

"What?"

"I planted a bomb inside," Tony insisted. He should've thought of this earlier. It was so much better than a fire.

"Yeah, a bomb. It's going to go off in thirty minutes."

Officer Gibbons tensed but didn't look convinced. Still, he looked troubled.

Peabody froze in apparent disbelief. "What nonsense," he said. "He didn't plant a bomb."

Sergeant Kline only sighed. He said to Tony, "You're in enough trouble as it is. Don't compound the situation."

"We've got to get inside," Tony insisted.

As if in response to this final plea, screams, shrieks, and cries rang out from inside.

Tony gasped. The situation inside was obviously escalating.

The outcry from inside continued, growing in volume.

At first, Tony thought he'd been the only one to hear the chorus of desperate voices. Just like with the beating heart. Just like seeing the black fog and the walls breathe. Soon, though, he realized everyone heard the commotion inside. They all stood frozen in time, staring at the place with looks of morbid fascination and dread on their faces.

"I told you something wasn't right," Officer Gibbons muttered, rubbing his gut as he did so.

"Would you call that probable cause, Sergeant?" Tony asked.

"It's nothing," Peabody said, voice shaky. "It's just the attractions inside starting up."

Tony grabbed Peabody. He shoved the owner of the horrible place back into the iron doors. "Is the place automated?" Spittle flew from his mouth as he yelled. "Well, is it?"

Peabody's eyes bugged out. Sweat ran down his face. His furtive glances traveled back and forth from Sergeant Kline to Officers Gibbons. "Are you going to let him treat me this way?"

"Answer the man," the sergeant ordered. "Is the place automated? Are those voices just recordings?"

Peabody's eyes suddenly went dark. His face contorted into an evil mask. "Consequences," he said, in a voice not his own but low, demonic. "I said there'd be consequences." Along with his words, his widening grin screamed of sinister intent.

Tony gasped. Even so, he held firm. He kept Peabody pinned against the doors.

"That's probable cause," Sergeant Kline barked. "Gibbons, place Mister Peabody under arrest. Get him out of here."

Somewhat hesitant, Officer Gibbons took hold of Peabody.

He led the man off.

"Consequences," Peabody growled.

Officer Gibbons threw Peabody into the backseat of a squad car, slamming the door shut.

The outcry from inside heightened in volume, in pitch.

"We need to get inside." Tony slammed the iron doors with the flat of his hand.

Seeing Peabody suddenly take on another persona, hearing the cries from inside, only served to intensify his panic.

"We need to get inside."

Gibbons returned with several more officers in tow. "What are we gonna do, Sarge?"

"Get a battering ram up here," the sergeant ordered.

"I'm not sure we have one," Officer Gibbons replied.

"Find one," Sergeant Kline ordered. "Check with the fire department. Be quick about it."

"Yes, sir."

Again, Tony slammed his hand in frustration against the iron doors. "We need to get inside."

That's when he felt an oddly warm sensation against his chest.

How could he be so stupid?

He had forgotten all about the copper key. The key that hung around his neck on a chain. If Penny was the key to what was happening within the walls of Fright House, then this key could be the answer to getting inside. After all, it had somehow transcended the limits of his vision, miraculously appeared in physical time and space, as a gift from the angel. It was extremely powerful.

Why hadn't he thought of it before now? It took the sudden warmth of the key against his skin to remind him of its existence. Was the key somehow communicating with him?

No matter. There was time to contemplate the implications of that later. Right now, he just needed to get inside.

"Wait," Tony yelled.

Officer Gibbons stopped in his tracks.

"What is it?" Sergeant Kline asked.

Tony took the key out from under his shirt. He pulled the chain from around his neck. "I think I have a way inside."

"Dammit, man. You had the key all along?" the sergeant barked.

"No time to explain, Sergeant." Tony put the key inside the

lock and said a prayer as he turned it. A *click* answered his prayers. With a rusted squeal, the iron doors swung open.

They were inside.

Chapter Sixty-Seven

Penny burst through the stairwell door into the first floor hallway.

The hallway she burst into was not of this time. Bright, white lights lit the way. Doctors and nurses walked the floor. Mental patients occupied the cells. Screaming. Shrieking. Rattling their cage doors.

Penny spun in circles. Disoriented. Confused. White wisps blew out with each rapid breath.

No one in the hallway paid her any mind. It was as if she didn't exist.

Still, she didn't know which way to turn. Where to run.

Shivering, she continued her out-of-control spin.

"Penny."

A child's voice rose above the din of the mental patients.

"Penny."

Penny spun toward the sound.

The pigtailed girl stood at the far end of the hallway. Behind her was the iron door that led to the lobby, which led to freedom.

Freedom into what time, into what reality?

"Penny," the girl called. "This way, Penny."

Penny froze, unable to move in either direction.

The little girl removed her head, holding it outstretched in her hands. A wicked grin spread across the face of the severed head. "Come play with me, Penny," the head said. "Come play with us all."

Penny shook her head in wild disbelief. Hysteria built within her, threatening to explode like a volcanic eruption.

"Come play with us," the little girl's head repeated.

The little girl threw her head. The head thumped and rolled toward Penny like a macabre bowling ball.

"No," Penny screamed. She grabbed her own head with both hands as if afraid it would dislodge and join the other head in play.

From behind came a loud ding that signaled the elevator's

arrival. In spite of her overwhelming terror of the oncoming head and the headless little girl, Penny wheeled toward the sound.

In that instant, she was plunged into her own time.

The hallway turned a garish red. The doctors and nurses disappeared. The cells were empty. The only sounds other than her racing breath and rapidly beating heart were the far-away wails of the poor, possessed souls and the swish of the elevator doors as they opened.

Penny's breath choked in her throat at the sight of Tory standing within the bright light of the elevator. She backed up a step as Tory moved into the hallway, the elevator doors closing behind him. The eerie scene playing out before her was all too familiar, all too reminiscent of the one with Jake, as Tory hefted up a large drill for her to see. The hum of the drill coming to life and the increasingly high-pitched squeal as Tory squeezed the drill's trigger, revving its motor, sent chills racing along her spine. Jake's drill was just a prop. The one Tory displayed, she knew would be all too real.

Still, she didn't move. Didn't run.

It wasn't until she saw the look of torment that twisted Tory's face into a maniacal mask that she turned on her heels. It wasn't until she heard the guttural growl that blasted out from somewhere deep within Tory that she ran for her life.

Chapter Sixty-Eight

Tony rushed across the dark, gloomy lobby to the iron door.

Sergeant Kline, Officer Gibbons, and three other policemen followed close behind. All five had their guns drawn.

The cries, screams, shrieks, and wails emanating from behind the iron door rose to new heights.

Tony's hands shook as he guided the copper key toward the iron door. Much to his dismay, he found no keyhole in which to place it. He found no door handle, either.

"Open it," the sergeant demanded.

"My God, no," Tony exclaimed. "No." He hit the iron door with the flat of his hand.

"What's wrong?" Officer Gibbons asked. "Why doesn't he open it?"

The outcry from within was at a fevered pitch, taunting them all.

"Dammit, man. Open it," Sergeant Kline demanded, again.

Tony slumped against the cold iron. "I can't," he muttered. "There's no place for the key. There's no handle."

"Stand aside," the sergeant barked.

For the first time, Tony did as he was told. Frustration and despair rattled his senses as he first watched the sergeant search for a keyhole and door handle that wasn't there, then watched the policeman, in desperation, throw his weight against the iron door.

The haunting, rising outcry from behind that iron door continued to taunt them.

How could they come this far, get this close, only to fail?

Fail they would, though. The copper key was apparently of no further use. There was no discernible way to open the iron door.

There had to be a way to open it. There had to be a way inside. All doors were meant to open.

"We have to get inside," Officer Gibbons said, taking up Tony's refrain. He joined the sergeant, both policemen throwing their weight into the door in the hopes of forcing it open. Their bodies thumped against the solid iron. Their grunts of effort and desperation filled the room.

There had to be a way inside.

Tony scanned his grim surroundings.

The place had been a mental hospital, an insane asylum. Of course there would've been security measures in place.

"You're wasting your time," Tony said.

The two policemen stopped their efforts.

"You're right," Sergeant Kline agreed. He turned to Officer Gibbons. "Find that battering ram. We need to get inside."

"No," Tony cautioned.

"You got a better idea?" the sergeant asked.

Tony nodded. "This was originally an insane asylum. Built long before computers or automation. So there must be a manual, secure door release or button of some kind. Somewhere. Close, too. We need to find it. Maybe it's on the wall. Maybe it's behind the reception counter. It's here. Somewhere. I'd bet my life on it."

Actually, he was betting more than his own life. He was betting the lives of everyone inside Fright House.

Chapter Sixty-Nine

Penny ran as fast as she could down the ghastly red hallway. Past the cells that once housed the criminally insane. Toward the iron door to the lobby that loomed just up ahead.

Her breath raced along with her. Blowing out into the frosty air.

Behind came the pounding footfalls that chased her. Behind came the piercingly shrill squeal of the drill. Behind came Tory, possessed, driven insane by his horrid surroundings.

He was gaining. His footsteps pounding. Coming faster.

Penny picked up her pace. The iron door got closer. She tripped. Fell. Flying face first through the air, she landed with a loud, painful thud onto the hard floor. Screaming, she slid on her stomach for several feet before coming to an abrupt stop.

Before she could regain her footing, before she could regain a semblance of composure or react in any way, a hand grabbed her by the shoulder and flipped her onto her back.

Penny screamed in response.

Tory loomed above. He raised the screeching drill and pointed the churning drill bit toward Penny's head.

Both of Penny's hands reflexively went up into a defensive posture, useless as it was. "Tory," she cried. "Stop."

Tory hesitated. Much like the apparition had earlier with Morgan.

"Don't do this, Tory," Penny pleaded.

A quizzical, pained expression pulled at Tory's face. Still, the drill continued to screech. The blood-caked bit churned ever closer.

"Don't let this place win," Penny continued.

In the end, she hadn't proven strong enough to save Morgan from his horrid fate. She hadn't proven strong enough to beat the savage psychic energy of the one-time asylum. This time, she had to be stronger. If she were to survive. If she were to save Tory and maybe even the possessed souls that had fallen victim to the asylum, she had to find the strength somewhere within her to defeat Fright House.

"Fight back, Tory. Fight back."

She concentrated all of her energy, all of her psychic force on Tory. He was the key to defeating Fright House. The key to both of their survival. He, too, had an intuitive strength, a paranormal sensitivity. After all, he had seen and spoken with his mother's ghost. Maybe it's why Fright House was able to use him, because he's sensitive. It was that intuitive nature in which *she* now had to connect. Between the two of them, they had to find the mental and spiritual toughness to thwart any of the asylum's malevolent plans.

The drill screeched. The bit moved closer.

"Fight it, Tory. Don't give in."

Disquiet and confusion marred Tory's face as he apparently continued to struggle with his inner demons. With great effort, as if grappling with the drill, he pulled the bit slightly back, away from Penny's head.

"That's it," Penny urged. "Fight it."

Tears welled in Tory's eyes. His lower lip trembled as the tears overflowed, running down his cheeks. His hands shook with exertion from an ongoing battle of wills for control of the drill.

"Be a good boy, Tory," Penny said, using the words of Tory's mother to connect. "Always make your mother proud."

The look of confounded turmoil on Tory's face disappeared. His body relaxed.

"I always try to be a good boy," Tory muttered.

The screech of the drill died.

"I always try to make her proud."

Tory lowered the drill. It dangled from his fingers; quiet and unthreatening.

Grinning, Penny sat up. They had won.

Then, she heard the loud buzz and a click. The iron door to the lobby burst inward, policemen rushing through it.

That's when everything ground into slow motion.

Tory turned toward the commotion. The drill fell from his fingers. Clanked against the hard floor.

Even so, a young cop raised his revolver. A cold blackness crept into his eyes.

"No," Penny cried.

The cop fired. Not at Tory. At Penny.

"No," Penny cried again.

Tory reacted quicker than Penny. Throwing himself in the line of fire. Taking the bullet meant for her.

Everything sped up again.

Tory landed in a heap in front of Penny. Body spasming. Choking on blood.

"Tory." Penny climbed to her knees and crawled across the floor. "Tory!" Kneeling next to Tory, she cradled his head in her arms.

"I try to be good," Tory croaked.

He went still, lifeless.

"Tory," Penny wept. "You are a good boy. Your mom would be so proud."

"Subdue him," someone yelled.

Penny choked back her sobs. Wiped away tears. Watched the commotion around her.

The young cop who shot the gun had been disarmed, subdued by two of his brethren. One was slapping handcuffs on the guy as an older cop approached. "Get Gibbons out of here," the older cop commanded.

"I didn't mean to do it," Gibbons cried. "I didn't mean to shoot him."

The two cops dragged Gibbons back through the lobby door, disappearing outside.

More cops rushed into the hallway, guns drawn. Firemen and paramedics followed.

An older man not in uniform ran to Penny and Tory's side. He knelt next to them. "My God," he said, looking down at Tory.

"He saved me," Penny whispered, choking back a sob. "In the end, he saved me."

The older man looked at Penny. "From what I saw, and from what I feel, you saved him, as well," he said. "Maybe not his life but definitely his soul."

Penny gave the older man a half-smile. She sniffed snot back up her nose, wiped away more tears. "Who are you?" she asked.

"My name's Tony Scout."

Two paramedics came to their aid. "We'll take care of him," one said.

Tony nodded in agreement. "Let's get you out of here, Miss Winters," he said. "Now."

"How do you know me?" Penny asked.

"I'll explain that later," Tony answered. "We've got to get you outside. That's the only way this madness will stop." He helped Penny to her feet.

Penny leaned heavily onto Tony as they made their way into the lobby and staggered through the front door.

Finally free of Fright House.

Chapter Seventy

Darkness had completely befallen the landscape. Fright House stood, a slain behemoth in the night. Harmlessly, its yellow lights twinkled. Its maniacal faces sign flashed. A line of cars behind a police barricade honked their horns and flashed their headlights.

Penny and Tony stared at the place from the safety of the parking lot, pandemonium reigning all around them.

The possessed victims that survived the tortures within the Halloween attraction staggered from inside, paramedics and firemen running to their aid. Policemen rushed around, apparently unsure of how to react, how to help. The young cop they had called Gibbons, the one who had done the shooting on behalf of Fright House, sat in the back of a squad car. Alone. Forlorn. Sobbing.

Penny aimlessly shook her head. "I'll never step foot in that place again," she declared.

Without looking her way, Tony responded, "If I have my way, no one will."

A fireman stopped next to Penny and Tony, taking in the Halloween attraction with them. As he stared at the building, he asked, "What happened here?"

Without tearing her gaze away from the place, Penny answered, "Evil. Pure evil."

Chapter Seventy-One

The room was small, square, spartan. Surrounded by video equipment and computers, Penny sat before a monitor, watching the final scene at Fright House play out on video. Next to her sat Harry Wong, the new Tech Specialist who had compiled all the footage taken over a year ago on that fateful Halloween into a cohesive, extended episode of *Paranormal Scene Investigations*. Together, they listened to Penny's voice-over.

"This is Penny Winters, the new Director of PSI. The show you have just witnessed is in memory of our fallen comrades: Gabriel Dent, Morgan Jones, Tom Chong, Lizzie Goodwin, Isabel Gold, and of course, Tory Jackson. They will always be a part of us, a part of PSI. Although they are no longer with us, Tony Scout, myself, and the rest of our new team of investigators will take up their banner, continue to seek out paranormal activity. We will continue to fight evil wherever it exists. Paranormal Scene Investigations will go on. The fight will never be over."

Harry pushed a button, ending the video. "What do you think?" he asked.

Penny eyed the Asian man. He wasn't quite as good a Tech Specialist as Cheech, but he was young. Okay, he was older than Penny herself but still young. He had great potential. He'd learn.

"Looks good, Harry," Penny said, forcing a smile but wanting nothing more than to put this episode behind her.

Just as she had done with her past. Having recently turned eighteen, she was free of worry concerning her identity or being forced back into her old life. Penelope Snow was officially dead as far as she was concerned. She *was* Penny Winters, now and forever. She had a new purpose in life too, being the head of PSI. With Tory leaving all of his money to PSI and with Tony the executor of the estate, she had no financial worries, either. Plus, having finally found a positive outlet for her psychic abilities, she didn't want to ever look back again. She wanted nothing more than to move forward in her new endeavors. Discovering new haunted locales. Fighting evil wherever it existed.

The door opened, and Tony stuck his head inside. "You

guys about finished in here?" he asked. "We have new ghosts to discover."

Penny scooted her chair back and stood. "You bet." She headed for the door. "Gather the team, Tony." Calling over her shoulder, she said, "Let's go, Harry."

She crossed the room and headed outside, her team of paranormal investigators in tow.

"Pasadena and Suicide Bridge await," Penny called.

Off they went into the night, eager to prove again that ghosts indeed existed.

Chapter Seventy-Two

Fright House stood, quiet and dark. The Halloween attraction was shut down due to a court order pending further investigation.

Inside its walls, deep within its empty bowels, hellish forces bided their time, waiting to be reawakened.

All they needed was the key.

About the Author:

Fred Wiehe is a member of the Horror Writers Association. He's the author of six other books besides *Fright House* and numerous short stories that have appeared in anthologies, magazines, and e-zines. His adult novel *Aleric: Monster Hunter* became an Amazon Bestseller in 2012. His collection of short stories for young adults, *Holiday Madness: 13 Dark Tales for Halloween, Christmas, & All Occasions,* became his publisher's #1 Bestseller for 2010.

Fred's now working on a YA novel *The In Between*, a screenplay based on his short story, *The Uglies*, and finishing a collection of short stories and poems entitled *The Collected Nightmares*.

To learn more, visit him at:
http://www.facebook.com/fred.wiehe
http://www.facebook.com/booksbyfredwiehe

Also from Damnation Books:

Storm Bay
by Gabe Thompson

eBook ISBN: 9781615727667
Print ISBN: 9781615727674

Young Adult Horror
Novel of 79,163 words

In a post-apocalyptic world, magic rules, zombies walk and werewolves roam the wilderness.

When Mikey LoPinto is bitten by a werewolf and infected with the werewolf virus, Riko Light and Mikey set out to find a cure. They meet a strange boy named Oz who leads them on a journey filled with cannibals, witches, demons and zombies. Oz and Riko find themselves falling in love while the clock runs out on finding a cure for Mikey and Oz fights off the deadly spell cast by his mother's Satanic Bible.

Also from Damnation Books:

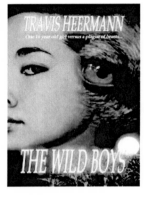

The Wild Boys
by Travis Heermann

eBook ISBN: 9781615728244
Print ISBN: 9781615728251

Young Adult Werewolf
Novel of 95,577 words

One sixteen-year-old girl versus a plague of beasts.

Can she stem the tide of a lycanthropocalypse?

When three younger boys show up on Mia's doorstep, naked and on the run, she is drawn into a shadow world where a series of strange disappearances heralds a slowly spreading plague of lycanthropy. Mia must save the three orphaned boys from their brutal Alpha, a man-beast who believes humans are food. A war is brewing for the top of the food chain. Mia doesn't know it yet, but she holds the key to the future of the human race.

Also available in audio.

Visit Damnation Books online at:

Our Blog—
http://www.damnationbooks.com/blog/

DB Reader's Yahoogroup—
http://groups.yahoo.com/group/DamnationBooks/

Twitter—
http://twitter.com/DamnationBooks

Google+—
https://plus.google.com/u/0/115524941844122973800

Facebook—
https://www.facebook.com/pages/Damnation-Books/80339241586

Tumblr—
http://eternalpress-damnationbooks.tumblr.com

Pinterest—
http://www.pinterest.com/EPandDB

Instagram—
http://instagram.com/eternalpress_damnationbooks

Youtube—
http://www.youtube.com/channel/
UC9mxZ4W-WaKHeML_f9-9CpA

Goodreads—
http://www.goodreads.com/DamnationBooks

Shelfari—
http://www.shelfari.com/damnationbooks

Library Thing—
http://www.librarything.com/DamnationBooks

HorrorWorld Forums—
http://horrorworld.org/phpBB3/viewforum.php?f=134

Our Ebay Store—
http://www.ebay.com/usr/ep-dbbooks

CPSIA information can be obtained
at www.ICGtesting.com
Printed in the USA
FSOW01n0805310315
6011FS